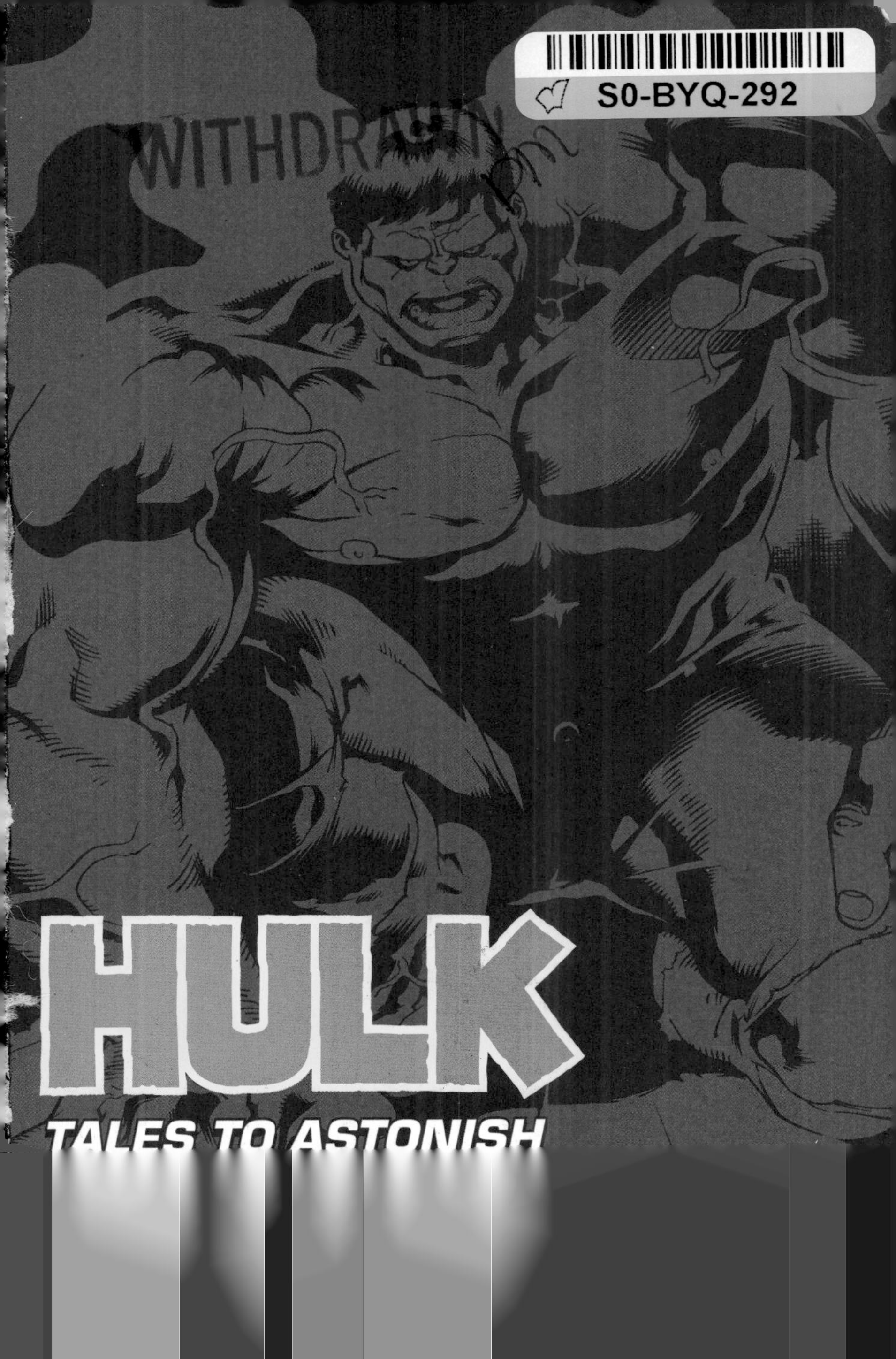

# HULK

## TALES TO ASTONISH

# HULK
## TALES TO ASTONISH


**WRITER:** PETER DAVID

**PENCILER:** JUAN SANTACRUZ

**INKER:** RAUL FERNANDEZ

**COLORIST:** ANGEL MARIN

**LETTERER:** DAVE SHARPE

**COVER ARTISTS:** SEAN GORDON MURPHY; DAVID NAKAYAMA & GURU eFX; JUAN SANTACRUZ & VICENTE CIFUENTES; AND TOM GRUMMETT, GARY MARTIN & MOOSE BAUMANN

**ASSISTANT EDITOR:** JORDAN D. WHITE

**EDITOR:** MARK PANICCIA

**COLLECTION EDITOR:** ALEX STARBUCK

**ASSISTANT EDITORS:** CORY LEVINE & JOHN DENNING

**EDITORS, SPECIAL PROJECT:** JENNIFER GRÜNWALD & MARK D. BEAZLEY

**SENIOR EDITOR, SPECIAL PROJECTS:** JEFF YOUNGQUIST

**SENIOR VICE PRESIDENT OF SALES:** DAVID GABRIEL

**PRODUCTION:** JERRON QUALITY COLOR

**EDITOR IN CHIEF:** JOE QUESADA

**PUBLISHER:** DAN BUCKLEY


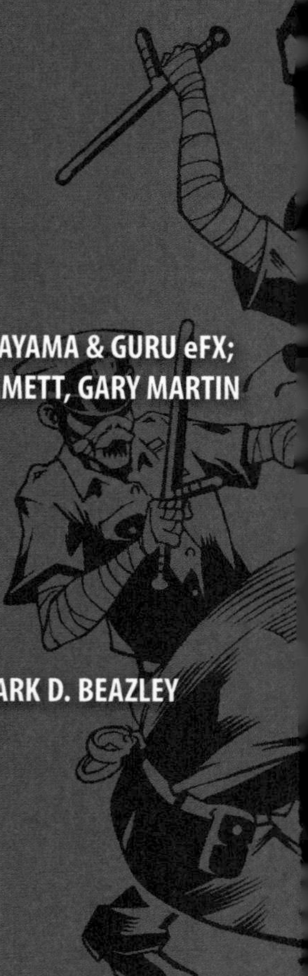

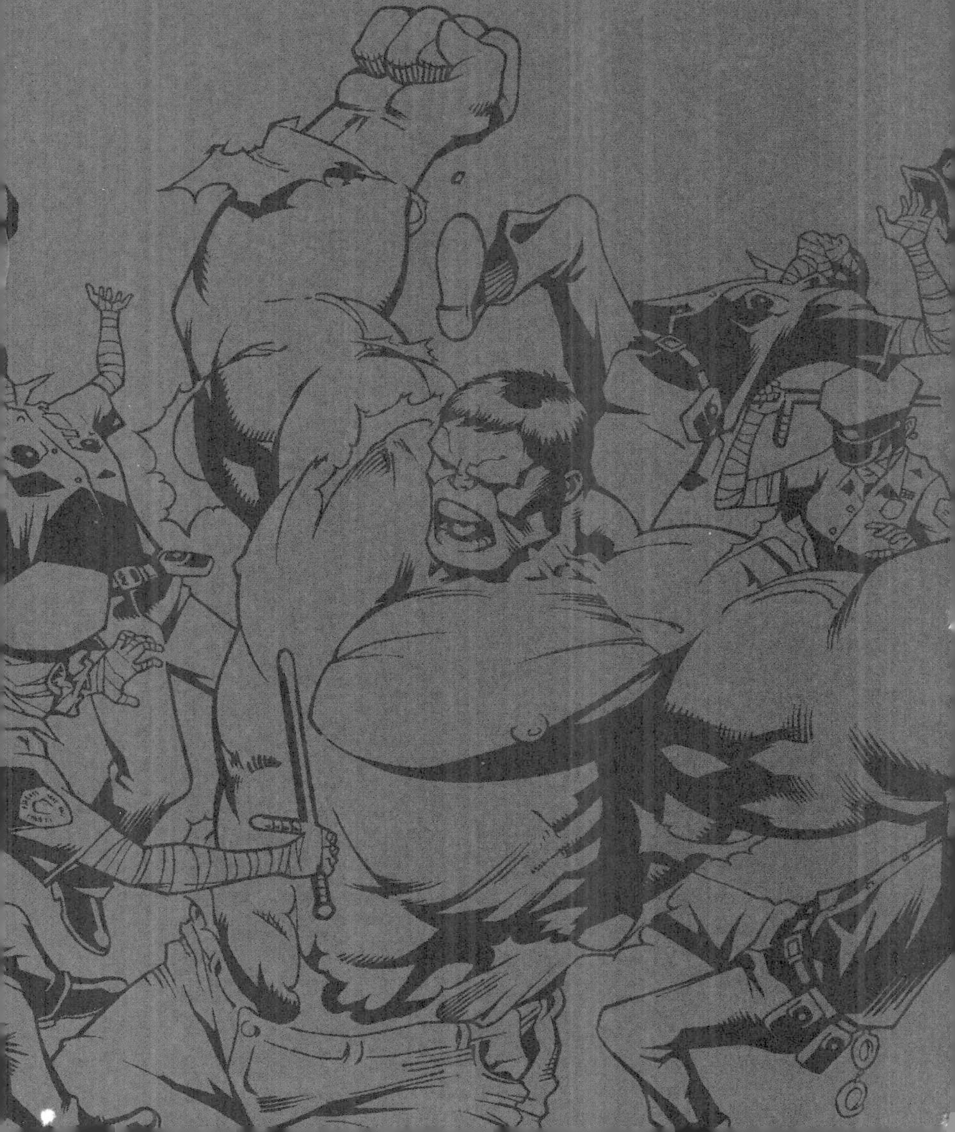

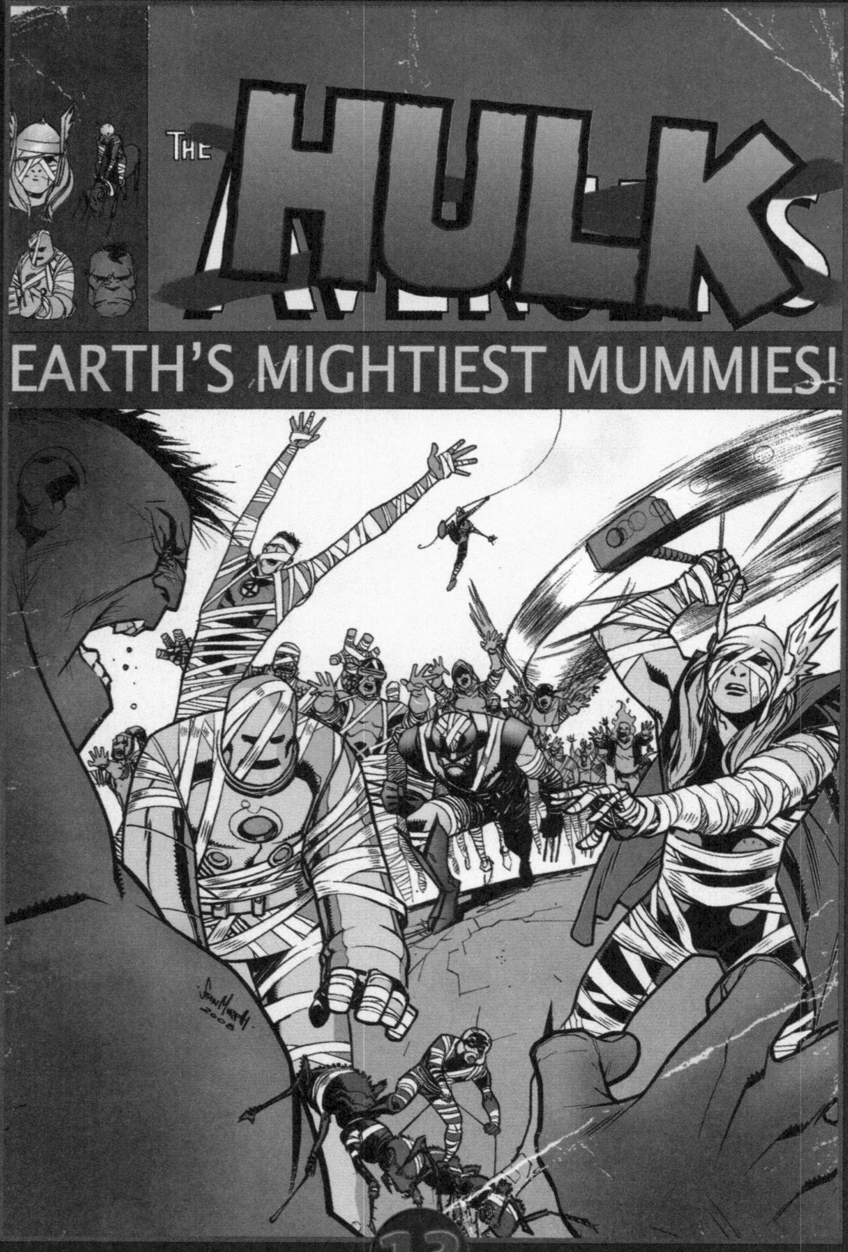
THE HULK
EARTH'S MIGHTIEST MUMMIES!
13

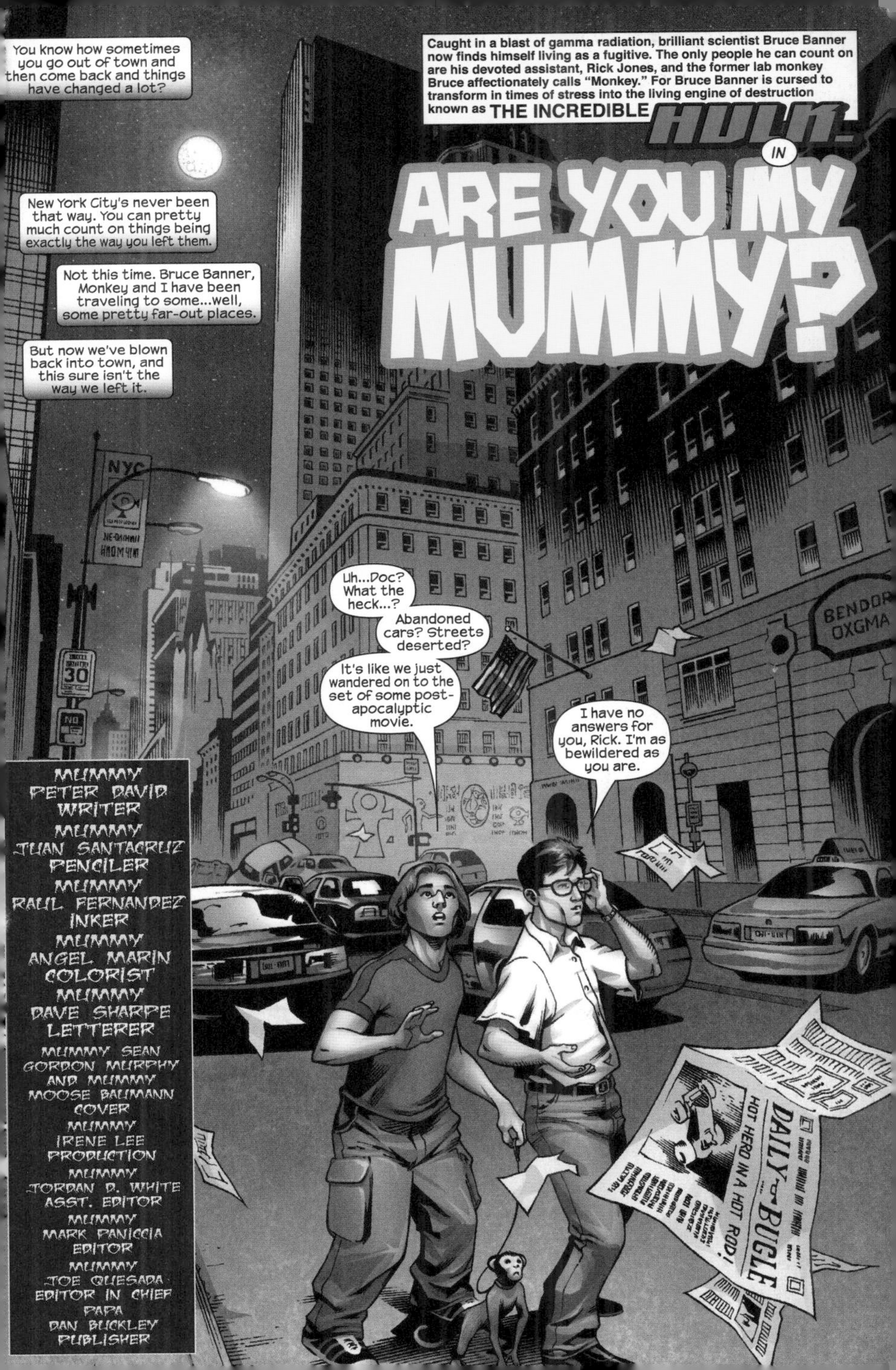

You know how sometimes you go out of town and then come back and things have changed a lot?
New York City's never been that way. You can pretty much count on things being exactly the way you left them.
Not this time. Bruce Banner, Monkey and I have been traveling to some...well, some pretty far-out places.
But now we've blown back into town, and this sure isn't the way we left it.
Caught in a blast of gamma radiation, brilliant scientist Bruce Banner now finds himself living as a fugitive. The only people he can count on are his devoted assistant, Rick Jones, and the former lab monkey Bruce affectionately calls "Monkey." For Bruce Banner is cursed to transform in times of stress into the living engine of destruction known as THE INCREDIBLE HULK.
IN
ARE YOU MY MUMMY?
Uh...Doc? What the heck...?
Abandoned cars? Streets deserted?
It's like we just wandered on to the set of some post-apocalyptic movie.
I have no answers for you, Rick. I'm as bewildered as you are.
NYC
30
BENDOR OXGMA
DAILY BUGLE
HOT HERO IN A HOT ROD!
MUMMY PETER DAVID WRITER
MUMMY JUAN SANTACRUZ PENCILER
MUMMY RAUL FERNANDEZ INKER
MUMMY ANGEL MARIN COLORIST
MUMMY DAVE SHARPE LETTERER
MUMMY SEAN GORDON MURPHY AND MUMMY MOOSE BAUMANN COVER
MUMMY IRENE LEE PRODUCTION
MUMMY JORDAN D. WHITE ASST. EDITOR
MUMMY MARK PANICCIA EDITOR
MUMMY JOE QUESADA EDITOR IN CHIEF
PAPA DAN BUCKLEY PUBLISHER

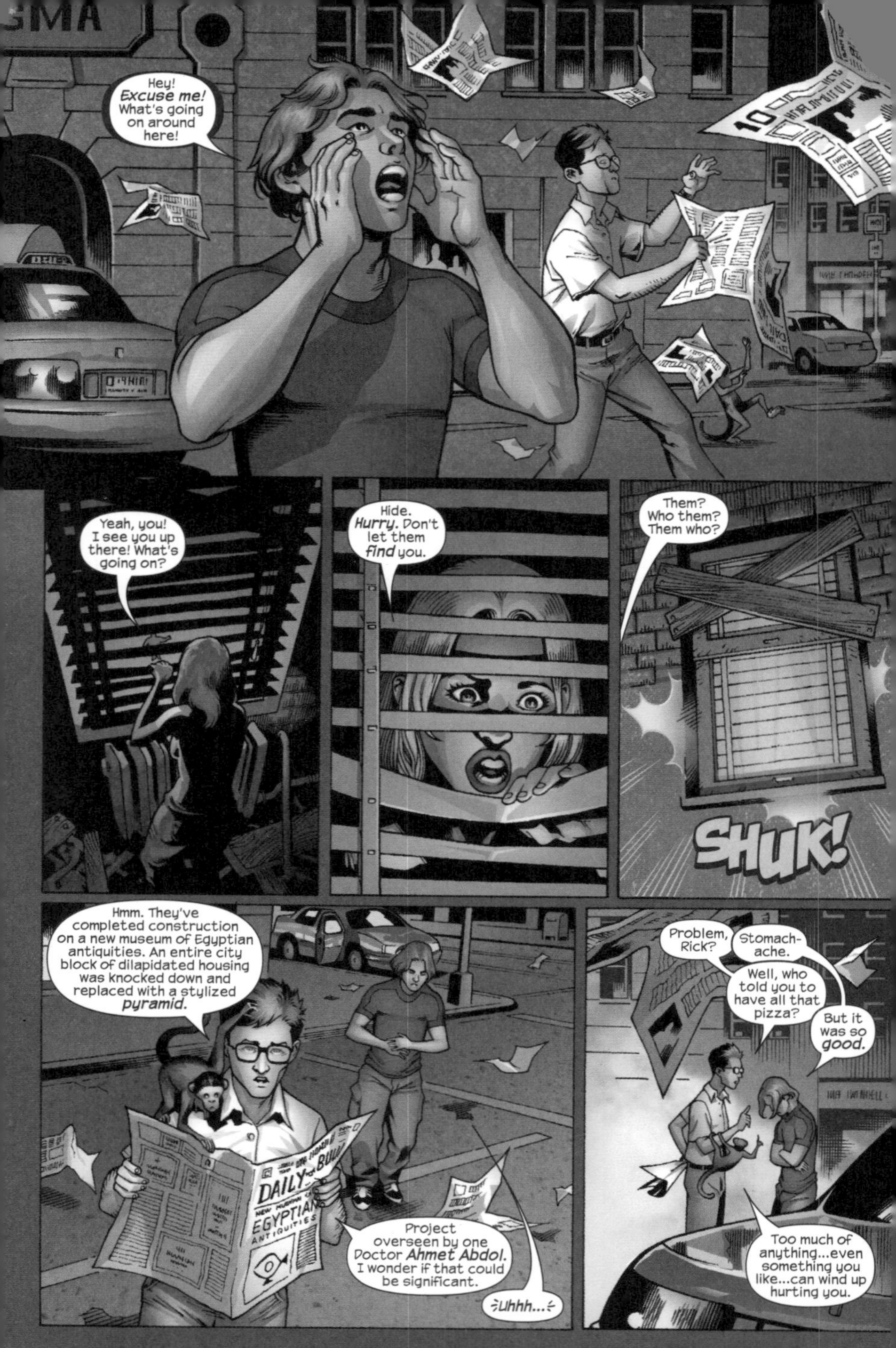
Hey! Excuse me! What's going on around here!
Yeah, you! I see you up there! What's going on?
Hide. Hurry. Don't let them find you.
Them? Who them? Them who?
SHUK!
Hmm. They've completed construction on a new museum of Egyptian antiquities. An entire city block of dilapidated housing was knocked down and replaced with a stylized pyramid.
DAILY BUGLE
EGYPTIAN ANTIQUITIES
Project overseen by one Doctor Ahmet Abdol. I wonder if that could be significant.
Uhhh...
Problem, Rick?
Stomach-ache.
Well, who told you to have all that pizza?
But it was so good.
Too much of anything...even something you like...can wind up hurting you.

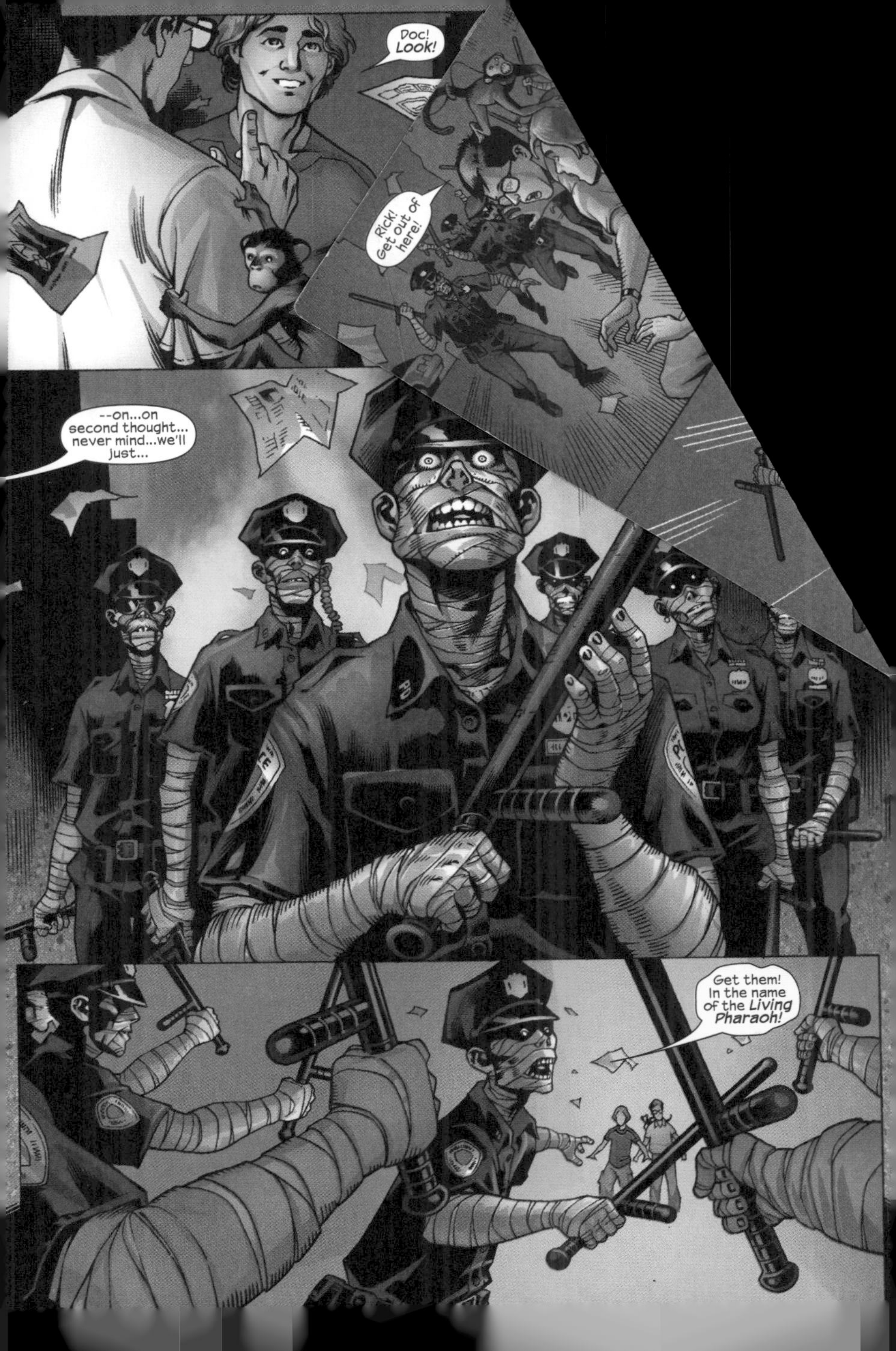
Doc! Look!
Rick! Get out of here!
--on...on second thought... never mind...we'll just...
Get them! In the name of the Living Pharaoh!

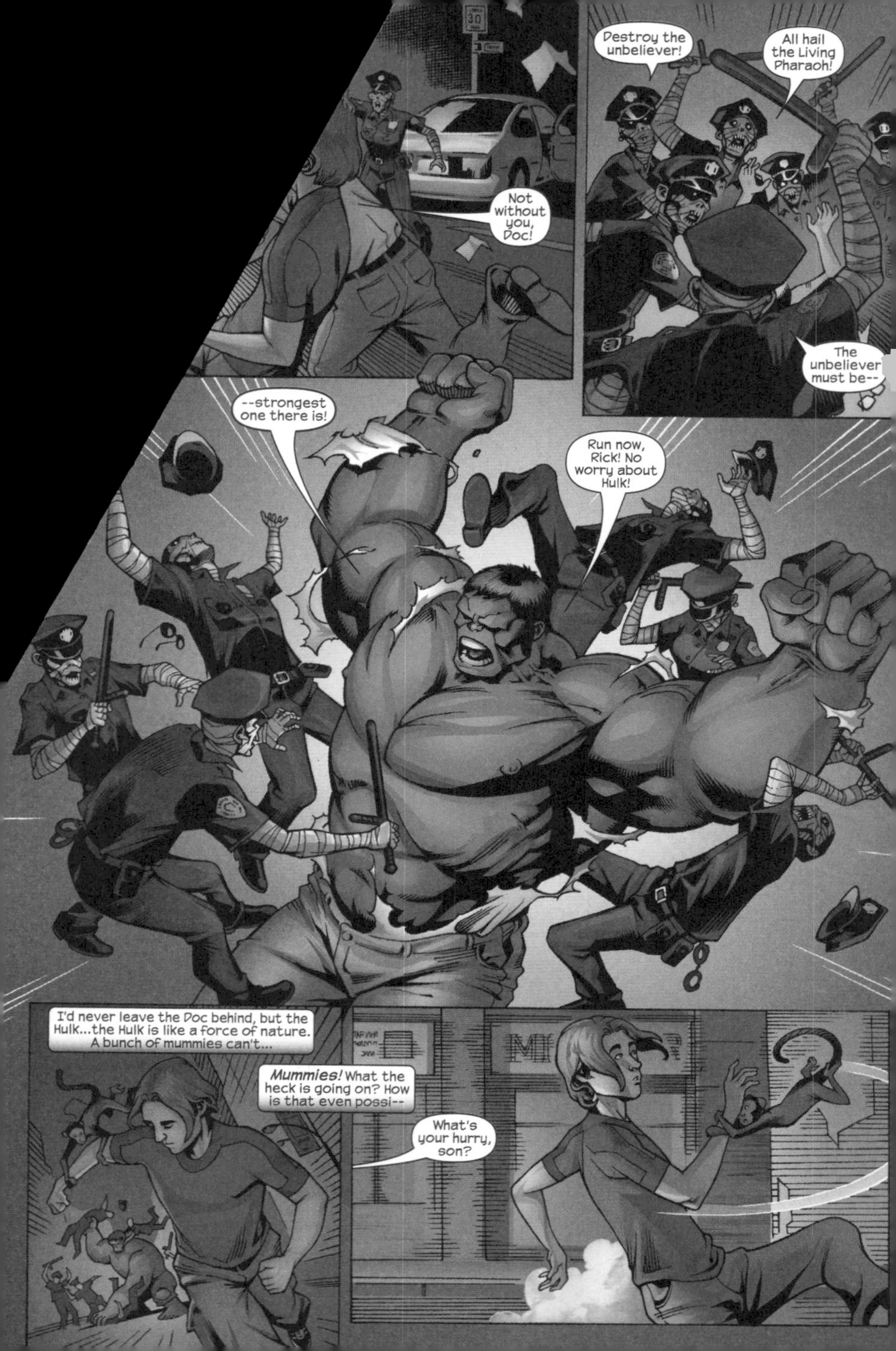
Not without you, Doc!
Destroy the unbeliever!
All hail the Living Pharaoh!
The unbeliever must be--
--strongest one there is!
Run now, Rick! No worry about Hulk!
I'd never leave the Doc behind, but the Hulk...the Hulk is like a force of nature. A bunch of mummies can't...
*Mummies!* What the heck is going on? How is that even possi--
What's your hurry, son?

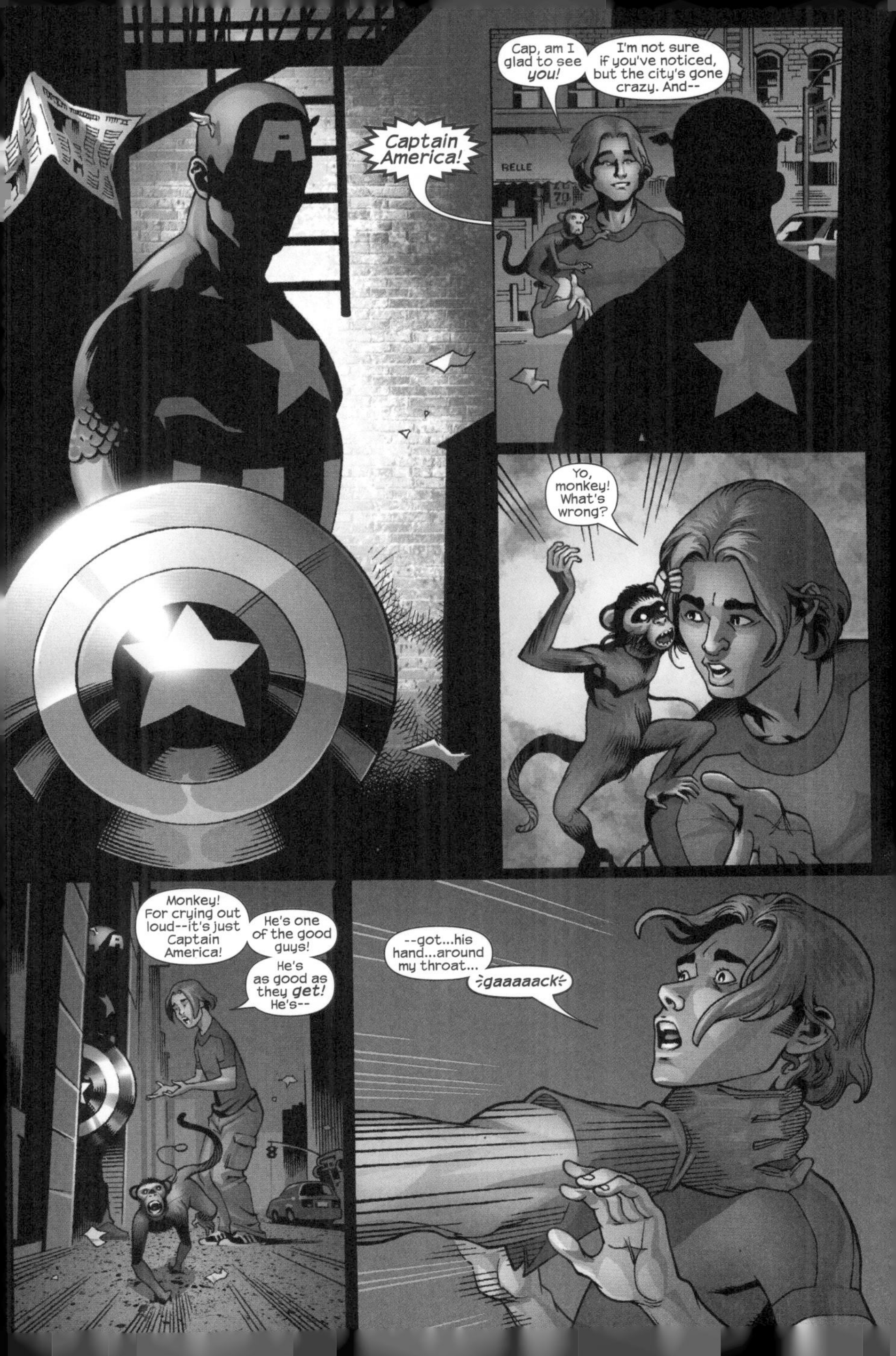
Captain America!
Cap, am I glad to see you!
I'm not sure if you've noticed, but the city's gone crazy. And--
Yo, monkey! What's wrong?
Monkey! For crying out loud--it's just Captain America!
He's one of the good guys!
He's as good as they get! He's--
--got...his hand...around my throat...
gaaaaack

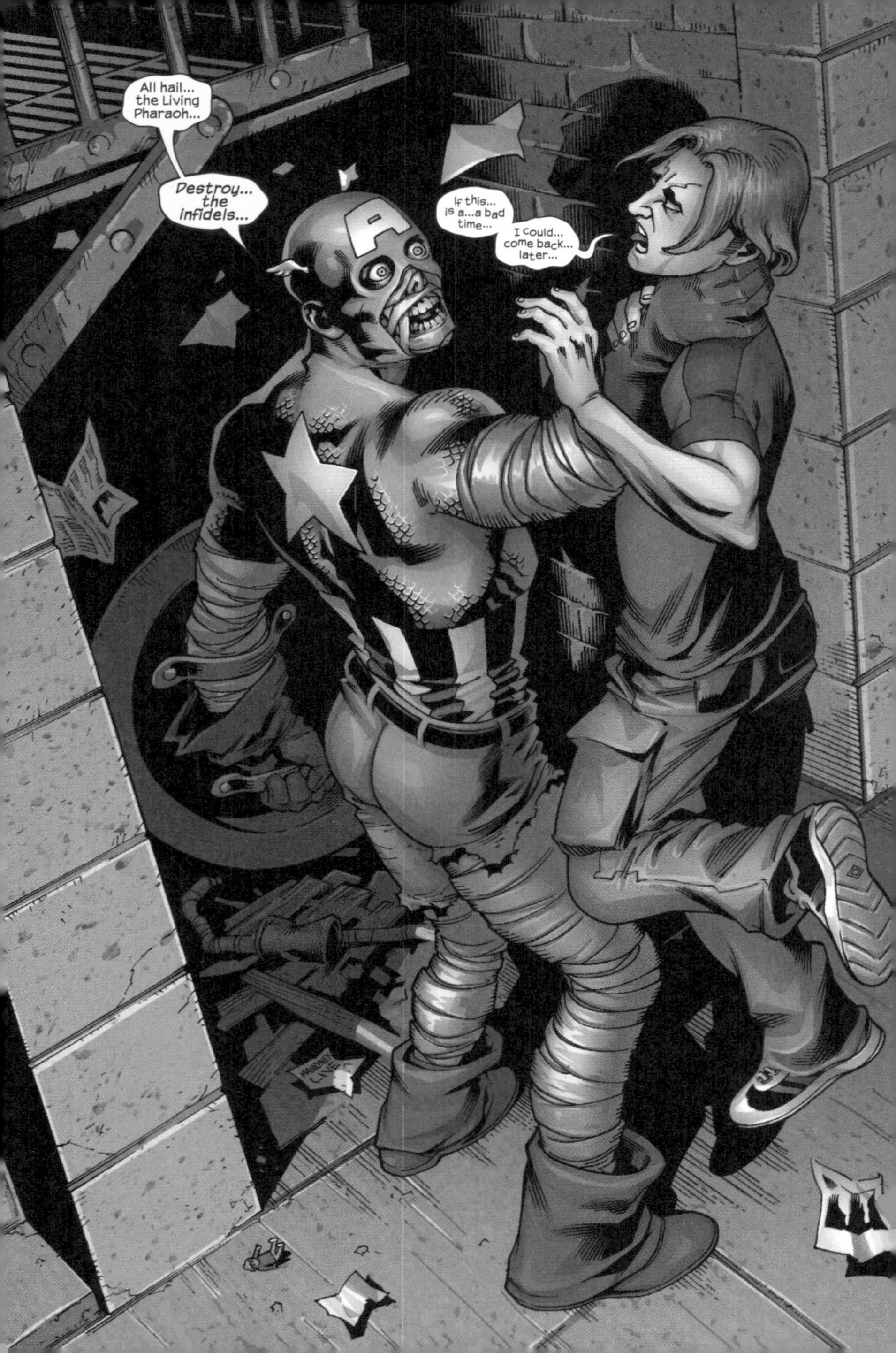
All hail... the Living Pharaoh...
Destroy... the infidels...
If this... is a...a bad time...
I could... come back... later...

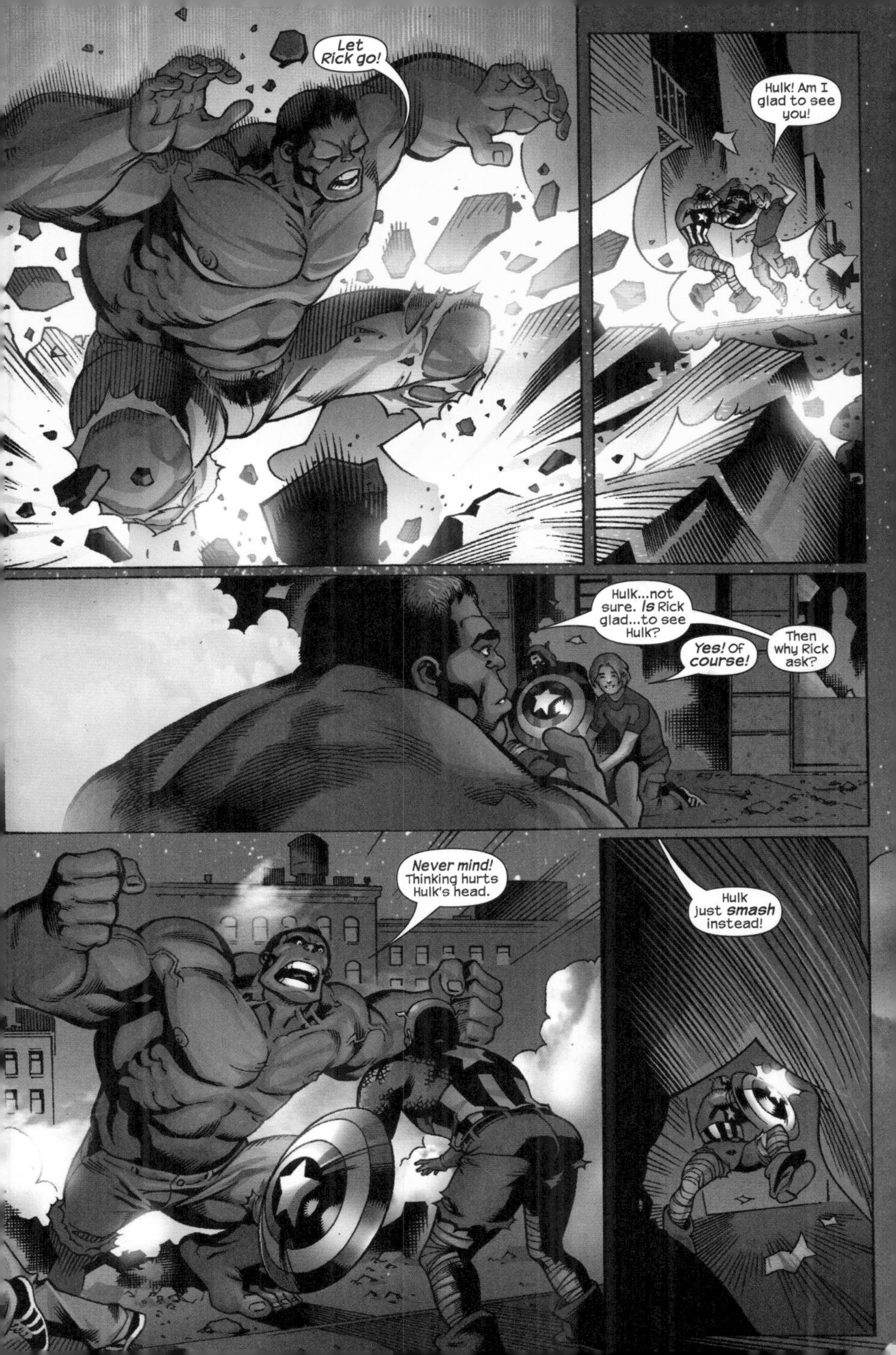
Let Rick go!
Hulk! Am I glad to see you!
Hulk...not sure. *Is* Rick glad...to see Hulk?
*Yes!* Of *course!*
Then why Rick ask?
*Never mind!* Thinking hurts Hulk's head.
Hulk just *smash* instead!

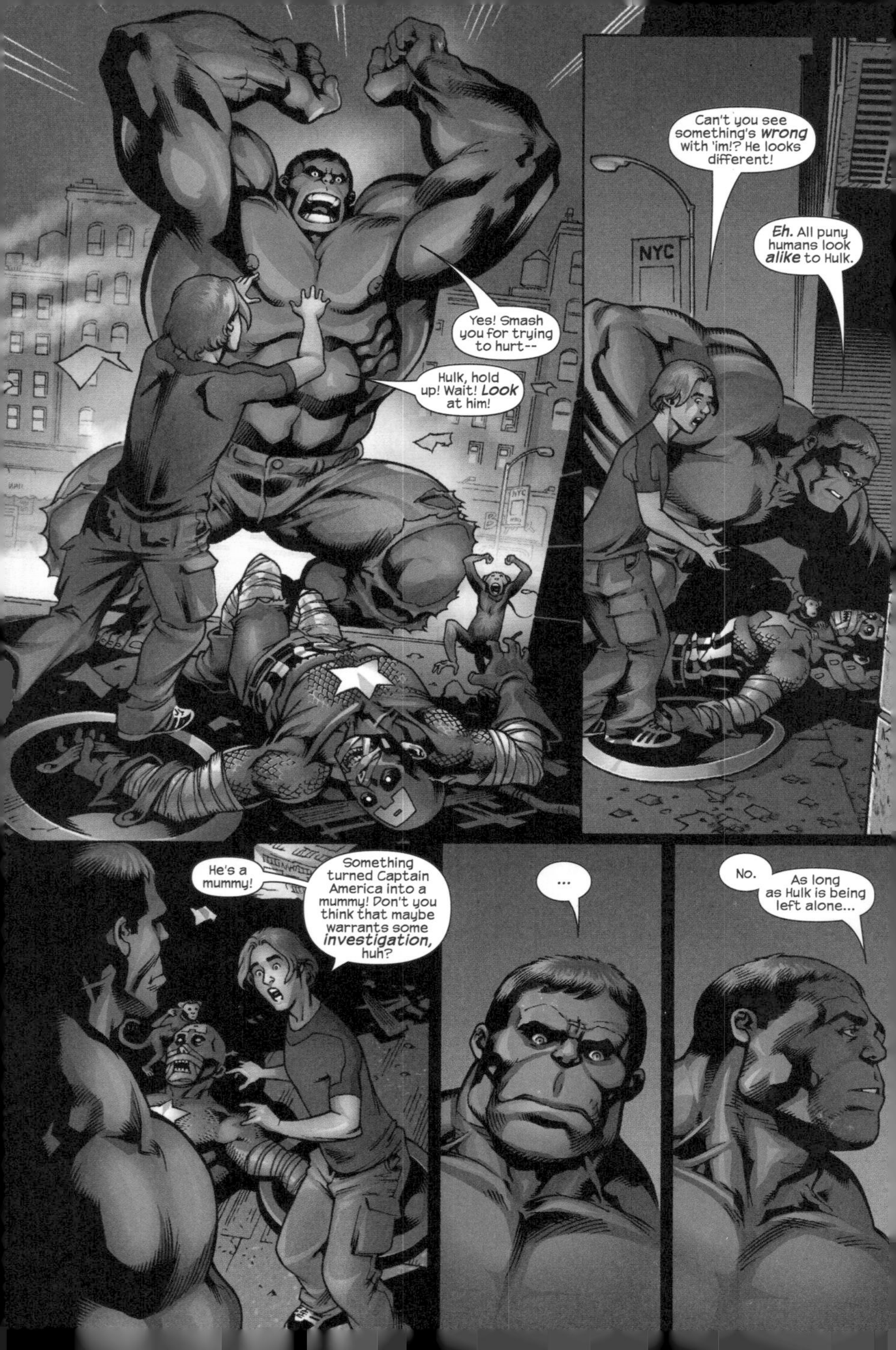
Yes! Smash you for trying to hurt--
Hulk, hold up! Wait! *Look* at him!
Can't you see something's ***wrong*** with 'im!? He looks different!
***Eh.*** All puny humans look ***alike*** to Hulk.
NYC
He's a mummy!
Something turned Captain America into a mummy! Don't you think that maybe warrants some ***investigation,*** huh?
...
No.
As long as Hulk is being left alone...

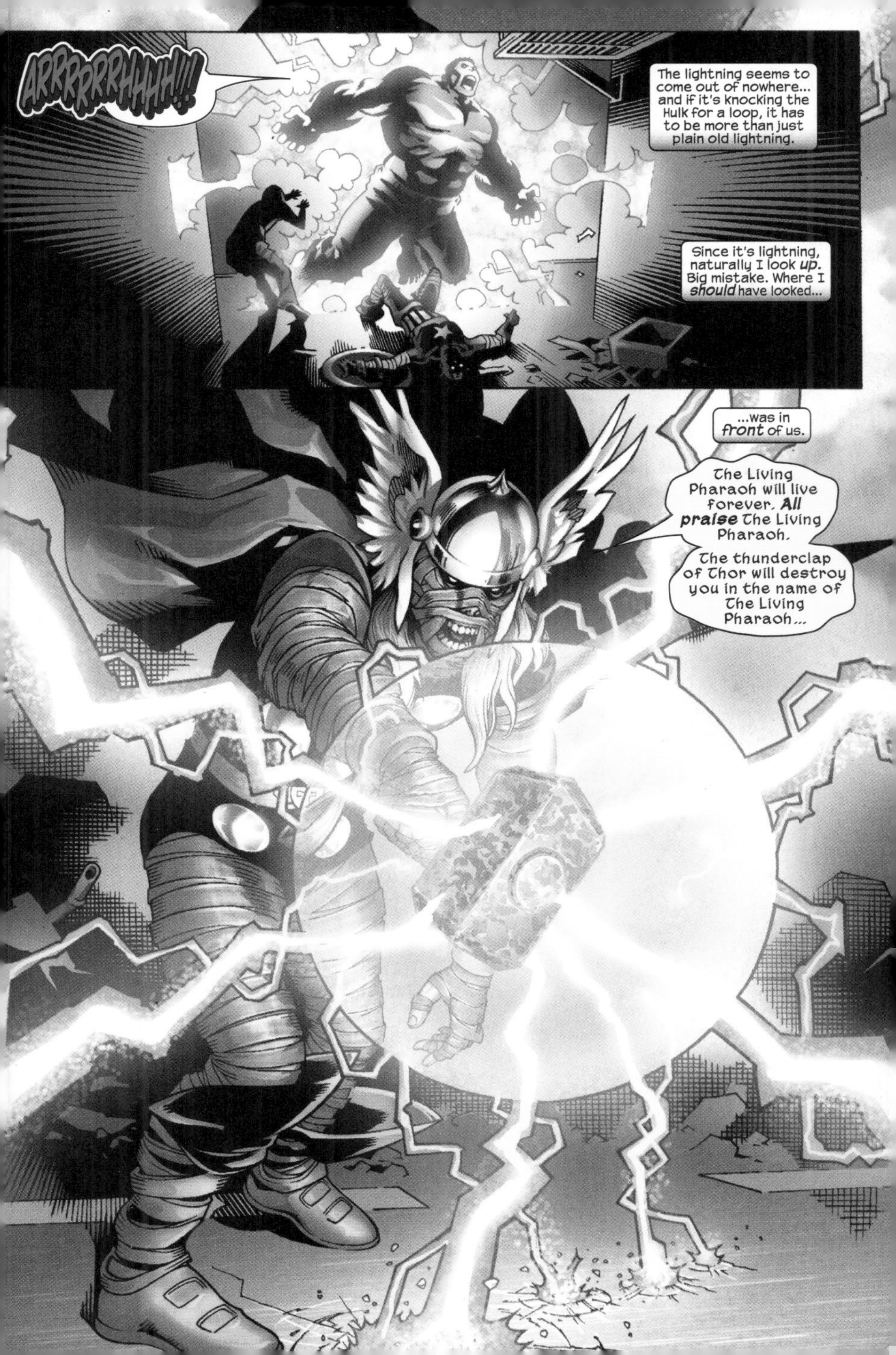
ARRRRRRHHHH!!!
The lightning seems to come out of nowhere... and if it's knocking the Hulk for a loop, it has to be more than just plain old lightning.
Since it's lightning, naturally I look *up.* Big mistake. Where I *should* have looked...
...was in *front* of us.
The Living Pharaoh will live forever. **All praise** The Living Pharaoh.
The thunderclap of Thor will destroy you in the name of The Living Pharaoh...

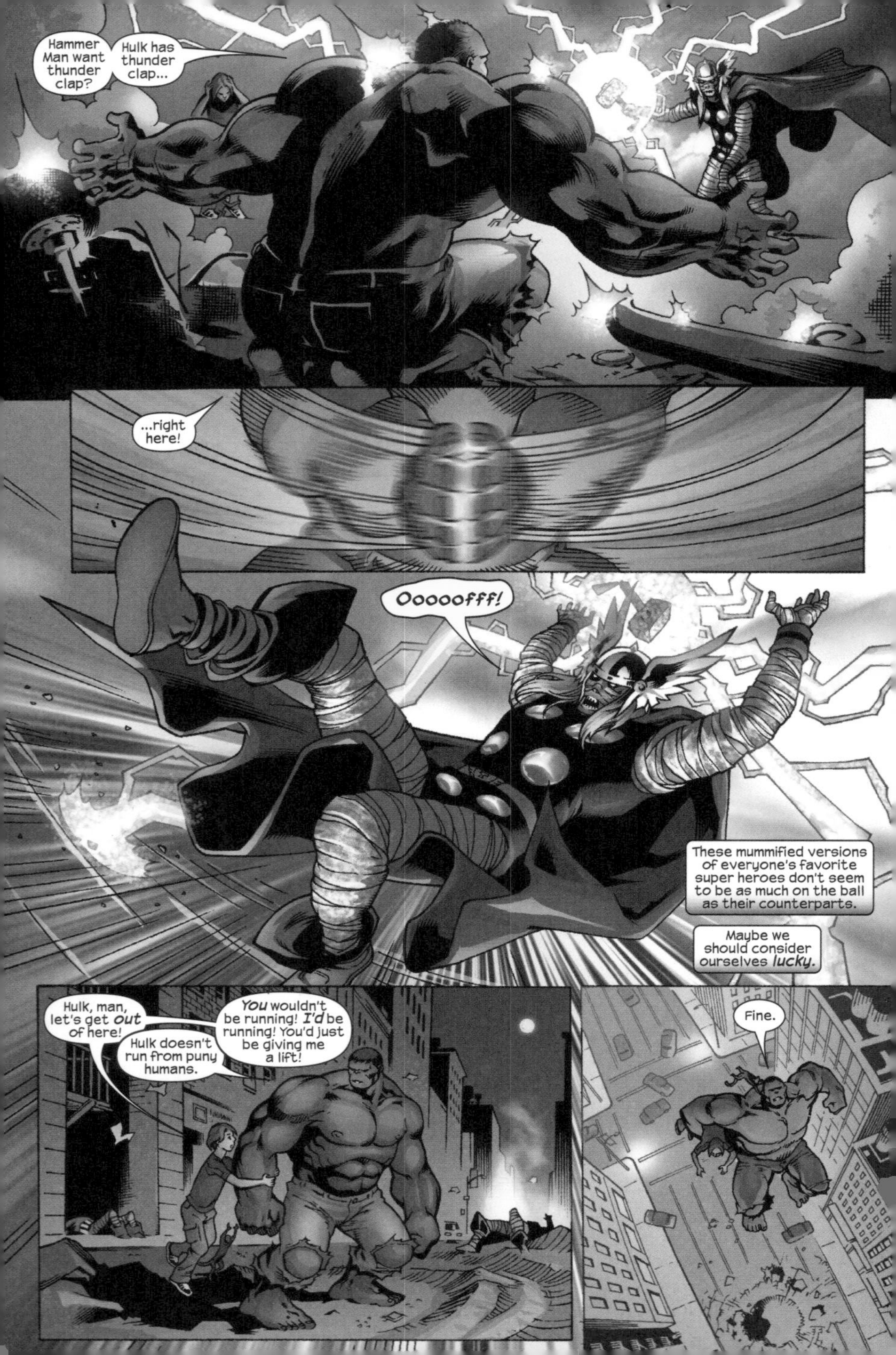
Hammer Man want thunder clap?
Hulk has thunder clap...
...right here!
Ooooofff!
These mummified versions of everyone's favorite super heroes don't seem to be as much on the ball as their counterparts.
Maybe we should consider ourselves lucky.
Hulk, man, let's get out of here!
Hulk doesn't run from puny humans.
You wouldn't be running! I'd be running! You'd just be giving me a lift!
Fine.

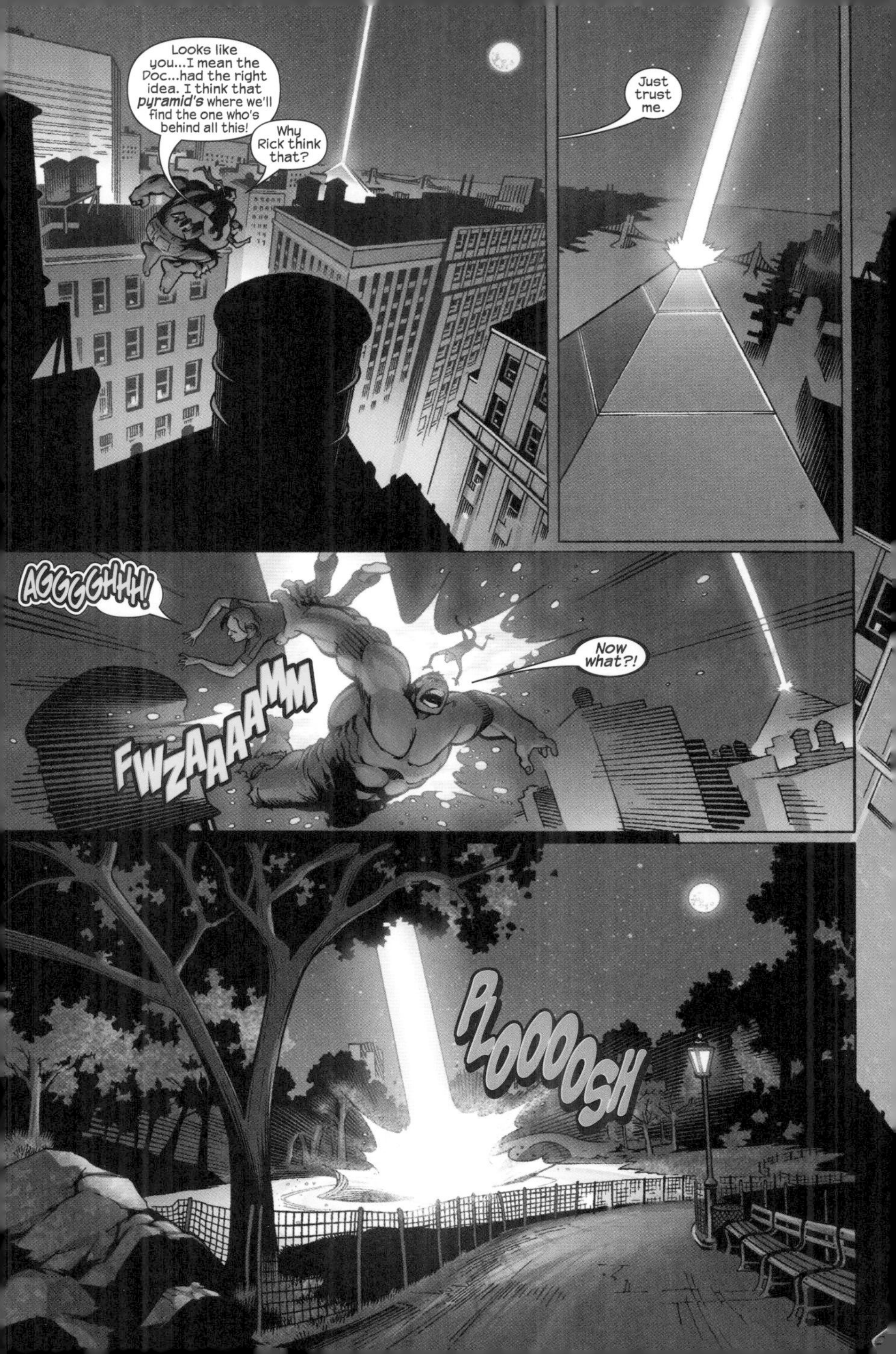
Looks like you...I mean the Doc...had the right idea. I think that *pyramid's* where we'll find the one who's behind all this!
Why Rick think that?
Just trust me.
AGGGGHHH!
FWZAAAAMMM
Now what?!
PLOOOOSH

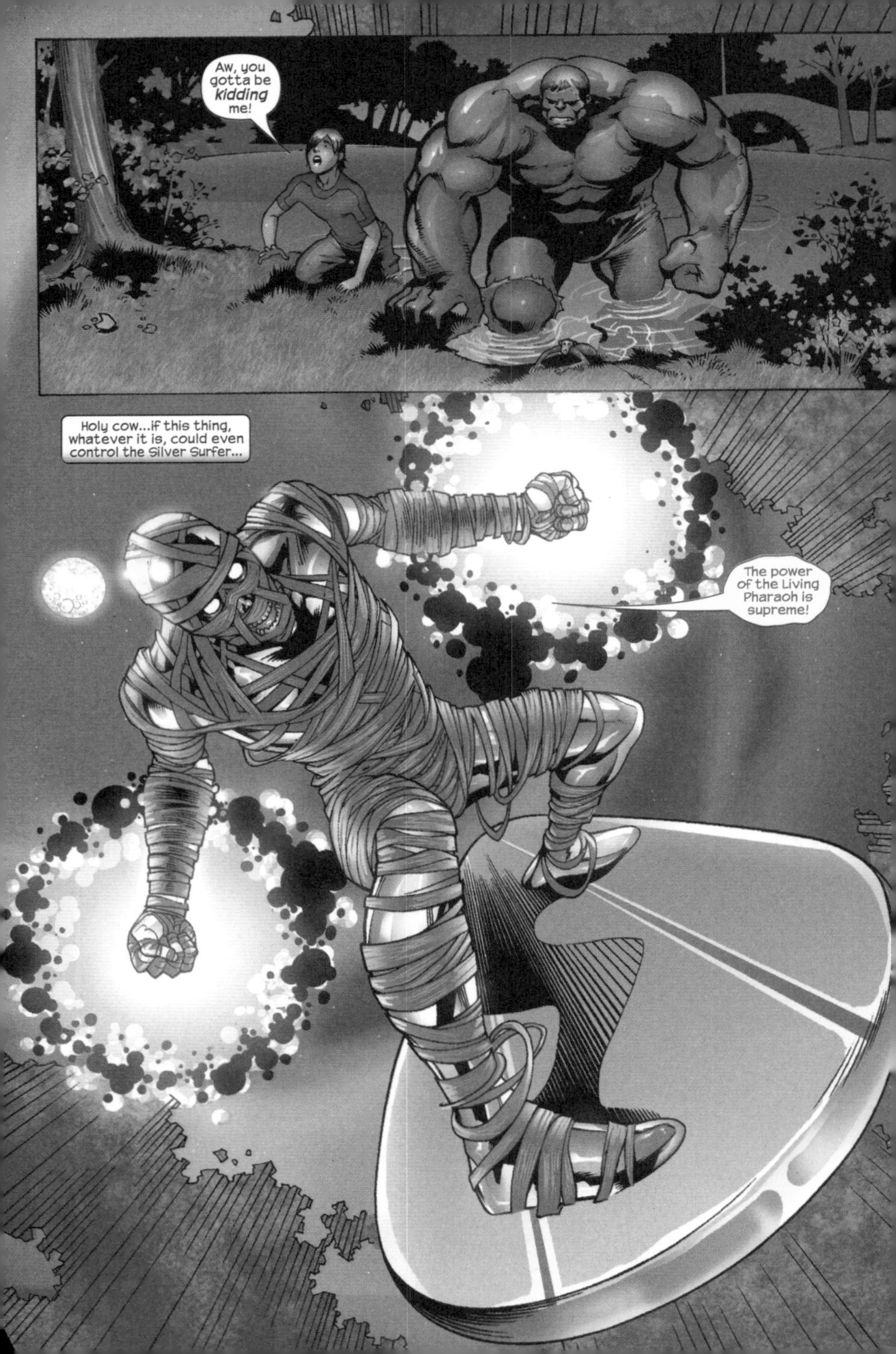
Aw, you gotta be *kidding* me!
Holy cow...if this thing, whatever it is, could even control the Silver Surfer...
The power of the Living Pharaoh is supreme!

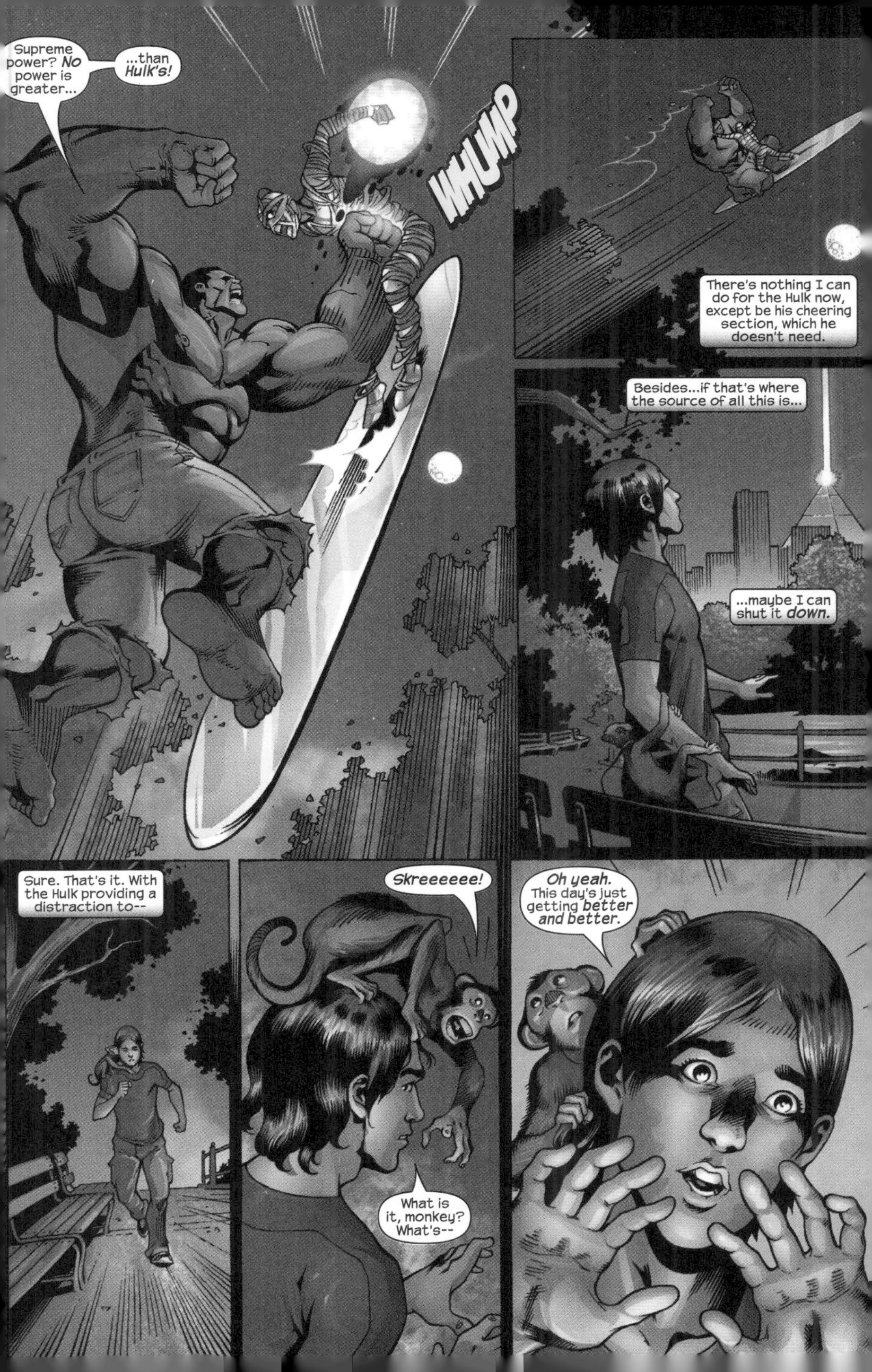
Supreme power? *No* power is greater...
...than *Hulk's!*
WHUMP
There's nothing I can do for the Hulk now, except be his cheering section, which he doesn't need.
Besides...if that's where the source of all this is...
...maybe I can shut it *down.*
Sure. That's it. With the Hulk providing a distraction to--
*Skreeeeeee!*
What is it, monkey? What's--
*Oh yeah.* This day's just getting *better and better.*

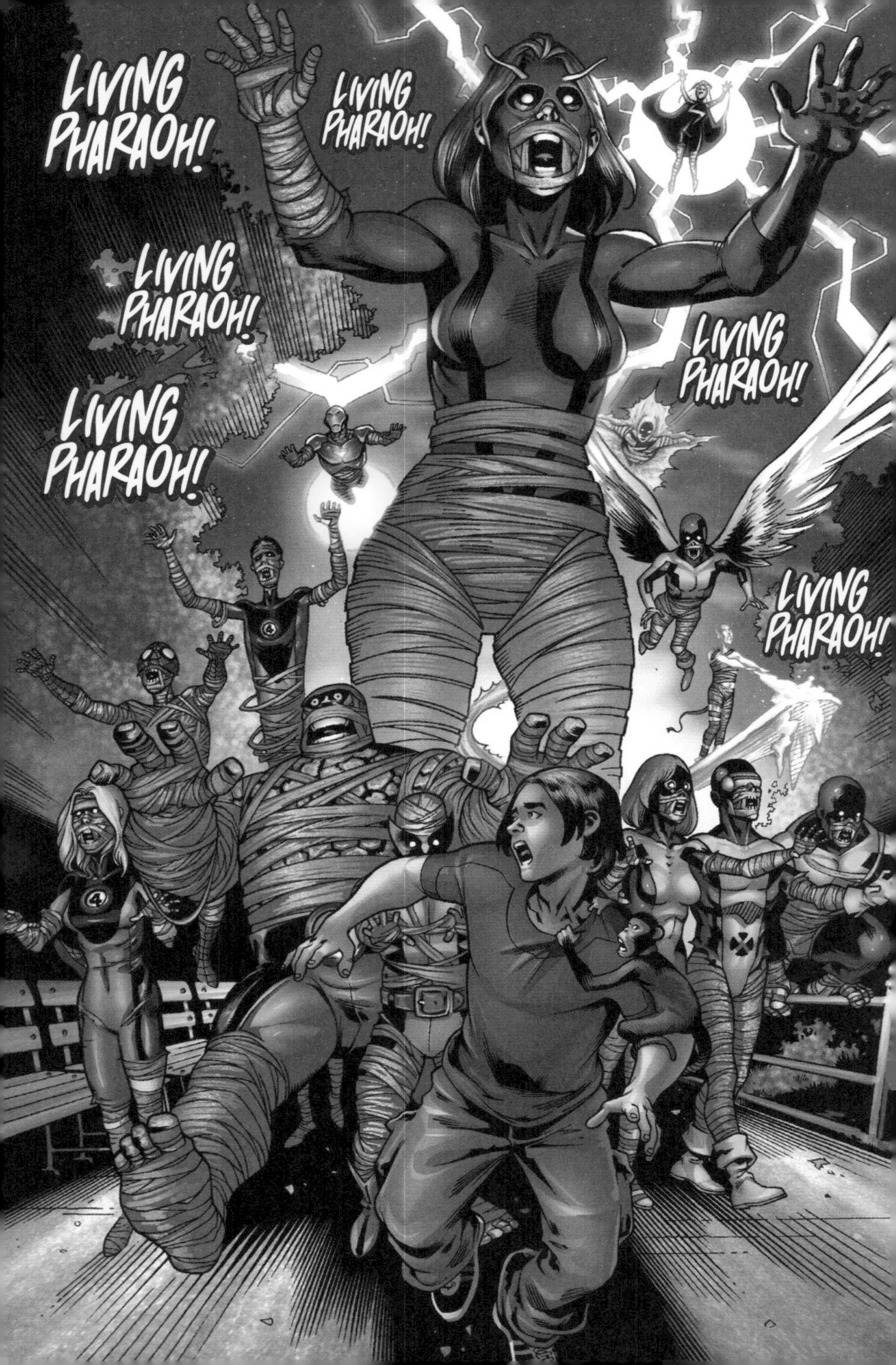
LIVING PHARAOH!
LIVING PHARAOH!
LIVING PHARAOH!
LIVING PHARAOH!
LIVING PHARAOH!
LIVING PHARAOH!

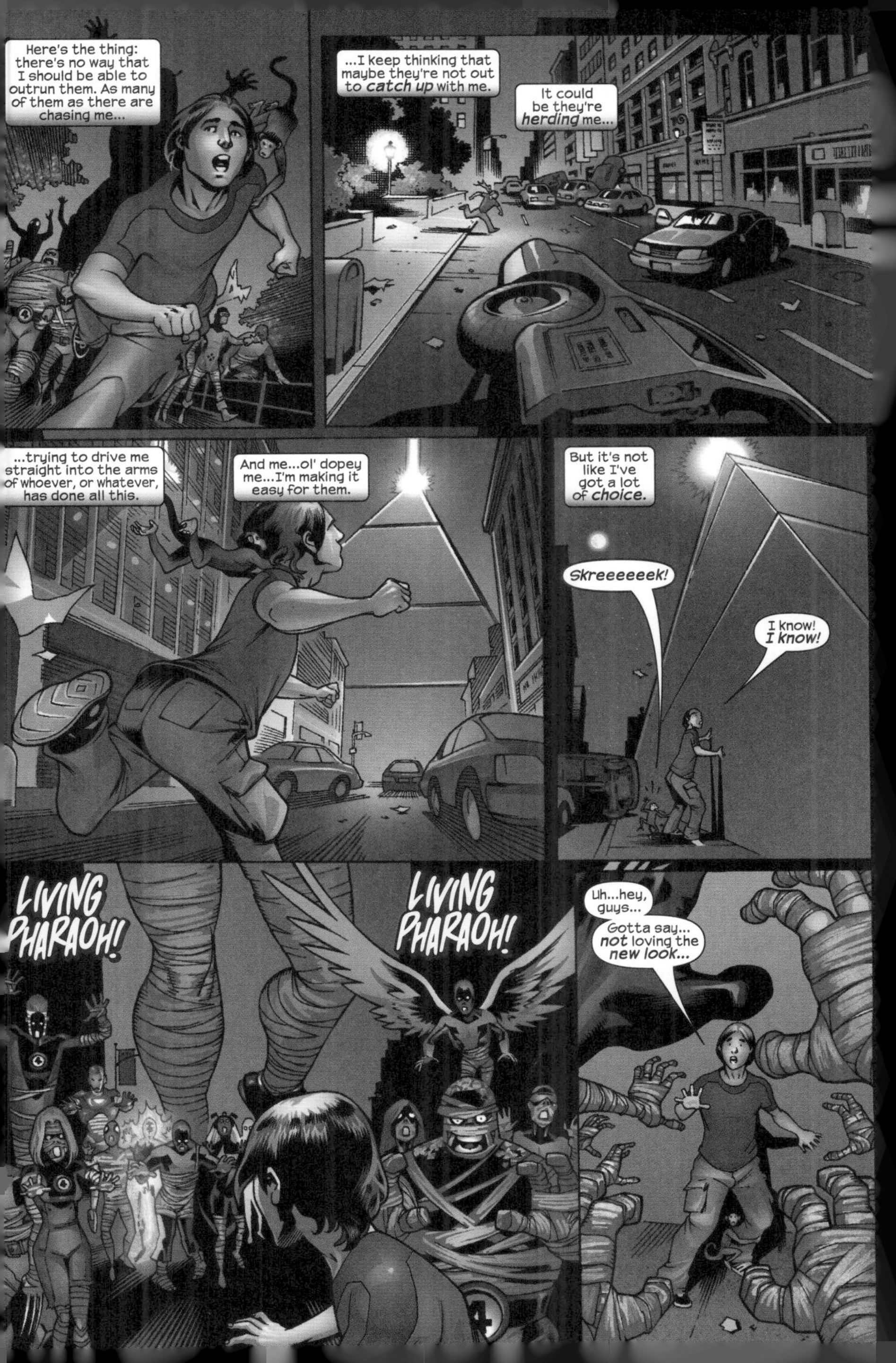

Here's the thing: there's no way that I should be able to outrun them. As many of them as there are chasing me...
...I keep thinking that maybe they're not out to catch up with me.
It could be they're herding me...
...trying to drive me straight into the arms of whoever, or whatever, has done all this.
And me...ol' dopey me...I'm making it easy for them.
But it's not like I've got a lot of choice.
Skreeeeeeek!
I know! I know!
LIVING PHARAOH!
LIVING PHARAOH!
Uh...hey, guys...
Gotta say... not loving the new look...

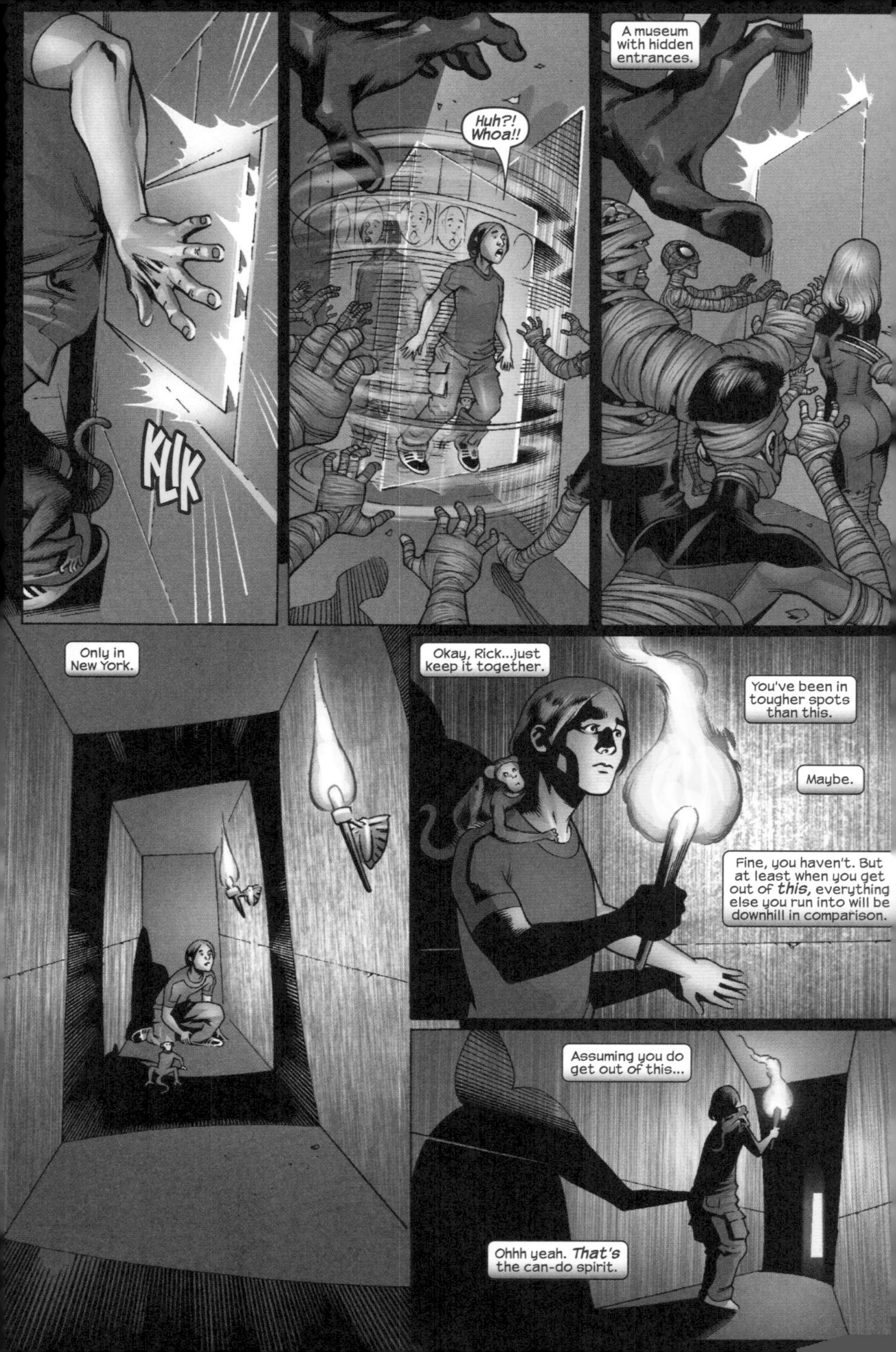
KLIK
Huh?! Whoa!!
A museum with hidden entrances.
Only in New York.
Okay, Rick...just keep it together.
You've been in tougher spots than this.
Maybe.
Fine, you haven't. But at least when you get out of *this,* everything else you run into will be downhill in comparison.
Assuming you do get out of this...
Ohhh yeah. *That's* the can-do spirit.

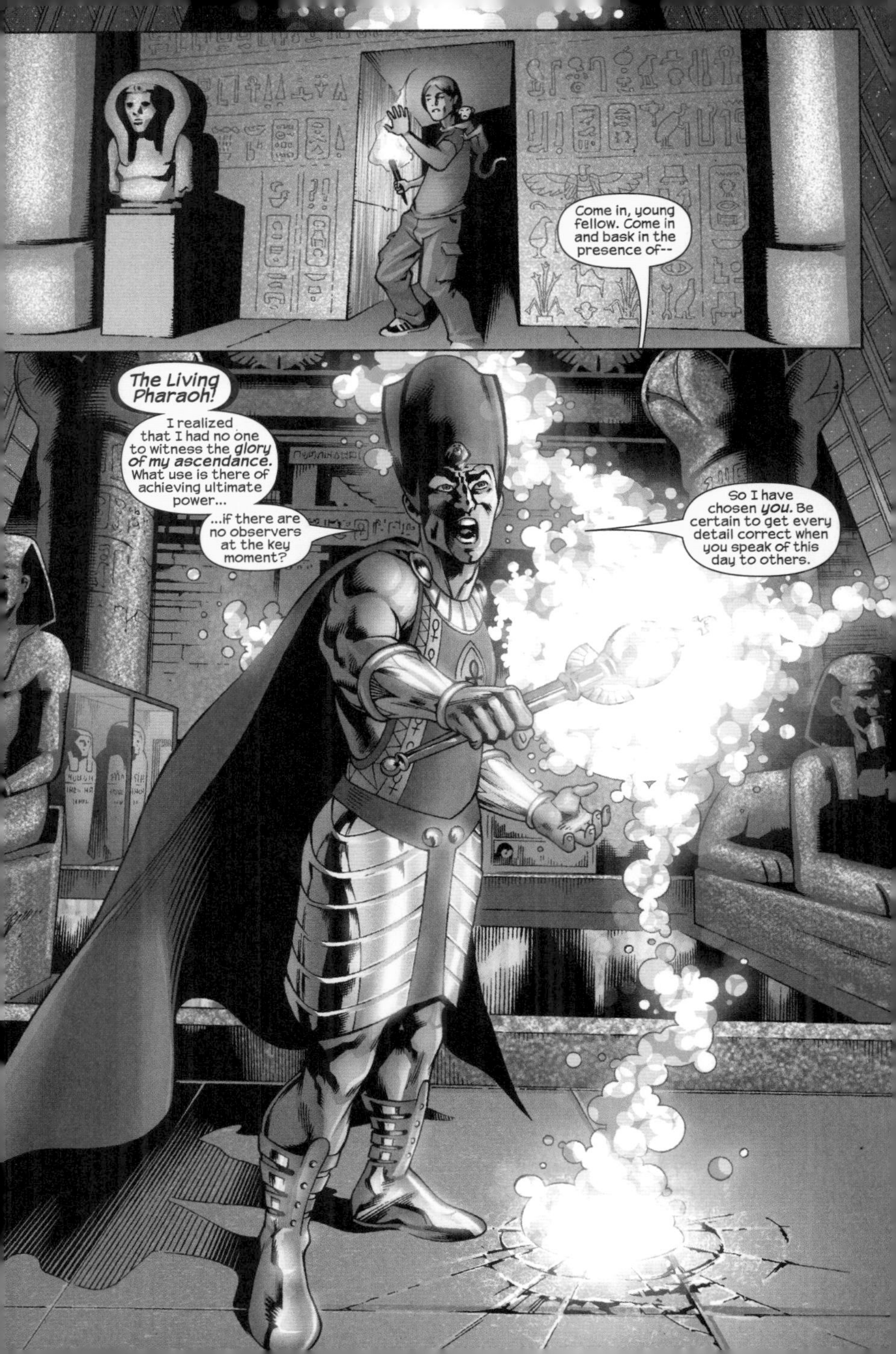

Come in, young fellow. Come in and bask in the presence of--
The Living Pharaoh!
I realized that I had no one to witness the *glory of my ascendance.* What use is there of achieving ultimate power...
...if there are no observers at the key moment?
So I have chosen *you.* Be certain to get every detail correct when you speak of this day to others.

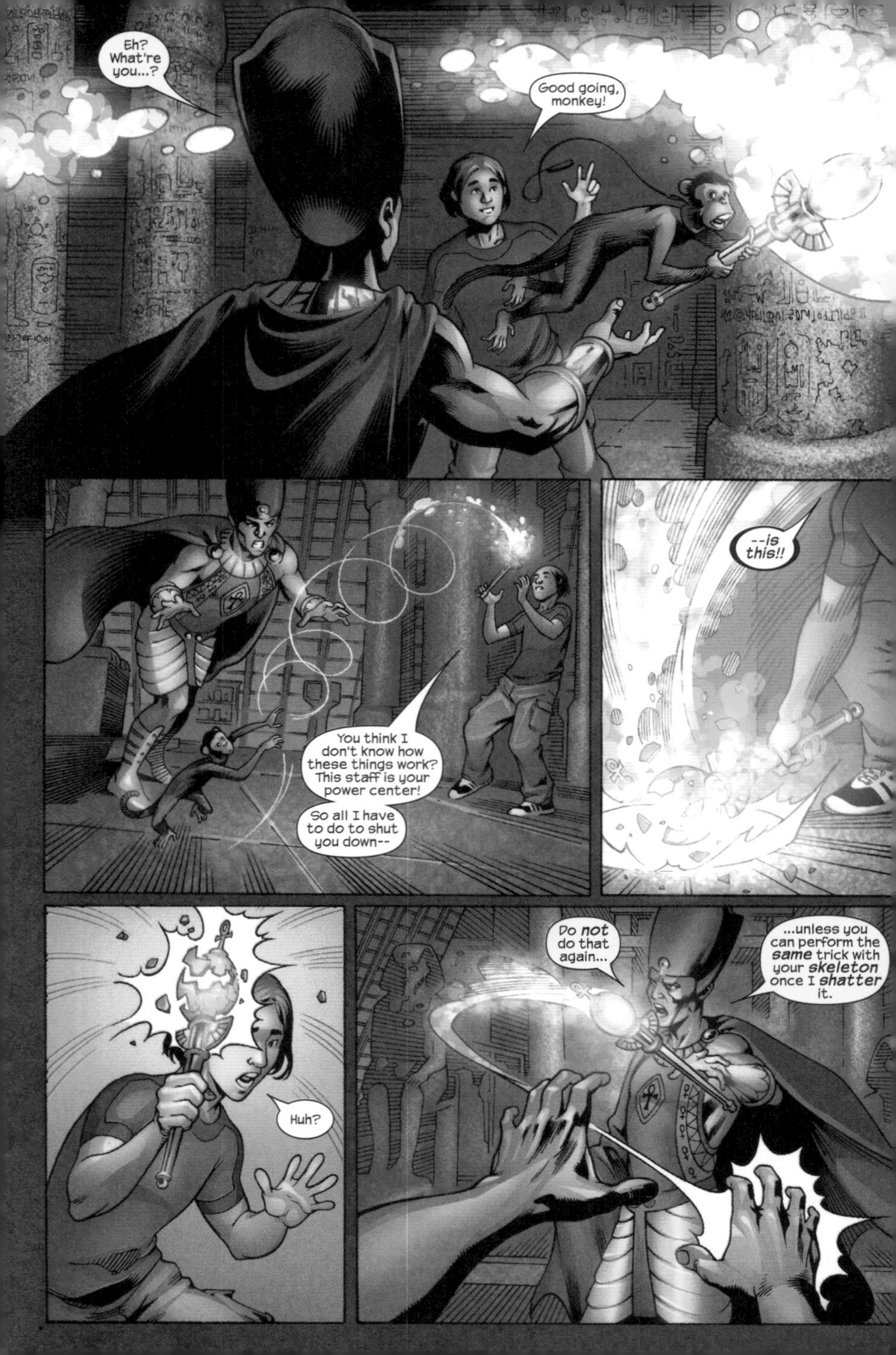
Eh? What're you...?
Good going, monkey!
You think I don't know how these things work? This staff is your power center!
So all I have to do to shut you down--
--is this!!
Huh?
Do not do that again...
...unless you can perform the same trick with your skeleton once I shatter it.

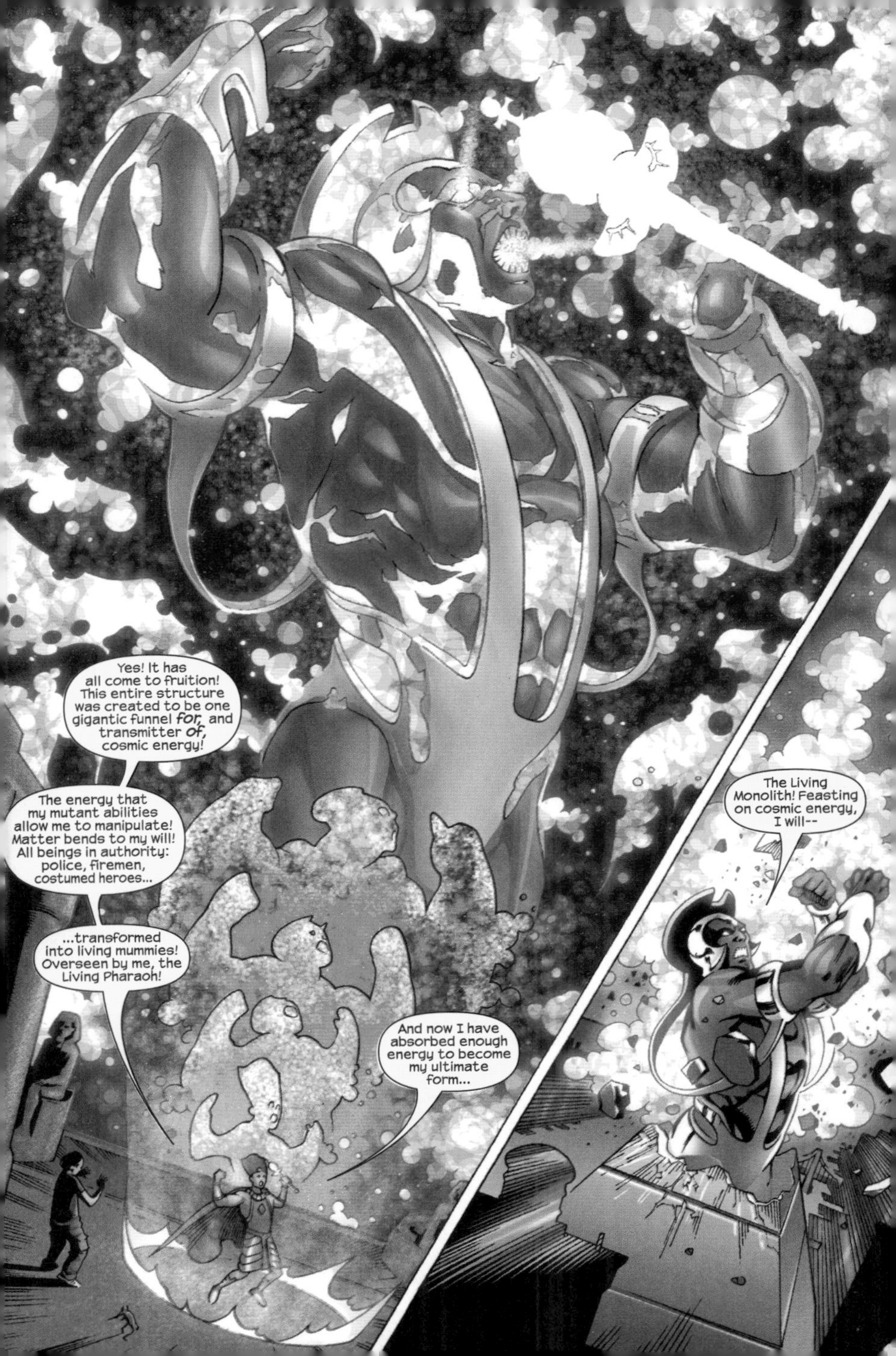
Yes! It has all come to fruition! This entire structure was created to be one gigantic funnel *for*, and transmitter *of*, cosmic energy!
The energy that my mutant abilities allow me to manipulate! Matter bends to my will! All beings in authority: police, firemen, costumed heroes...
...transformed into living mummies! Overseen by me, the Living Pharaoh!
And now I have absorbed enough energy to become my ultimate form...
The Living Monolith! Feasting on cosmic energy, I will--

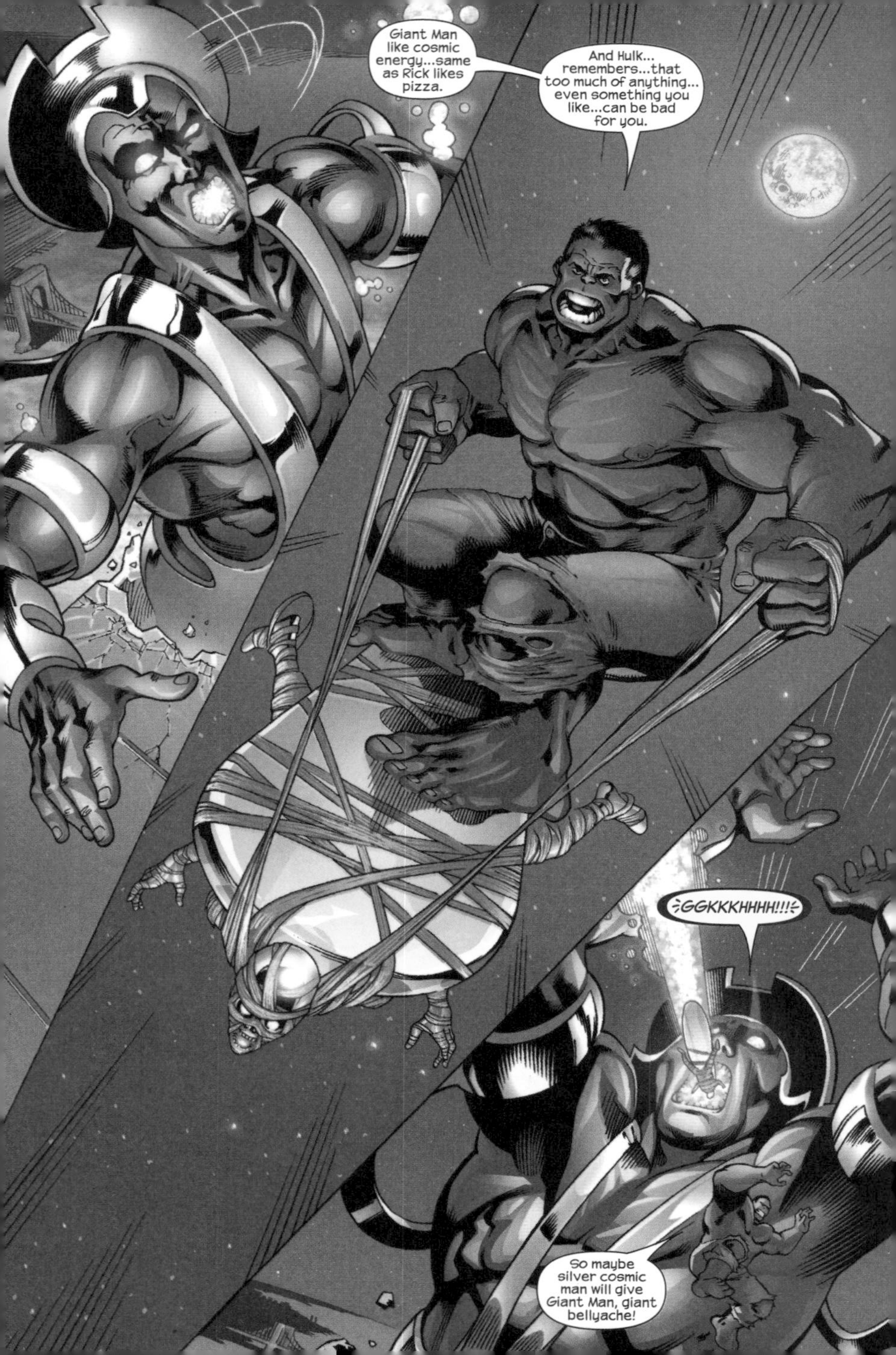
Giant Man like cosmic energy...same as Rick likes pizza.
And Hulk... remembers...that too much of anything... even something you like...can be bad for you.
GGKKKHHHH!!!
So maybe silver cosmic man will give Giant Man, giant bellyache!

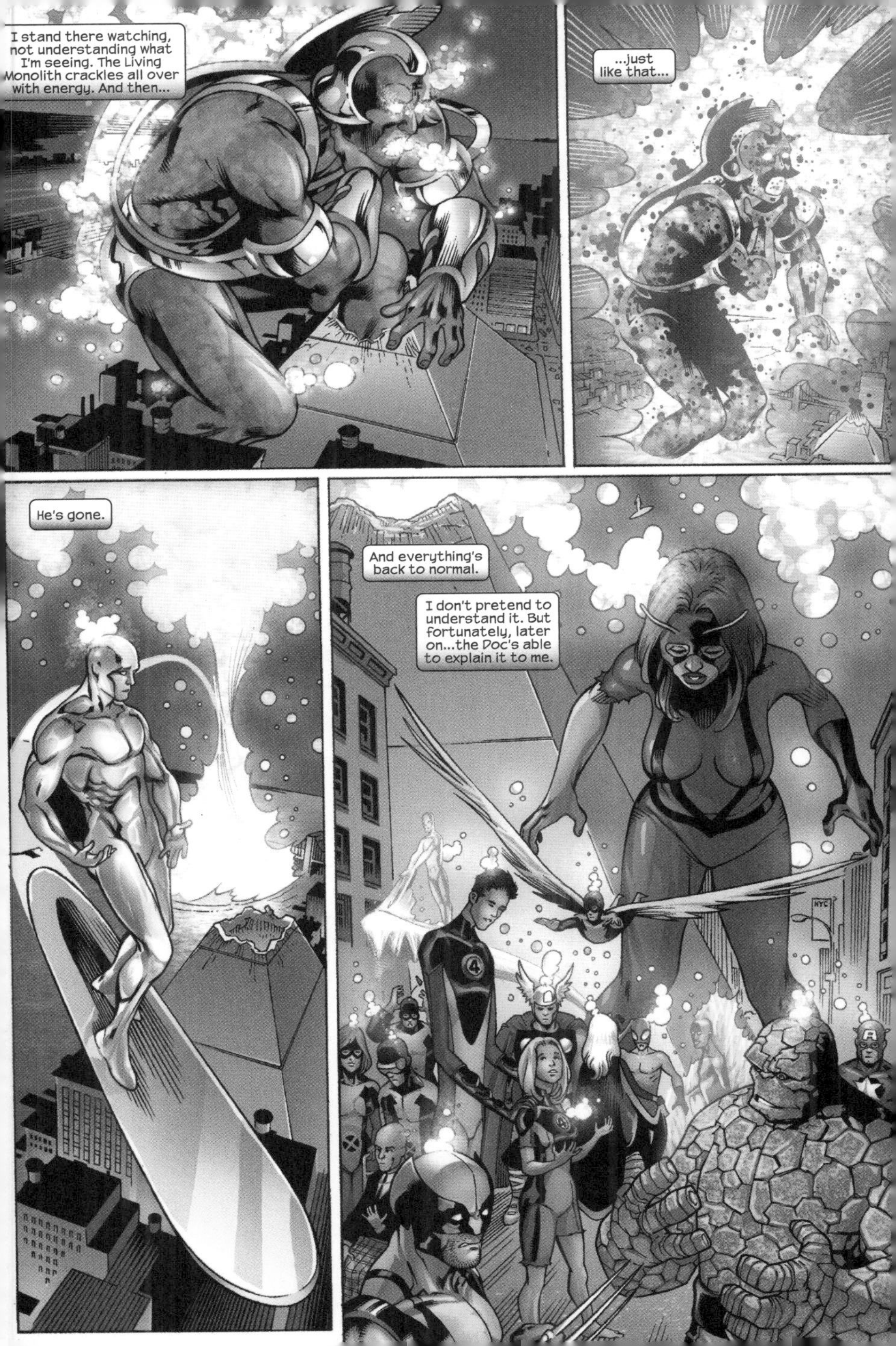

I stand there watching, not understanding what I'm seeing. The Living Monolith crackles all over with energy. And then...
...just like that...
He's gone.
And everything's back to normal.
I don't pretend to understand it. But fortunately, later on...the Doc's able to explain it to me.

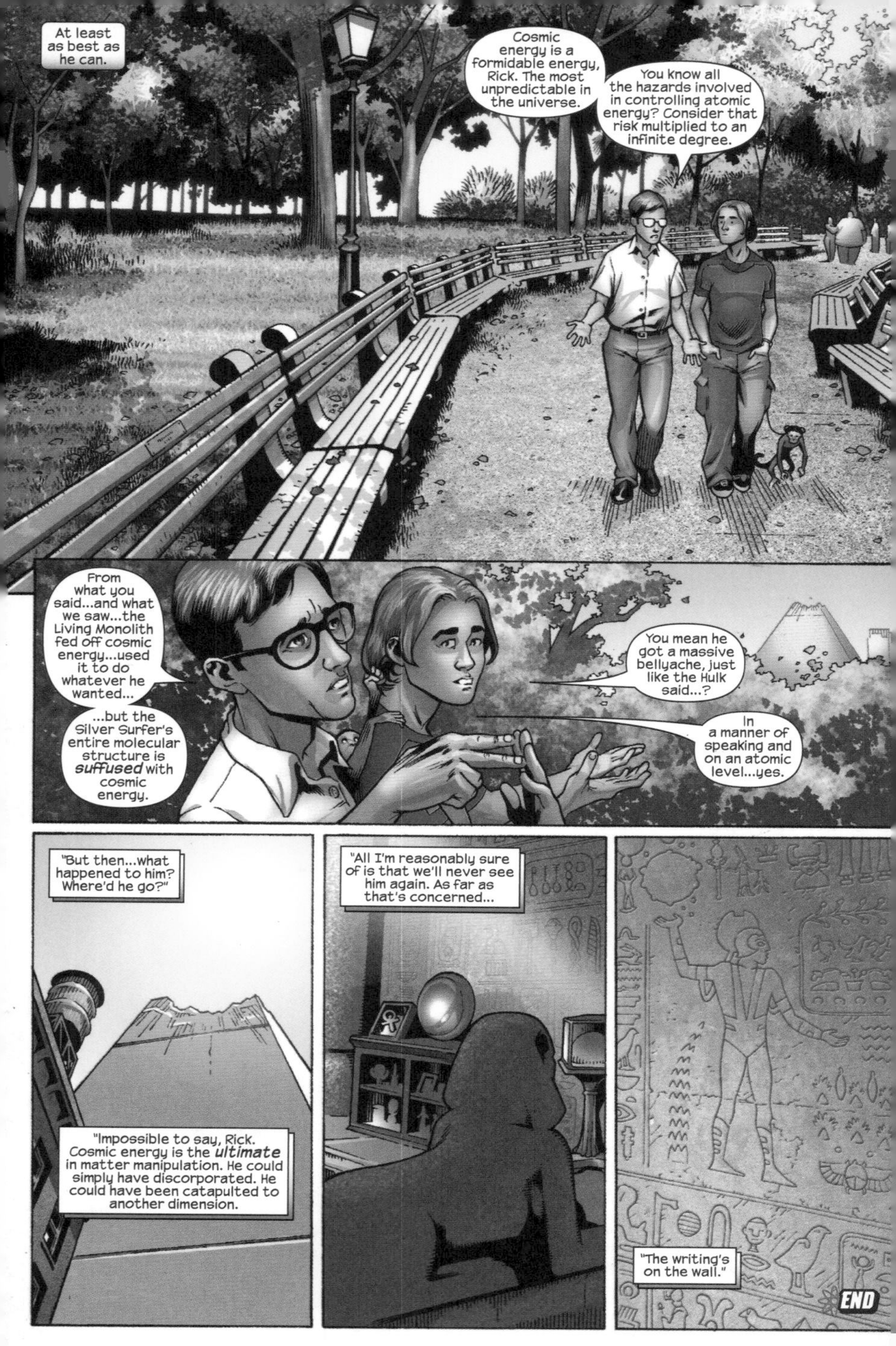

At least as best as he can.
Cosmic energy is a formidable energy, Rick. The most unpredictable in the universe.
You know all the hazards involved in controlling atomic energy? Consider that risk multiplied to an infinite degree.
From what you said...and what we saw...the Living Monolith fed off cosmic energy...used it to do whatever he wanted...
...but the Silver Surfer's entire molecular structure is *suffused* with cosmic energy.
You mean he got a massive bellyache, just like the Hulk said...?
In a manner of speaking and on an atomic level...yes.
"But then...what happened to him? Where'd he go?"
"Impossible to say, Rick. Cosmic energy is the *ultimate* in matter manipulation. He could simply have discorporated. He could have been catapulted to another dimension.
"All I'm reasonably sure of is that we'll never see him again. As far as that's concerned...
"The writing's on the wall."
END

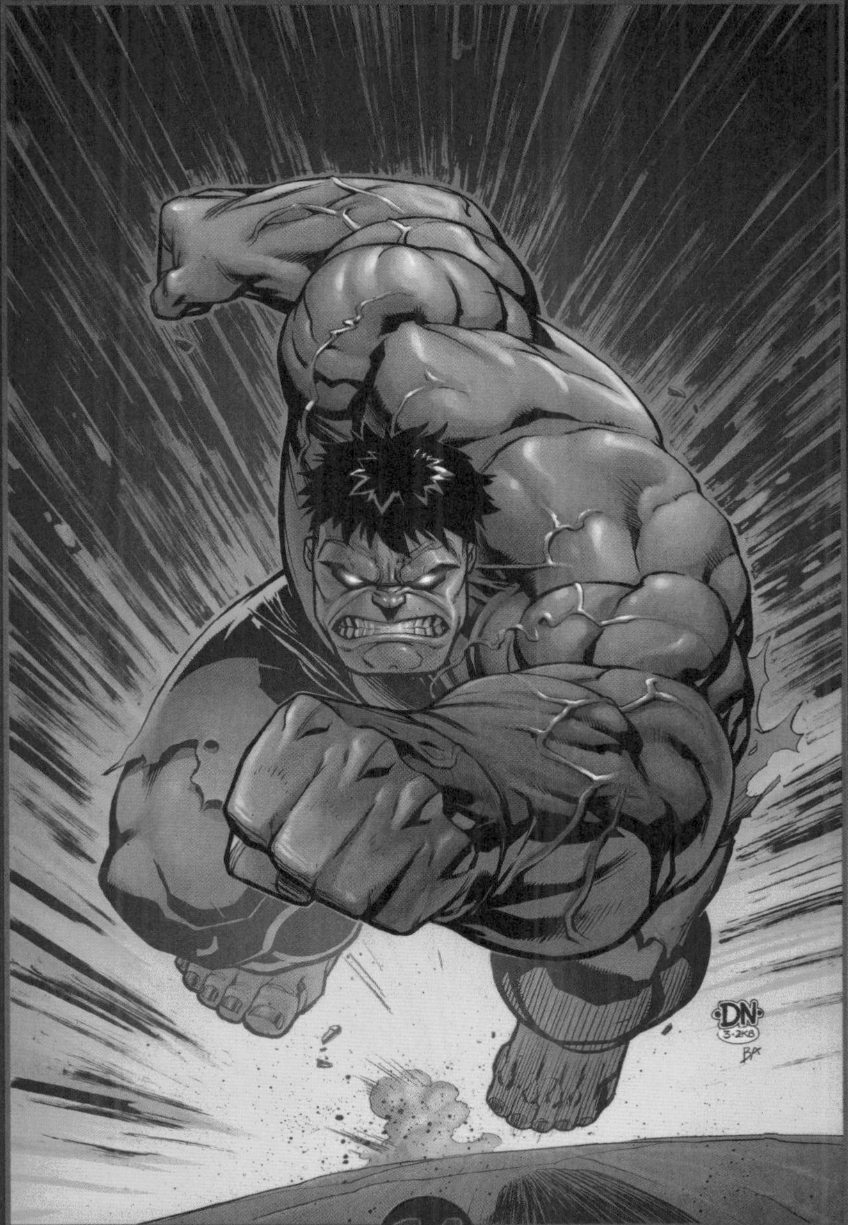

14

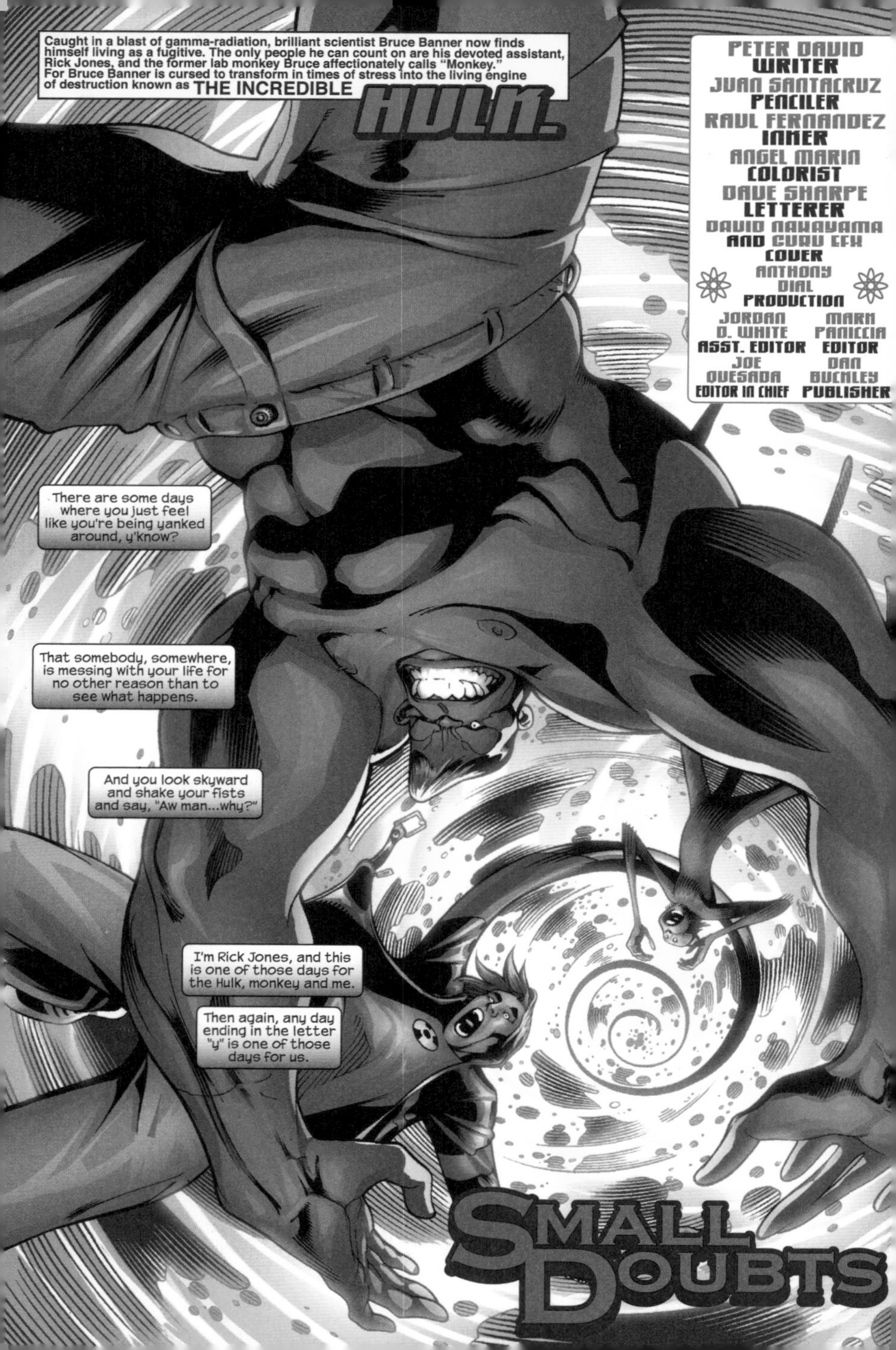
Caught in a blast of gamma-radiation, brilliant scientist Bruce Banner now finds himself living as a fugitive. The only people he can count on are his devoted assistant, Rick Jones, and the former lab monkey Bruce affectionately calls "Monkey." For Bruce Banner is cursed to transform in times of stress into the living engine of destruction known as THE INCREDIBLE HULK.
PETER DAVID WRITER
JUAN SANTACRUZ PENCILER
RAUL FERNANDEZ INKER
ANGEL MARIN COLORIST
DAVE SHARPE LETTERER
DAVID NAKAYAMA AND GURU EFX COVER
ANTHONY DIAL PRODUCTION
JORDAN D. WHITE ASST. EDITOR
MARK PANICCIA EDITOR
JOE QUESADA EDITOR IN CHIEF
DAN BUCKLEY PUBLISHER
There are some days where you just feel like you're being yanked around, y'know?
That somebody, somewhere, is messing with your life for no other reason than to see what happens.
And you look skyward and shake your fists and say, "Aw man...why?"
I'm Rick Jones, and this is one of those days for the Hulk, monkey and me.
Then again, any day ending in the letter "y" is one of those days for us.
SMALL DOUBTS

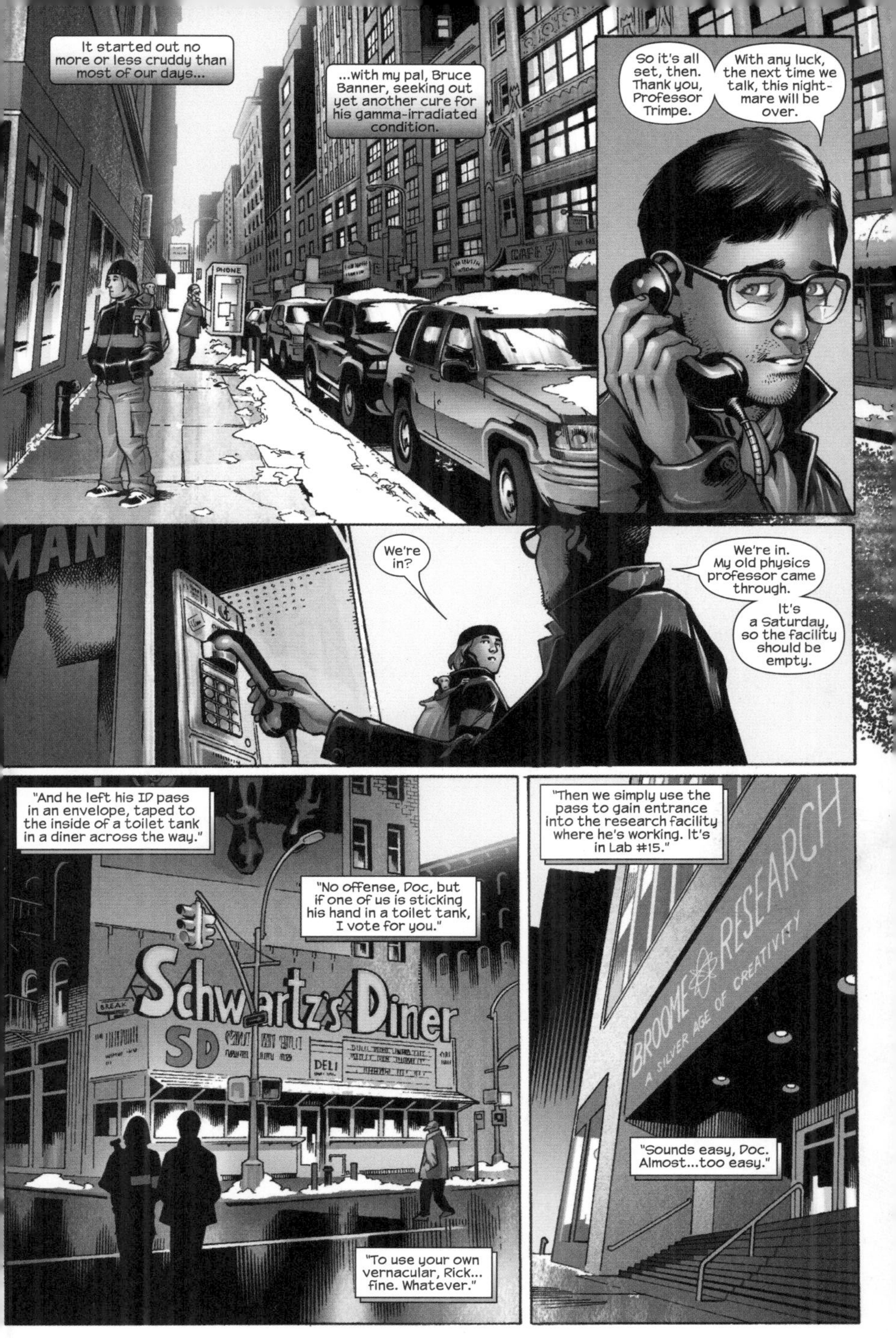
It started out no more or less cruddy than most of our days...
...with my pal, Bruce Banner, seeking out yet another cure for his gamma-irradiated condition.
PHONE
So it's all set, then. Thank you, Professor Trimpe.
With any luck, the next time we talk, this night-mare will be over.
We're in?
We're in. My old physics professor came through.
It's a Saturday, so the facility should be empty.
"And he left his ID pass in an envelope, taped to the inside of a toilet tank in a diner across the way."
"No offense, Doc, but if one of us is sticking his hand in a toilet tank, I vote for you."
Schwartz's Diner
SD
DELI
"To use your own vernacular, Rick... fine. Whatever."
"Then we simply use the pass to gain entrance into the research facility where he's working. It's in Lab #15."
BROOME RESEARCH
A SILVER AGE OF CREATIVITY
"Sounds easy, Doc. Almost...too easy."

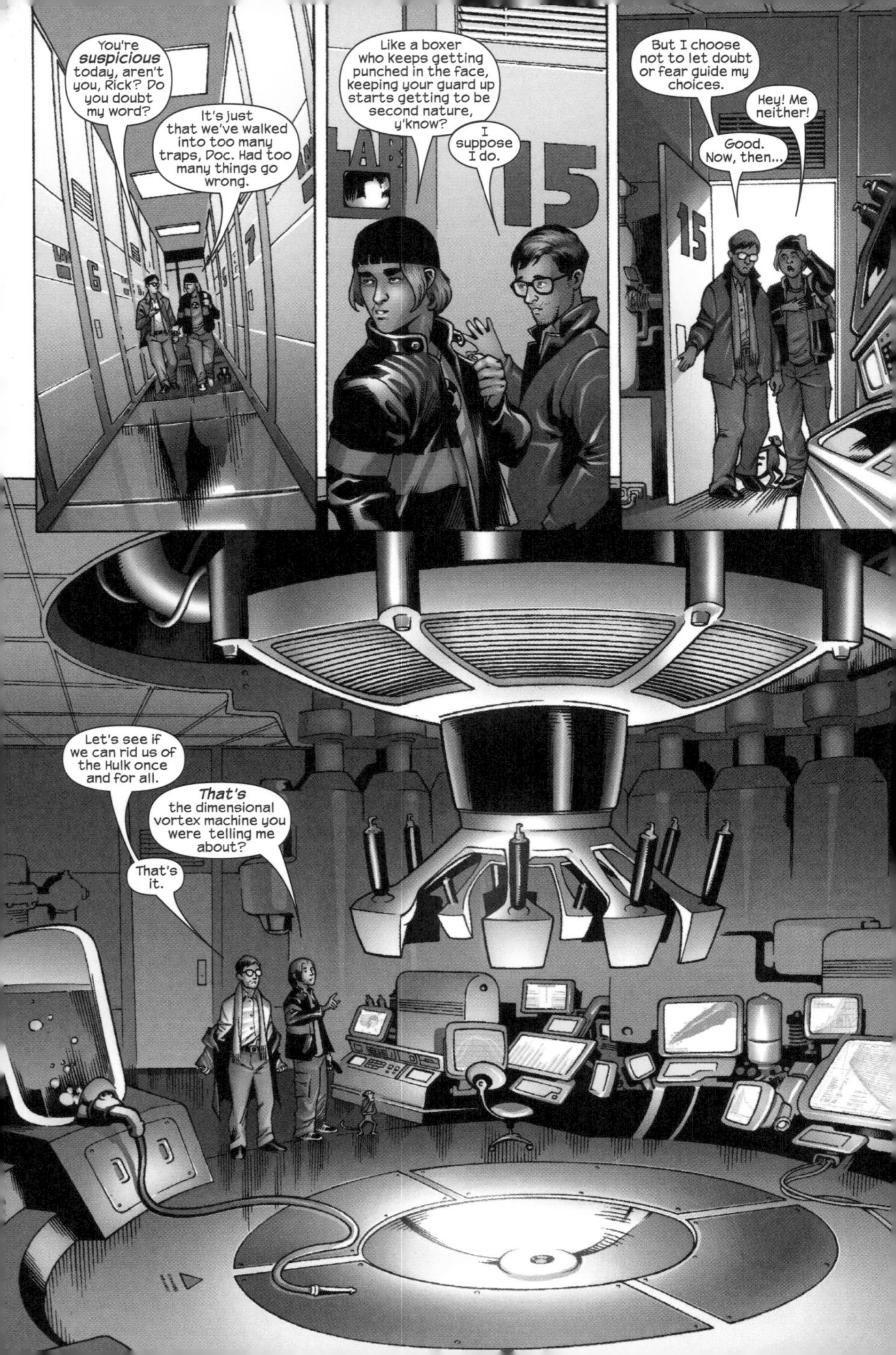
You're *suspicious* today, aren't you, Rick? Do you doubt my word?
It's just that we've walked into too many traps, Doc. Had too many things go wrong.
Like a boxer who keeps getting punched in the face, keeping your guard up starts getting to be second nature, y'know?
I suppose I do.
LAB 15
But I choose not to let doubt or fear guide my choices.
Hey! Me neither!
Good. Now, then...
Let's see if we can rid us of the Hulk once and for all.
*That's* the dimensional vortex machine you were telling me about?
That's it.

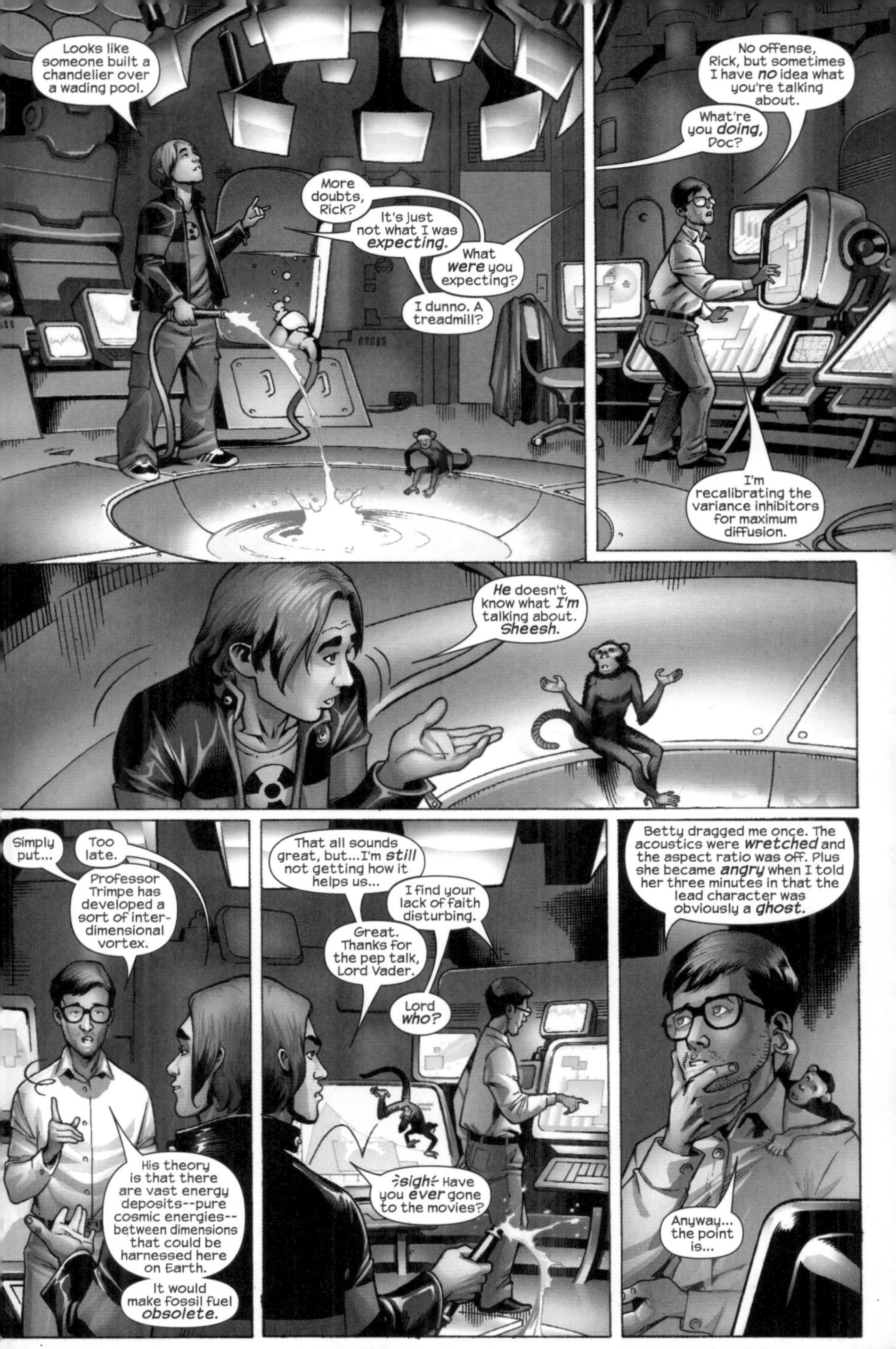
Looks like someone built a chandelier over a wading pool.
More doubts, Rick?
It's just not what I was *expecting.*
What *were* you expecting?
I dunno. A treadmill?
No offense, Rick, but sometimes I have *no* idea what you're talking about.
What're you *doing,* Doc?
I'm recalibrating the variance inhibitors for maximum diffusion.
*He* doesn't know what *I'm* talking about. *Sheesh.*
Simply put...
Too late.
Professor Trimpe has developed a sort of inter-dimensional vortex.
His theory is that there are vast energy deposits--pure cosmic energies--between dimensions that could be harnessed here on Earth.
It would make fossil fuel *obsolete.*
That all sounds great, but...I'm *still* not getting how it helps us...
I find your lack of faith disturbing.
Great. Thanks for the pep talk, Lord Vader.
Lord *who?*
*sigh* Have you *ever* gone to the movies?
Betty dragged me once. The acoustics were *wretched* and the aspect ratio was off. Plus she became *angry* when I told her three minutes in that the lead character was obviously a *ghost.*
Anyway... the point is...

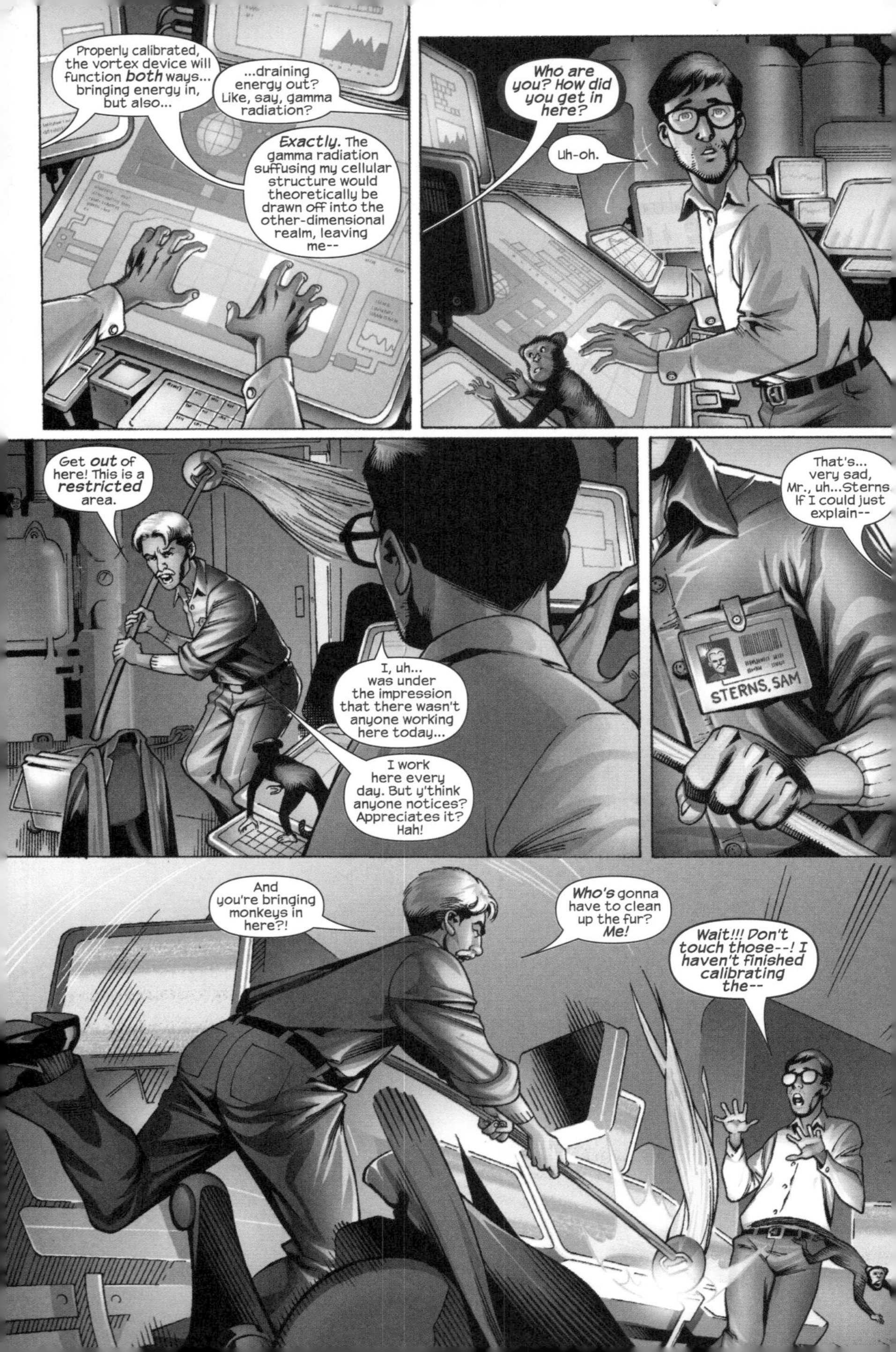
Properly calibrated, the vortex device will function *both* ways... bringing energy in, but also...
...draining energy out? Like, say, gamma radiation?
*Exactly.* The gamma radiation suffusing my cellular structure would theoretically be drawn off into the other-dimensional realm, leaving me--
*Who are you? How did you get in here?*
Uh-oh.
Get *out* of here! This is a *restricted* area.
I, uh... was under the impression that there wasn't anyone working here today...
I work here every day. But y'think anyone notices? Appreciates it? Hah!
That's... very sad, Mr., uh...Sterns. If I could just explain--
STERNS, SAM
And you're bringing monkeys in here?!
*Who's* gonna have to clean up the fur? *Me!*
*Wait!!! Don't touch those--! I haven't finished calibrating the--*

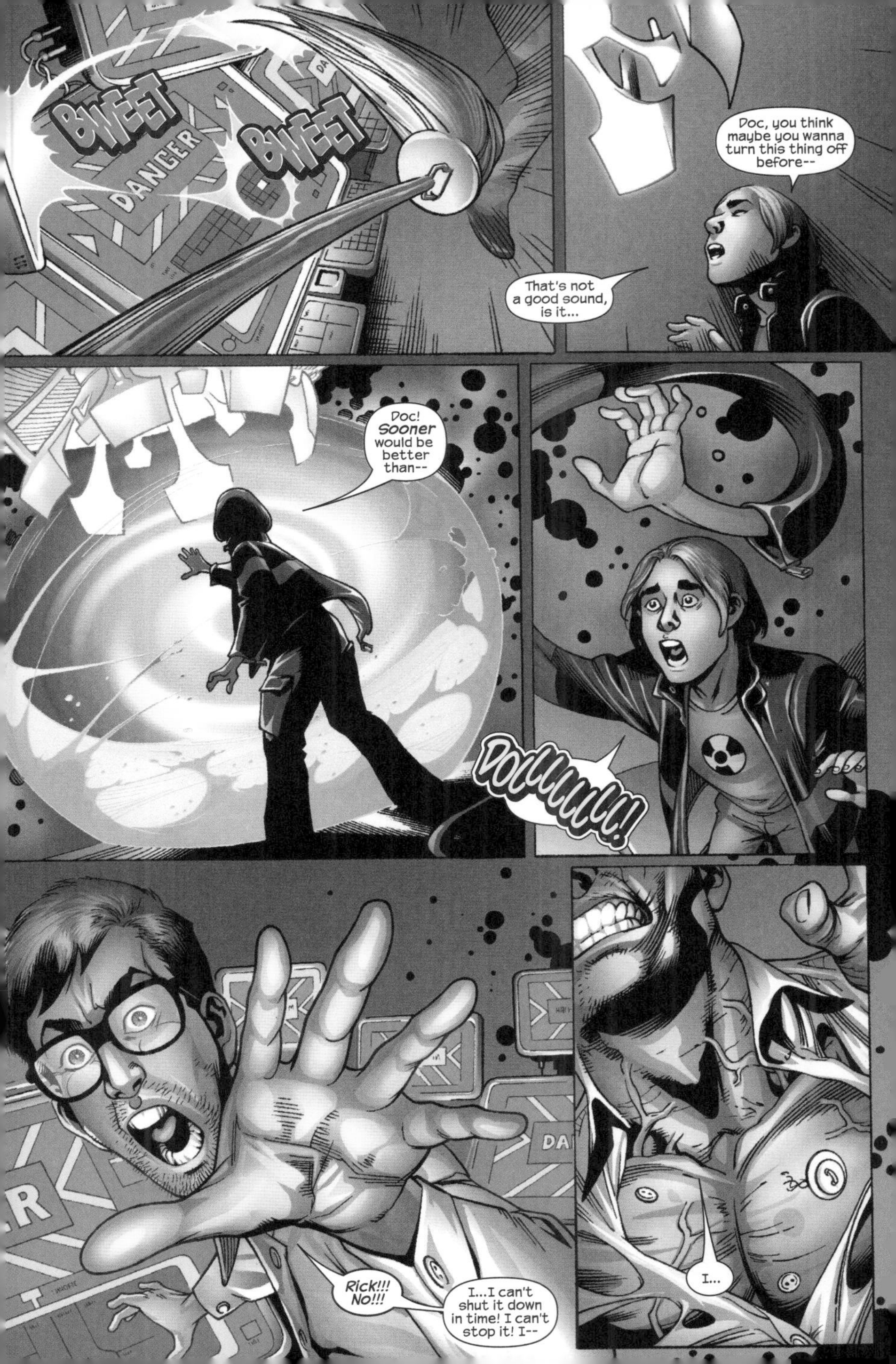
BWEET
BWEET
DANGER
Doc, you think maybe you wanna turn this thing off before--
That's not a good sound, is it...
Doc! *Sooner* would be better than--
DOLLLLLLL!
Rick!!! No!!!
I...I can't shut it down in time! I can't stop it! I--
I...

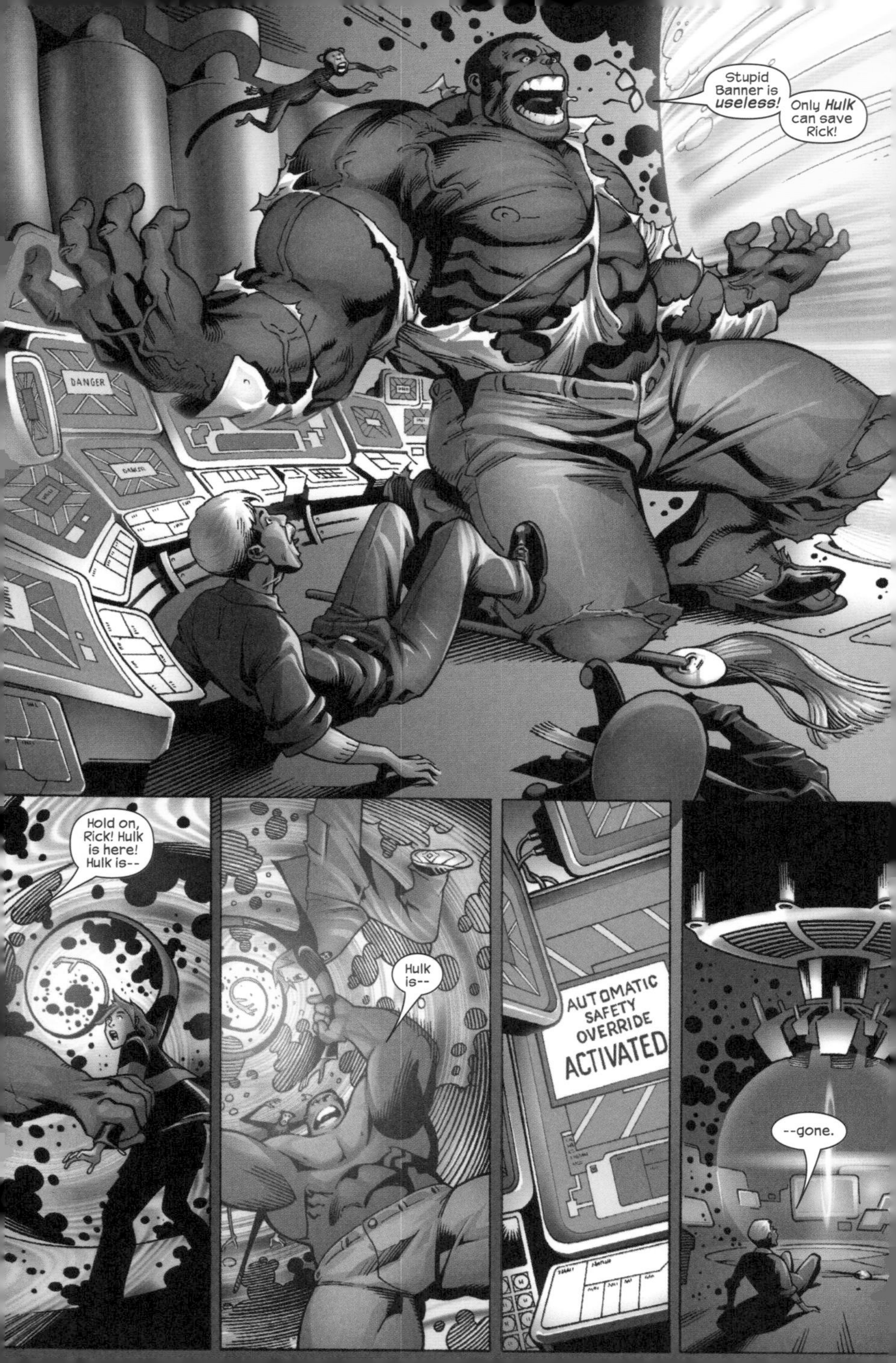
Stupid Banner is useless!
Only Hulk can save Rick!
DANGER
Hold on, Rick! Hulk is here! Hulk is--
Hulk is--
AUTOMATIC SAFETY OVERRIDE ACTIVATED
--gone.

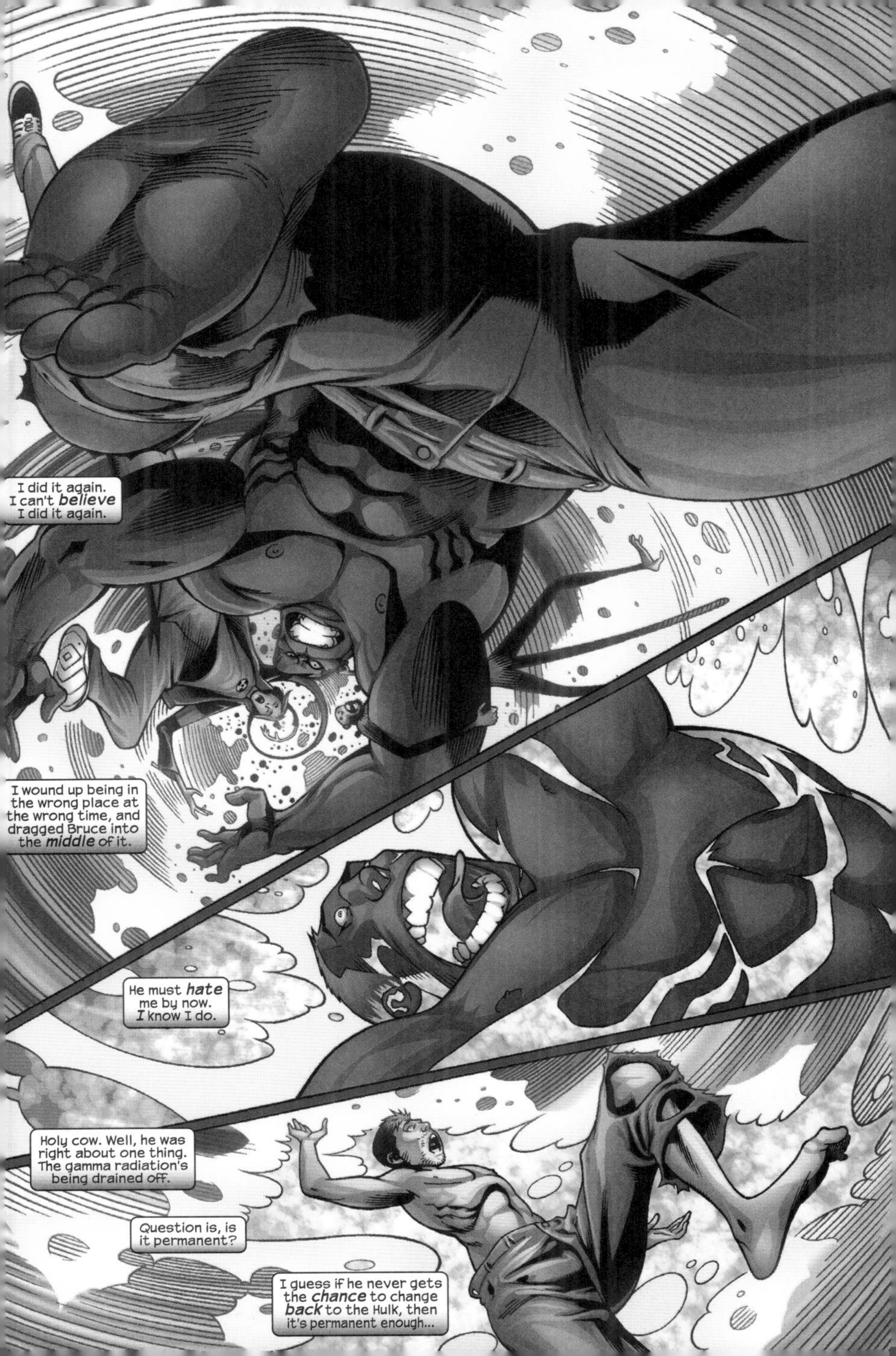

I did it again. I can't *believe* I did it again.
I wound up being in the wrong place at the wrong time, and dragged Bruce into the *middle* of it.
He must *hate* me by now. *I* know I do.
Holy cow. Well, he was right about one thing. The gamma radiation's being drained off.
Question is, is it permanent?
I guess if he never gets the *chance* to change *back* to the Hulk, then it's permanent enough...

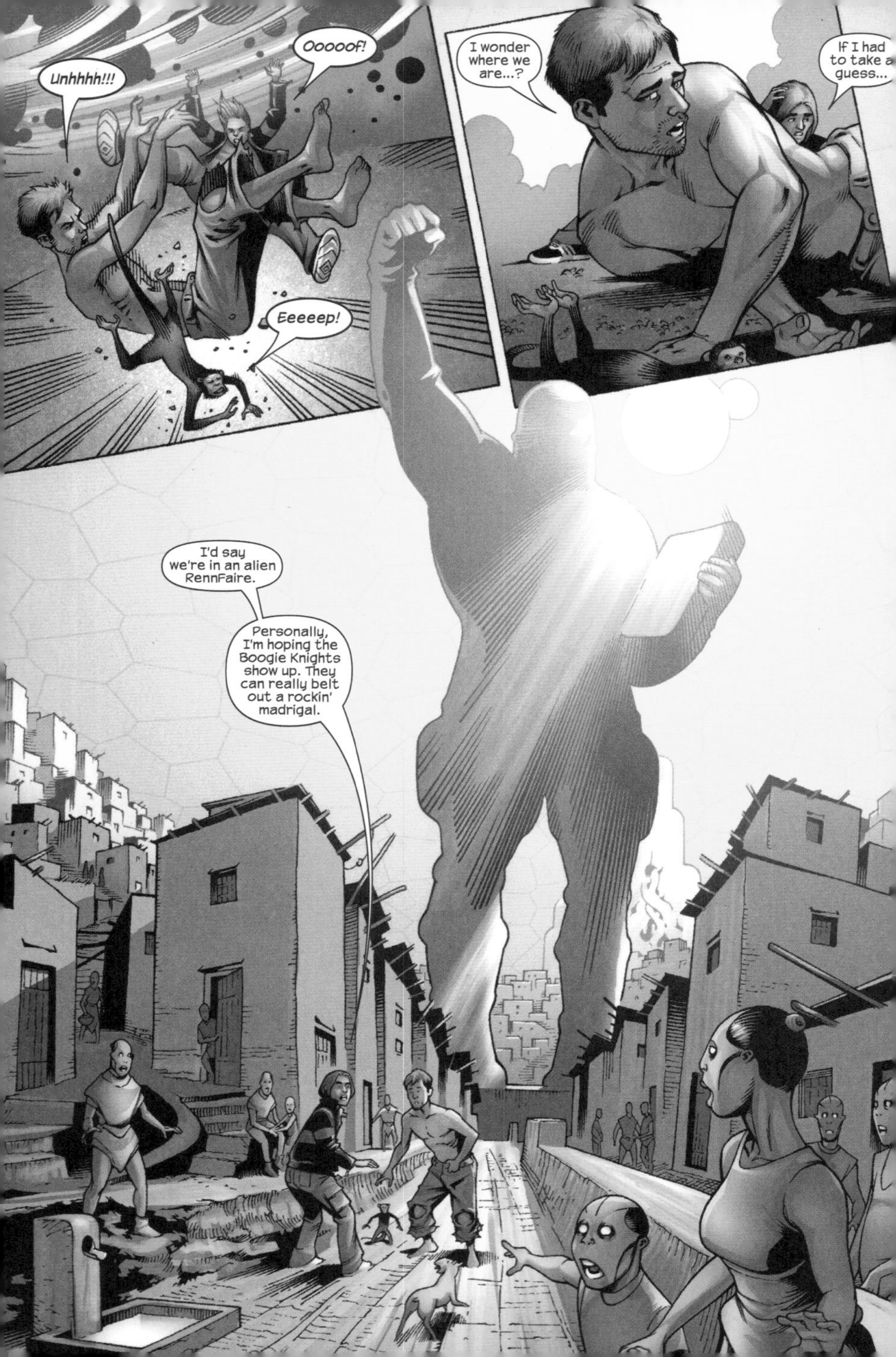
Unhhhh!!!
Oooooof!
Eeeeep!
I wonder where we are...?
If I had to take a guess...
I'd say we're in an alien RennFaire.
Personally, I'm hoping the Boogie Knights show up. They can really belt out a rockin' madrigal.

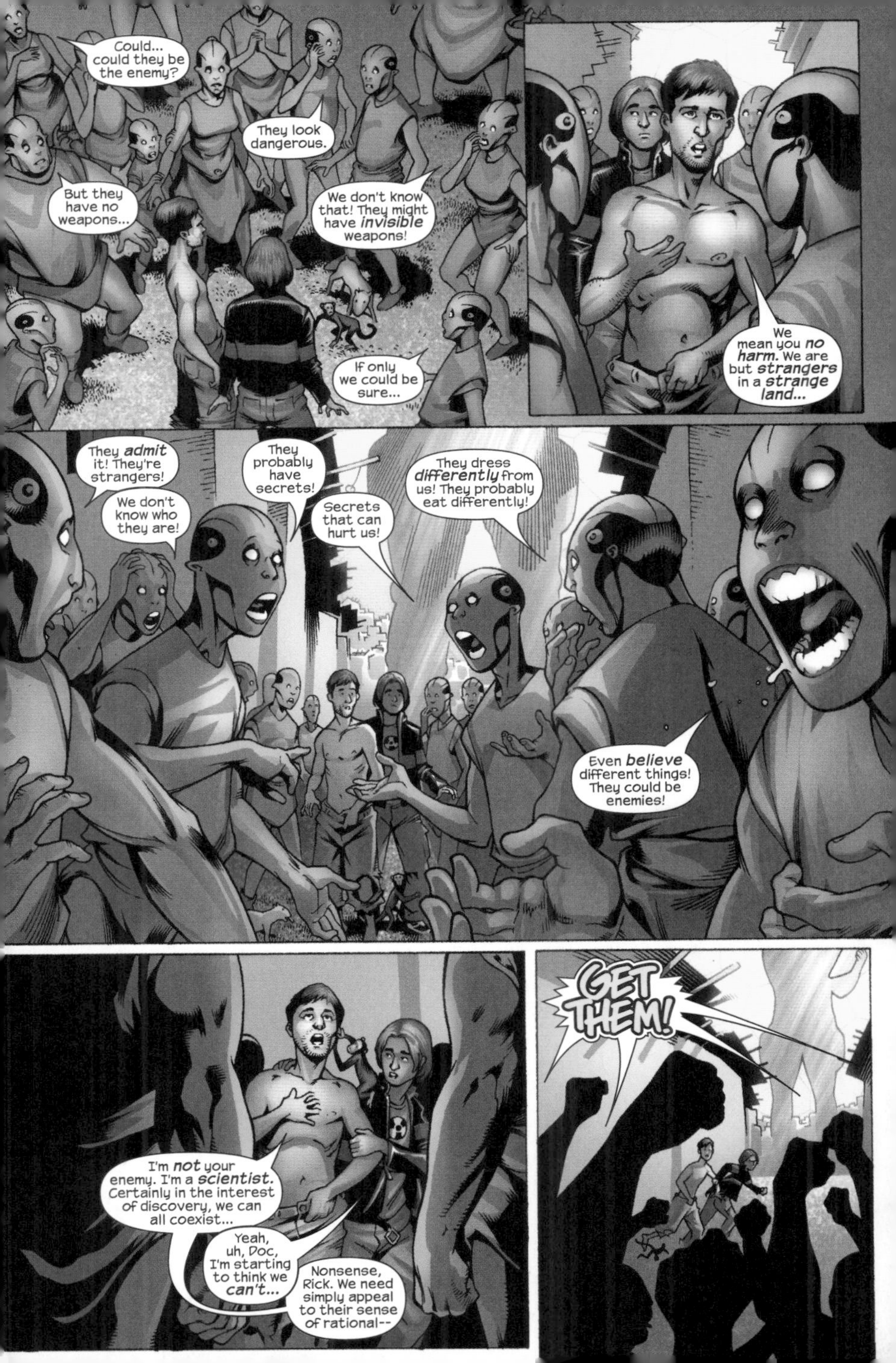
Could... could they be the enemy?
They look dangerous.
But they have no weapons...
We don't know that! They might have invisible weapons!
If only we could be sure...
We mean you no harm. We are but strangers in a strange land...
They admit it! They're strangers!
We don't know who they are!
They probably have secrets!
Secrets that can hurt us!
They dress differently from us! They probably eat differently!
Even believe different things! They could be enemies!
I'm not your enemy. I'm a scientist. Certainly in the interest of discovery, we can all coexist...
Yeah, uh, Doc, I'm starting to think we can't...
Nonsense, Rick. We need simply appeal to their sense of rational--
GET THEM!

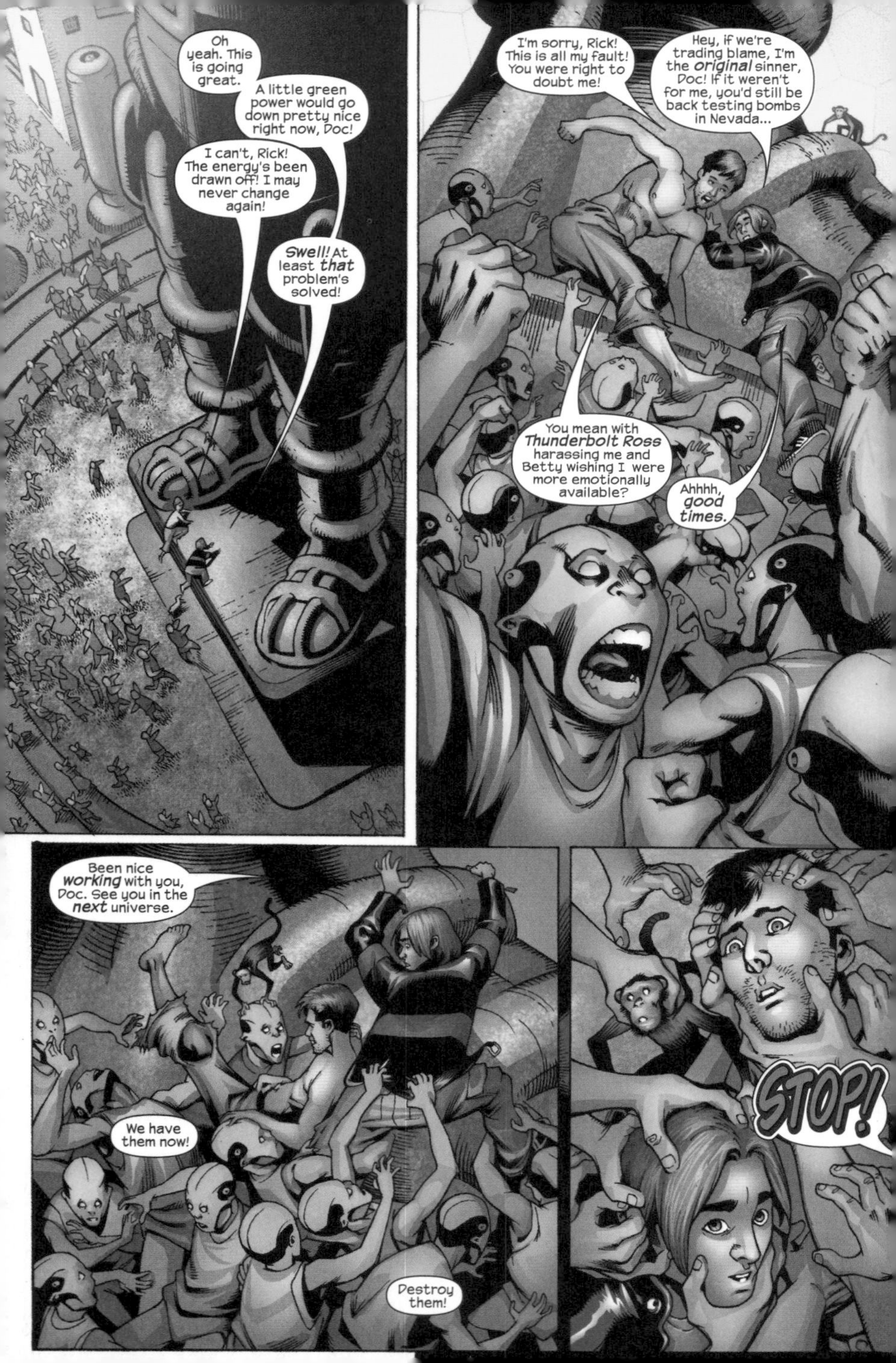

Oh yeah. This is going great.
A little green power would go down pretty nice right now, Doc!
I can't, Rick! The energy's been drawn off! I may never change again!
Swell! At least that problem's solved!
I'm sorry, Rick! This is all my fault! You were right to doubt me!
Hey, if we're trading blame, I'm the original sinner, Doc! If it weren't for me, you'd still be back testing bombs in Nevada...
You mean with Thunderbolt Ross harassing me and Betty wishing I were more emotionally available?
Ahhhh, good times.
Been nice working with you, Doc. See you in the next universe.
We have them now!
Destroy them!
STOP!

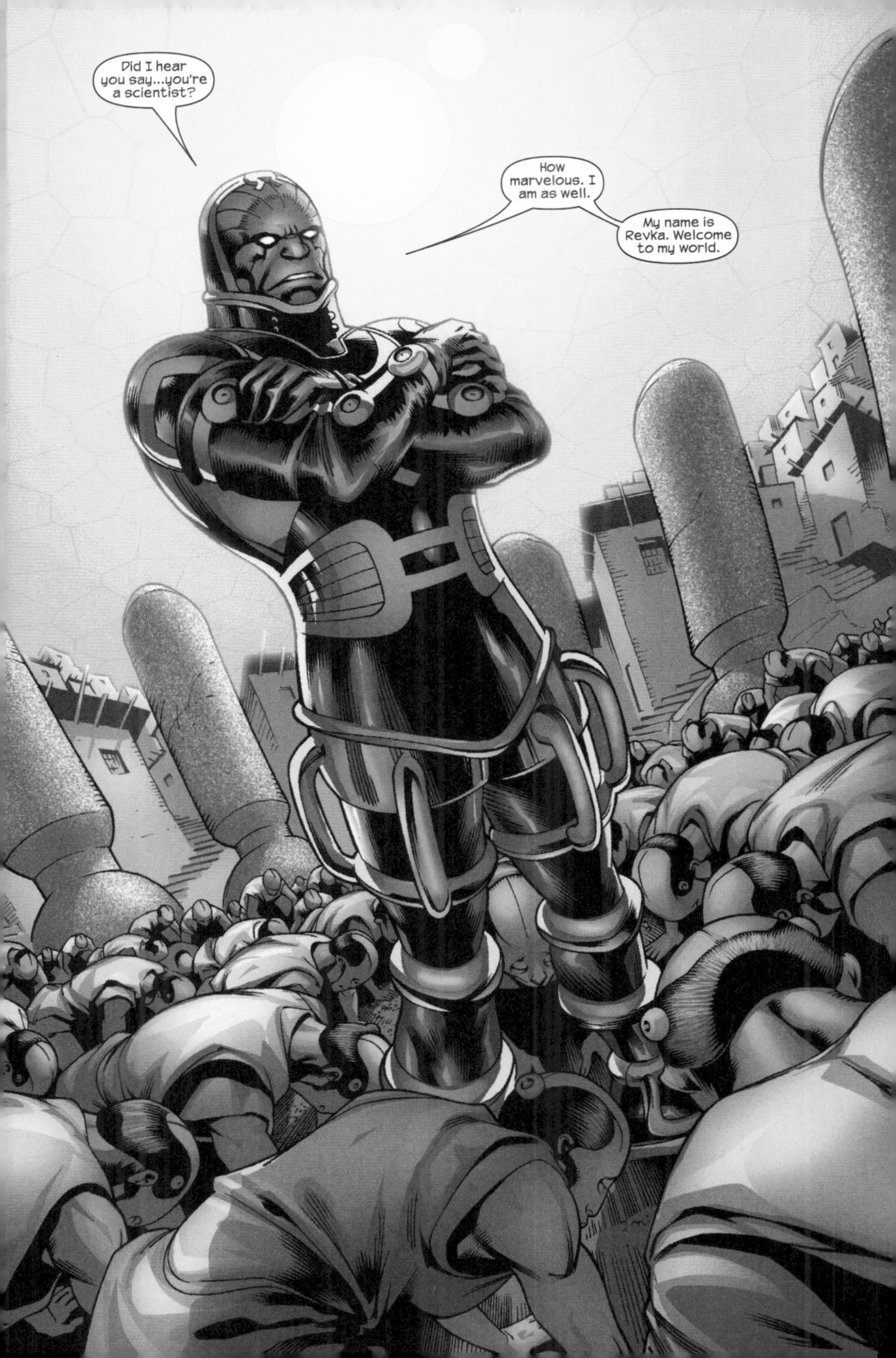
Did I hear you say...you're a scientist?
How marvelous. I am as well.
My name is Revka. Welcome to my world.

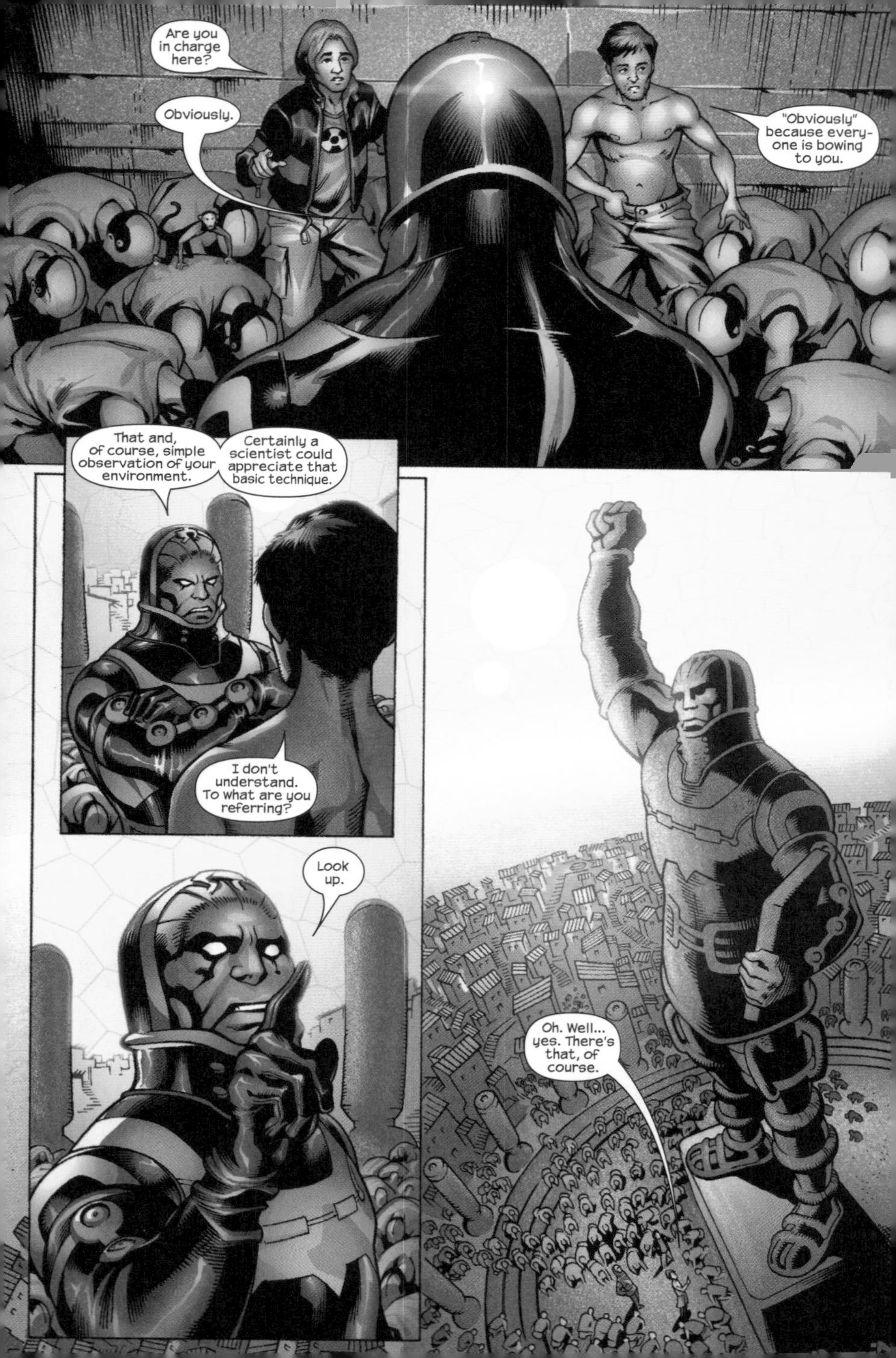
Are you in charge here?
Obviously.
"Obviously" because every-one is bowing to you.
That and, of course, simple observation of your environment.
Certainly a scientist could appreciate that basic technique.
I don't understand. To what are you referring?
Look up.
Oh. Well... yes. There's that, of course.

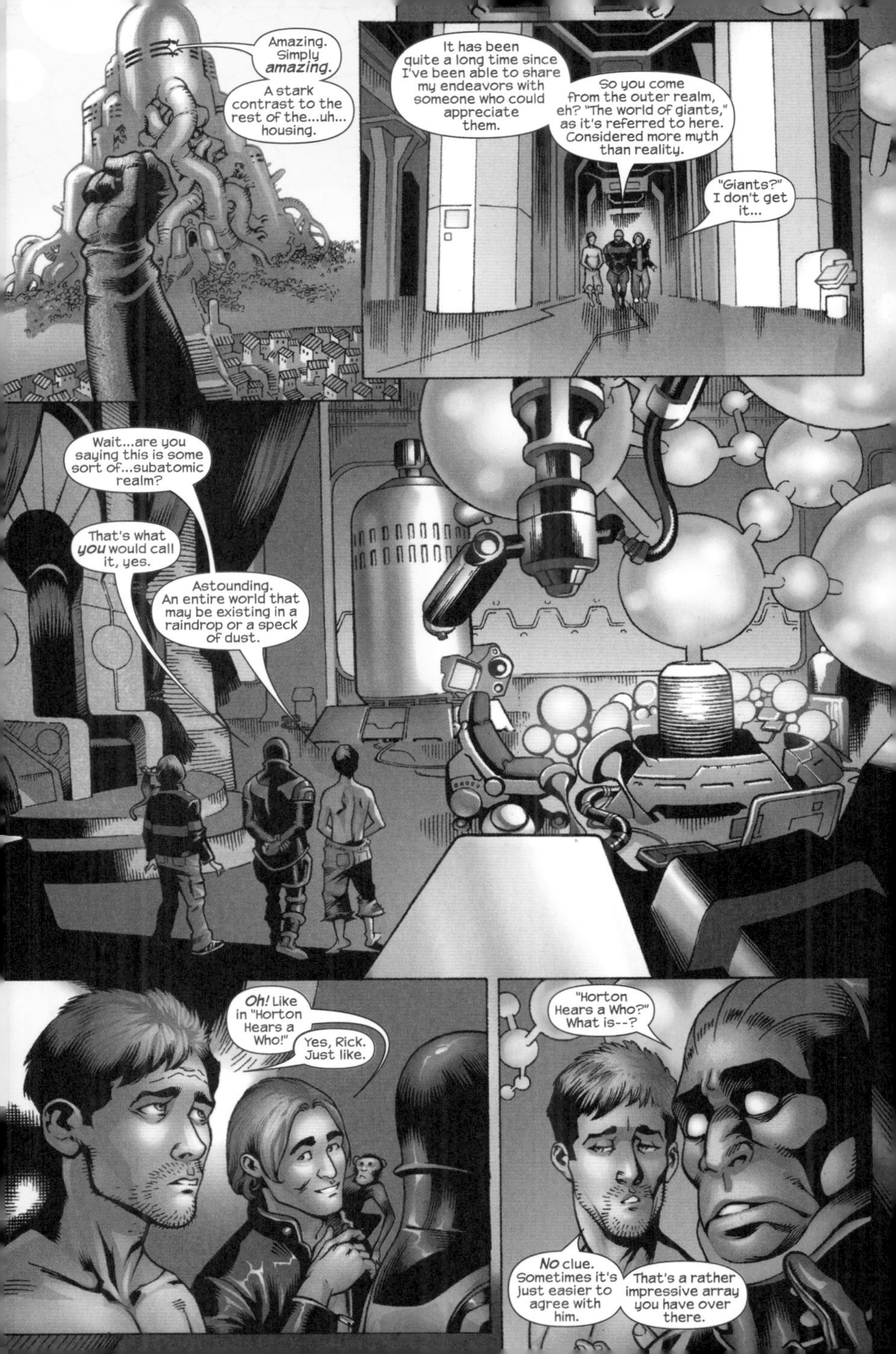

Amazing. Simply *amazing.*
A stark contrast to the rest of the...uh... housing.
It has been quite a long time since I've been able to share my endeavors with someone who could appreciate them.
So you come from the outer realm, eh? "The world of giants," as it's referred to here. Considered more myth than reality.
"Giants?" I don't get it...
Wait...are you saying this is some sort of...subatomic realm?
That's what *you* would call it, yes.
Astounding. An entire world that may be existing in a raindrop or a speck of dust.
*Oh!* Like in "Horton Hears a Who!"
Yes, Rick. Just like.
"Horton Hears a Who?" What is--?
*No* clue. Sometimes it's just easier to agree with him.
That's a rather impressive array you have over there.

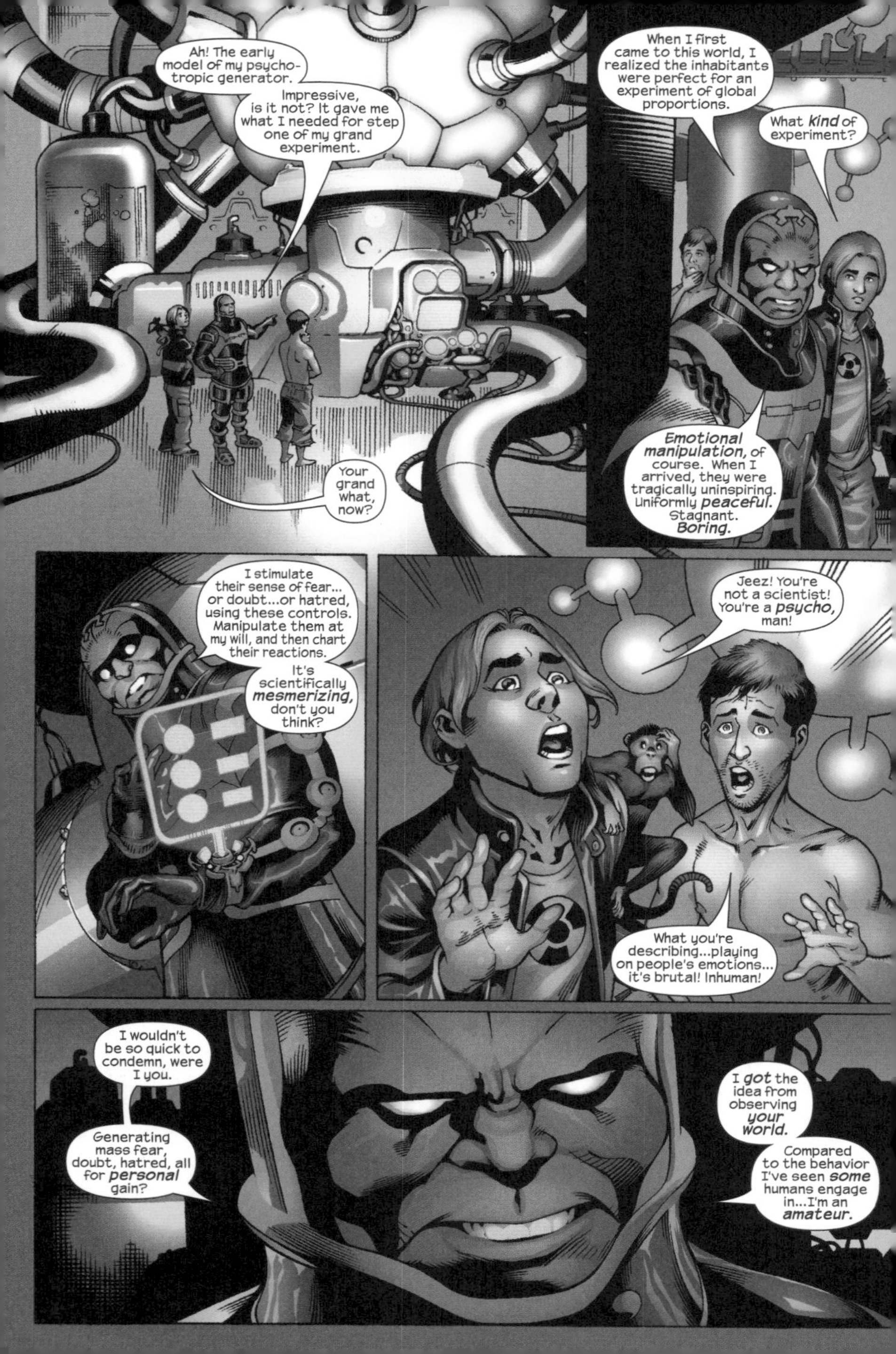
Ah! The early model of my psycho-tropic generator.
Impressive, is it not? It gave me what I needed for step one of my grand experiment.
Your grand what, now?
When I first came to this world, I realized the inhabitants were perfect for an experiment of global proportions.
What *kind* of experiment?
*Emotional manipulation*, of course. When I arrived, they were tragically uninspiring. Uniformly *peaceful.* Stagnant. *Boring.*
I stimulate their sense of fear... or doubt...or hatred, using these controls. Manipulate them at my will, and then chart their reactions.
It's scientifically *mesmerizing,* don't you think?
Jeez! You're not a scientist! You're a *psycho,* man!
What you're describing...playing on people's emotions... it's brutal! Inhuman!
I wouldn't be so quick to condemn, were I you.
Generating mass fear, doubt, hatred, all for *personal* gain?
I *got* the idea from observing *your world.*
Compared to the behavior I've seen *some* humans engage in...I'm an *amateur.*

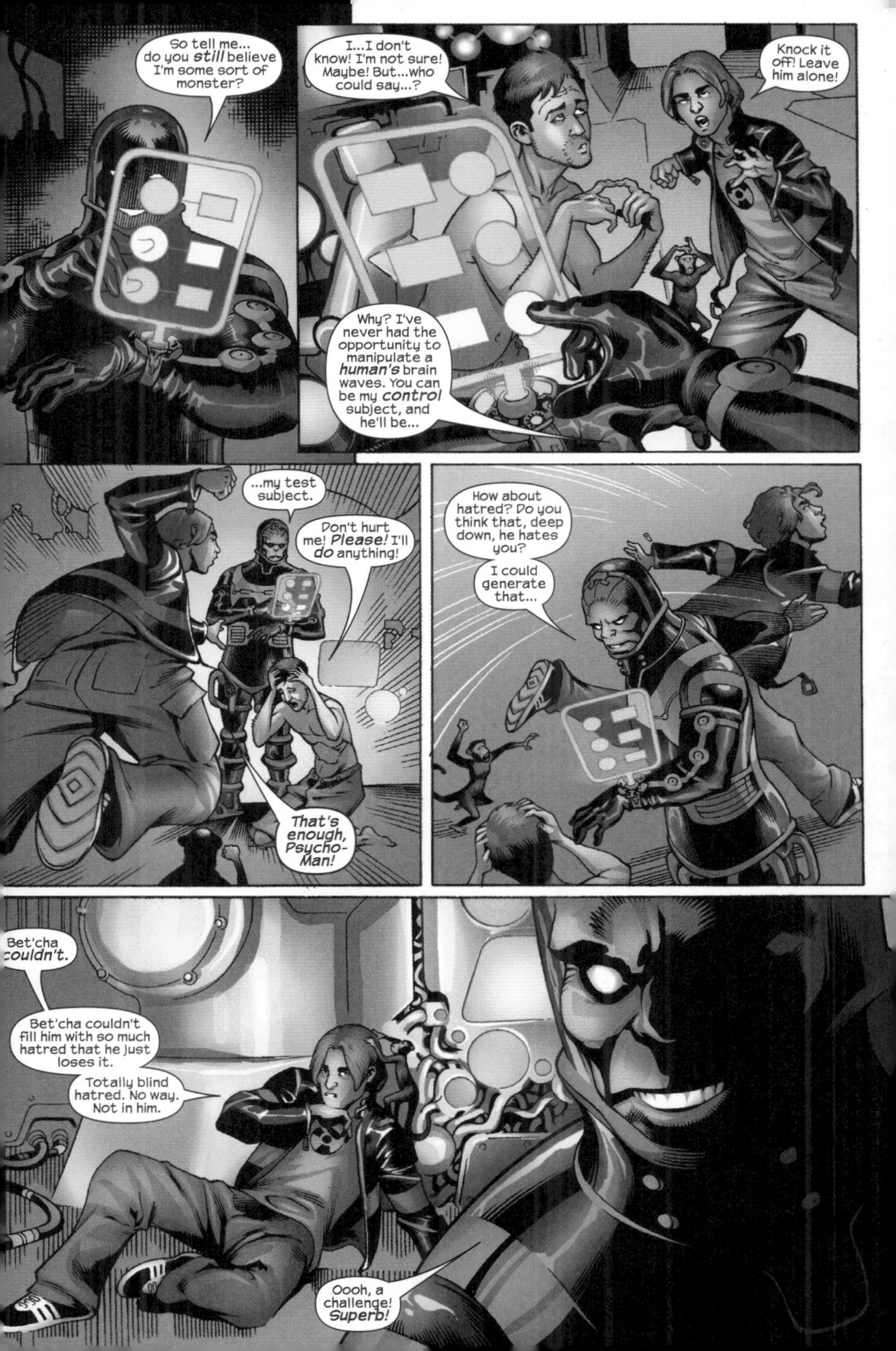
So tell me... do you *still* believe I'm some sort of monster?
I...I don't know! I'm not sure! Maybe! But...who could say...?
Knock it off! Leave him alone!
Why? I've never had the opportunity to manipulate a *human's* brain waves. You can be my *control* subject, and he'll be...
...my test subject.
Don't hurt me! *Please!* I'll *do* anything!
*That's enough, Psycho-Man!*
How about hatred? Do you think that, deep down, he hates you?
I could generate that...
Bet'cha ***couldn't.***
Bet'cha couldn't fill him with so much hatred that he just loses it.
Totally blind hatred. No way. Not in him.
Oooh, a challenge! ***Superb!***

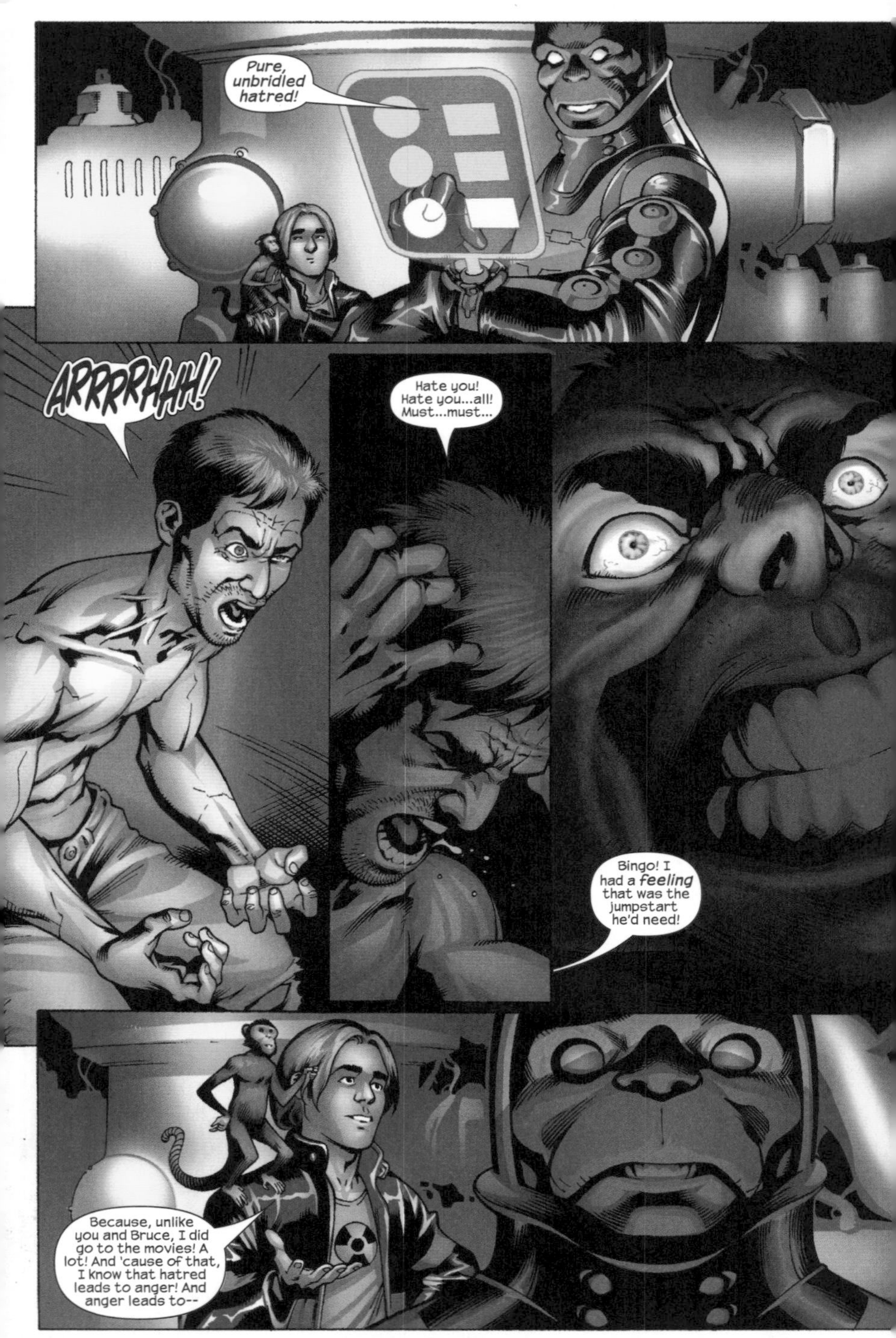
Pure, unbridled hatred!
ARRRRHHH!
Hate you! Hate you...all! Must...must...
Bingo! I had a *feeling* that was the jumpstart he'd need!
Because, unlike you and Bruce, I did go to the movies! A lot! And 'cause of that, I know that hatred leads to anger! And anger leads to--

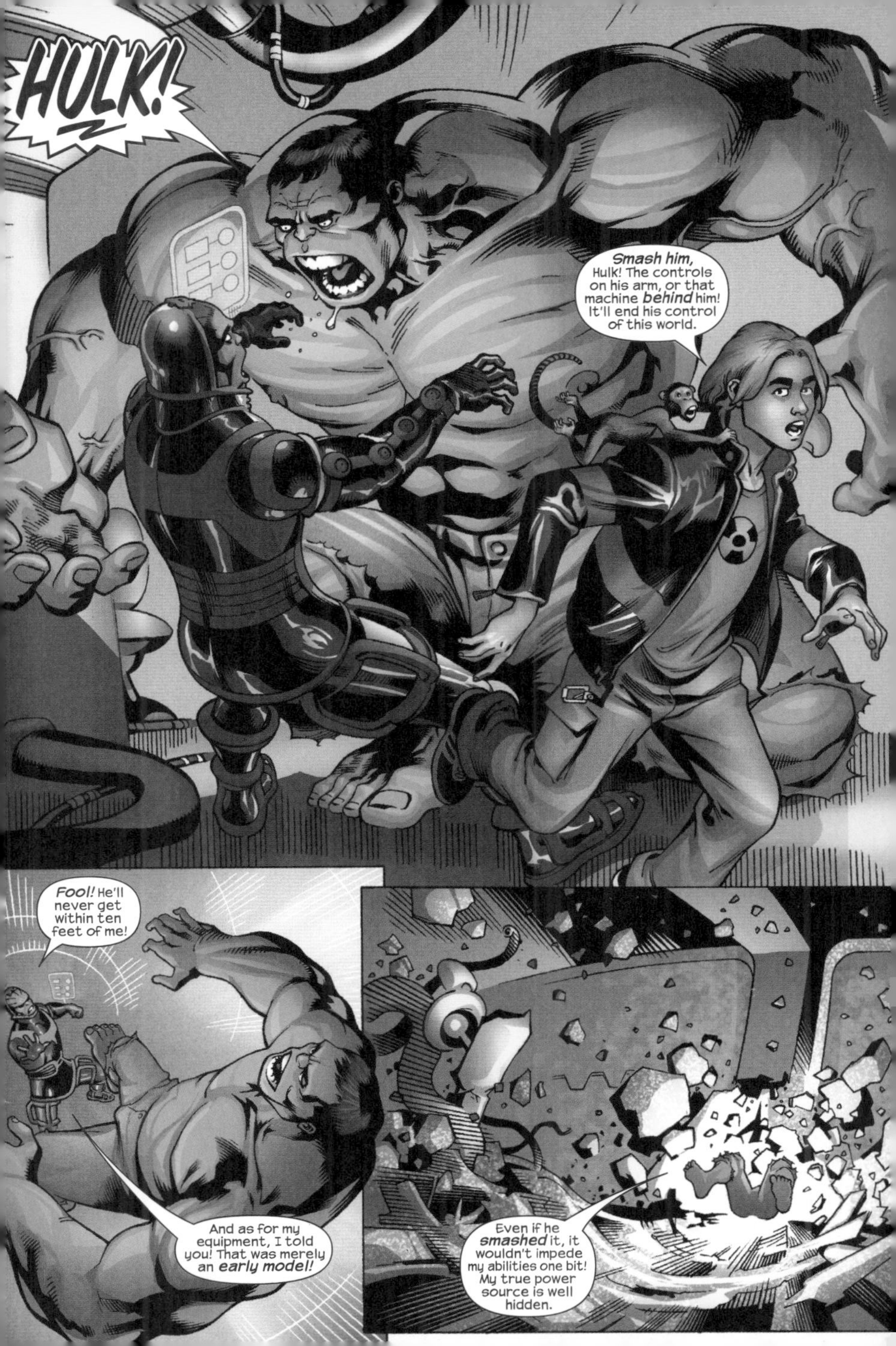
HULK!
Smash him, Hulk! The controls on his arm, or that machine behind him! It'll end his control of this world.
Fool! He'll never get within ten feet of me!
And as for my equipment, I told you! That was merely an early model!
Even if he smashed it, it wouldn't impede my abilities one bit! My true power source is well hidden.

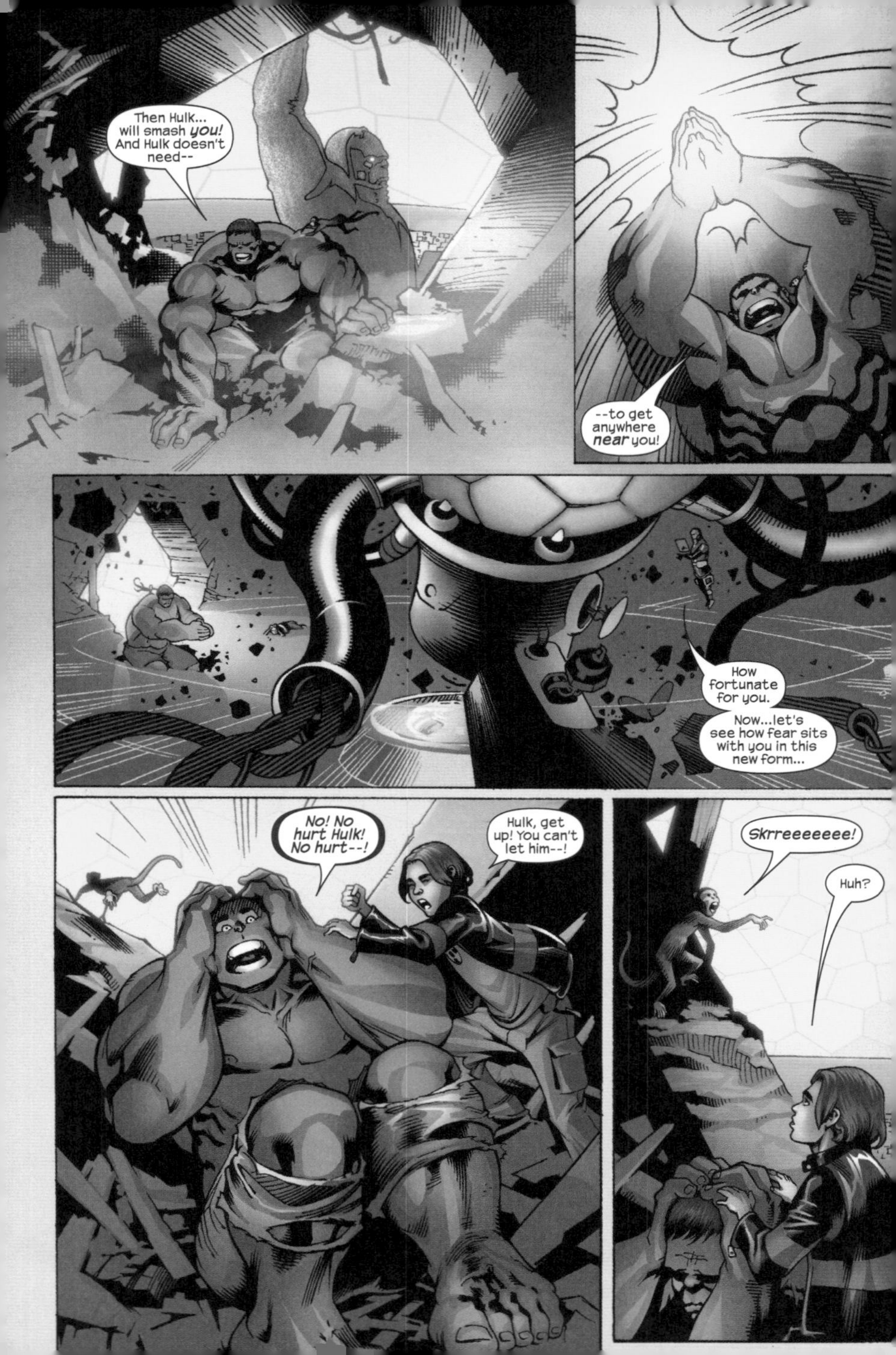
Then Hulk... will smash *you!* And Hulk doesn't need--
--to get anywhere *near* you!
How fortunate for you.
Now...let's see how fear sits with you in this new form...
*No! No hurt Hulk! No hurt--!*
Hulk, get up! You can't let him--!
*Skrreeeeeeee!*
Huh?

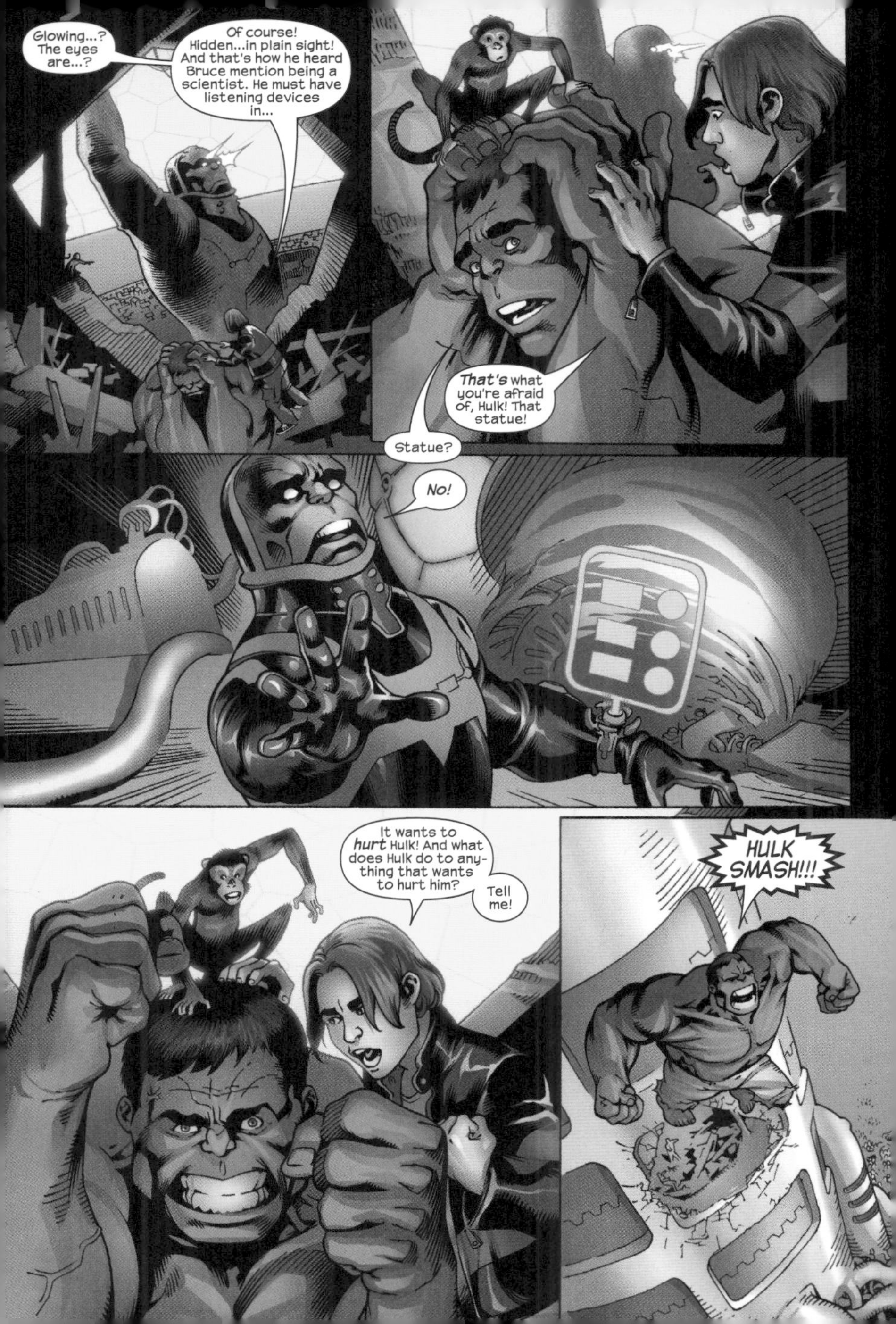
Glowing...? The eyes are...?
Of course! Hidden...in plain sight! And that's how he heard Bruce mention being a scientist. He must have listening devices in...
That's what you're afraid of, Hulk! That statue!
Statue?
No!
It wants to hurt Hulk! And what does Hulk do to anything that wants to hurt him?
Tell me!
HULK SMASH!!!

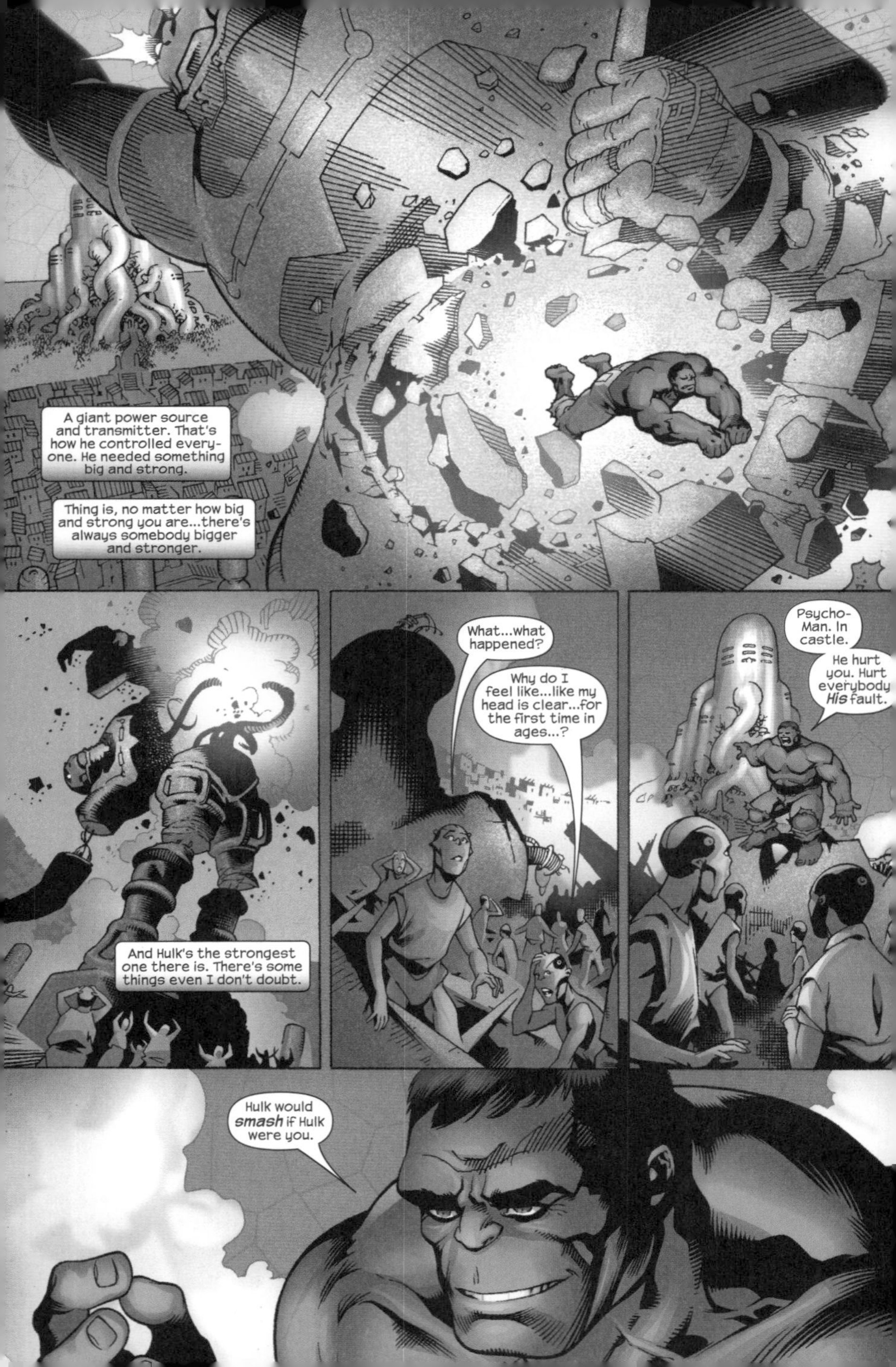
A giant power source and transmitter. That's how he controlled every-one. He needed something big and strong.
Thing is, no matter how big and strong you are...there's always somebody bigger and stronger.
And Hulk's the strongest one there is. There's some things even I don't doubt.
What...what happened?
Why do I feel like...like my head is clear...for the first time in ages...?
Psycho-Man. In castle.
He hurt you. Hurt everybody. *His* fault.
Hulk would *smash* if Hulk were you.

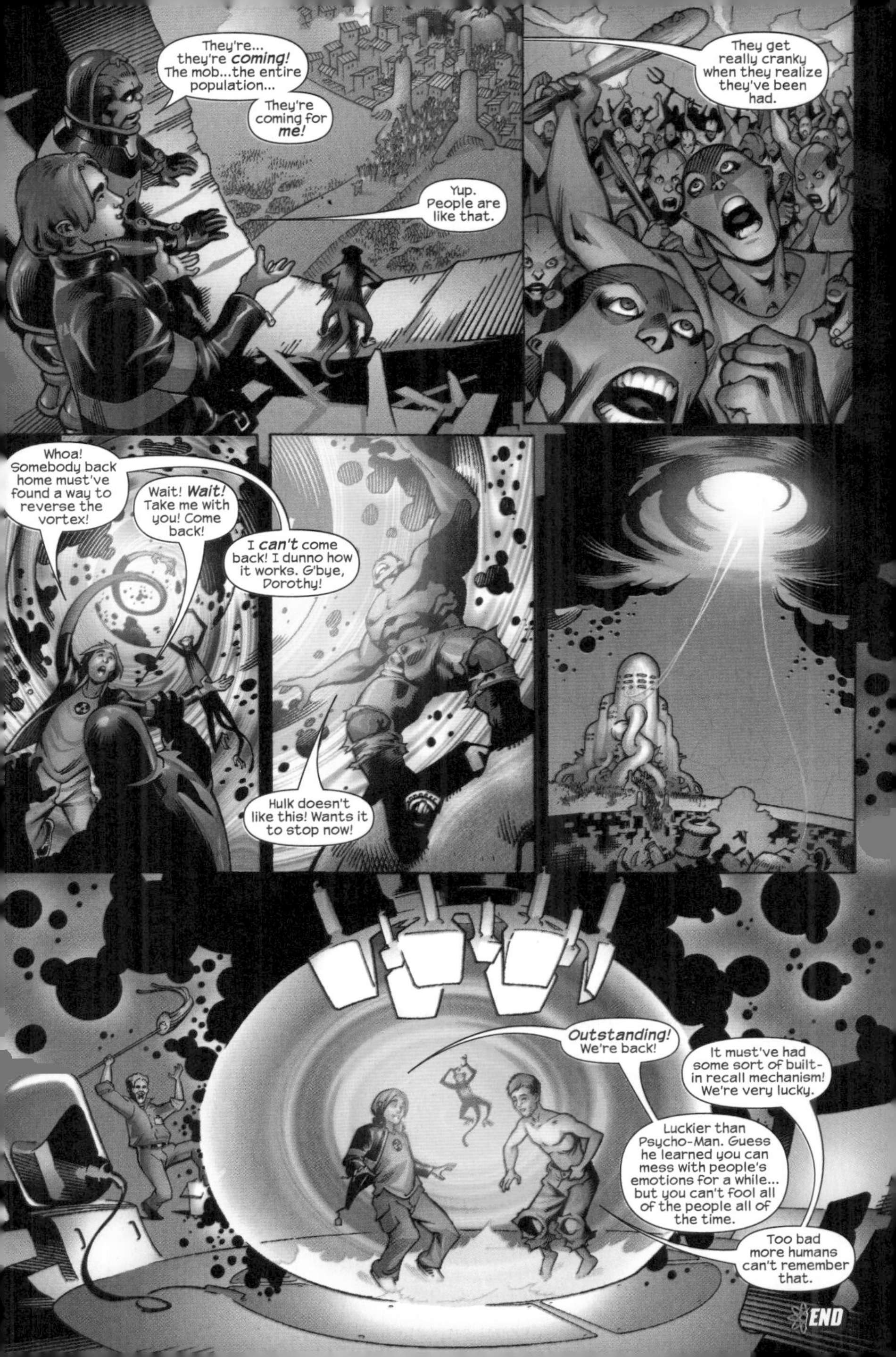
They're... they're *coming!* The mob...the entire population...
They're coming for *me!*
Yup. People are like that.
They get really cranky when they realize they've been had.
Whoa! Somebody back home must've found a way to reverse the vortex!
Wait! *Wait!* Take me with you! Come back!
I *can't* come back! I dunno how it works. G'bye, Dorothy!
Hulk doesn't like this! Wants it to stop now!
*Outstanding!* We're back!
It must've had some sort of built-in recall mechanism! We're very lucky.
Luckier than Psycho-Man. Guess he learned you can mess with people's emotions for a while... but you can't fool all of the people all of the time.
Too bad more humans can't remember that.
END

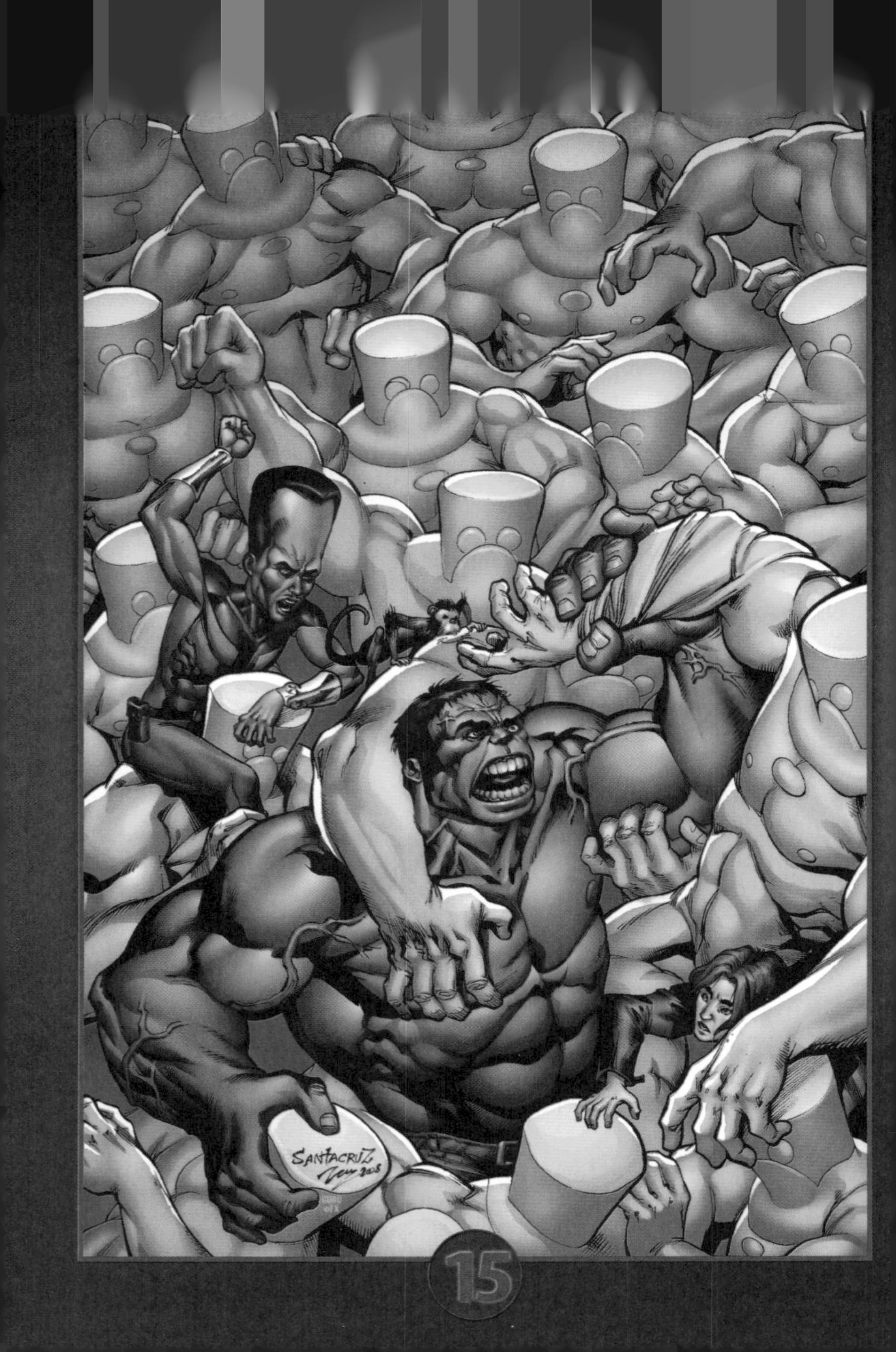
SANTACRUZ

15

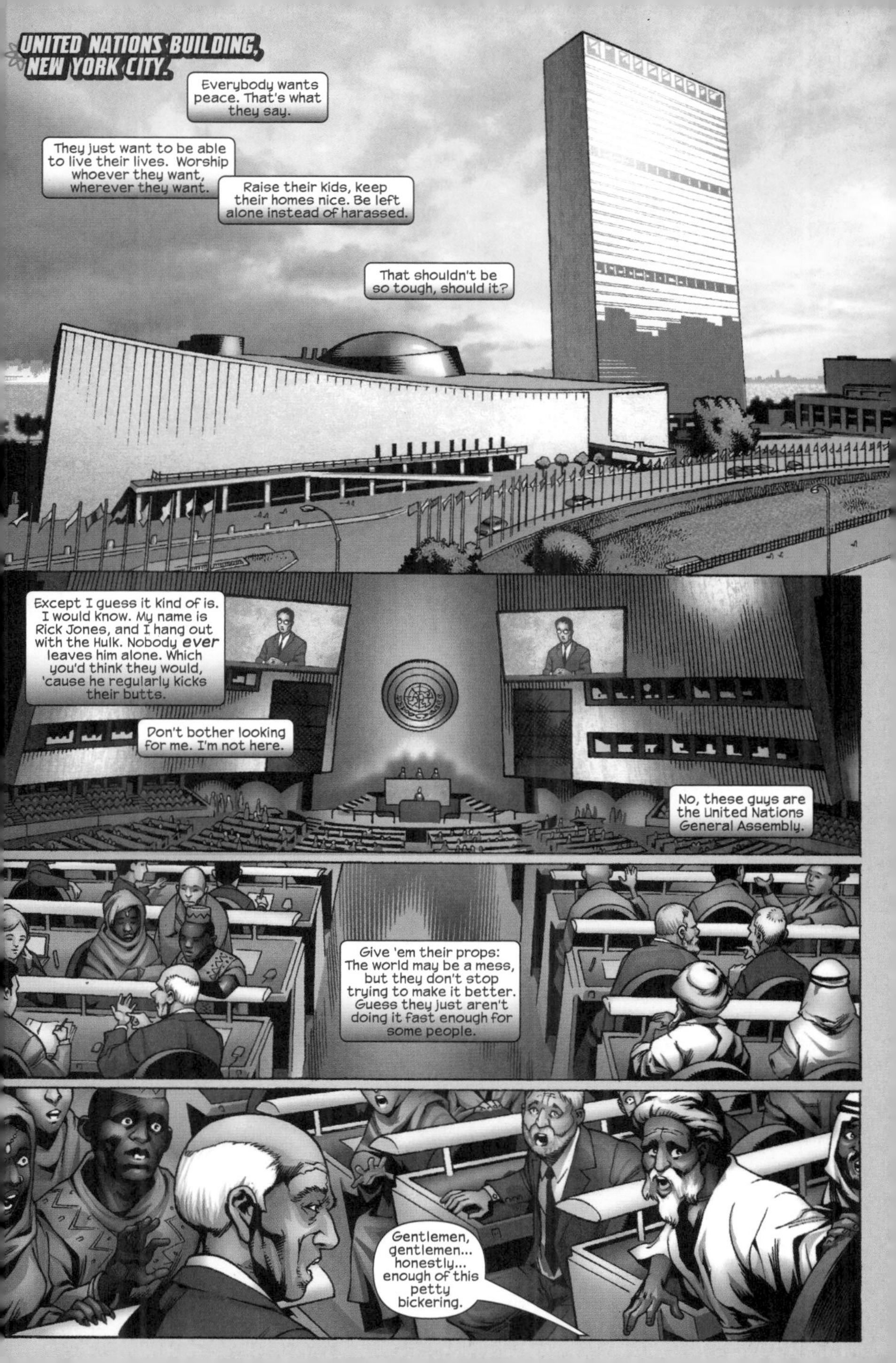
UNITED NATIONS BUILDING, NEW YORK CITY.
Everybody wants peace. That's what they say.
They just want to be able to live their lives. Worship whoever they want, wherever they want.
Raise their kids, keep their homes nice. Be left alone instead of harassed.
That shouldn't be so tough, should it?
Except I guess it kind of is. I would know. My name is Rick Jones, and I hang out with the Hulk. Nobody *ever* leaves him alone. Which you'd think they would, 'cause he regularly kicks their butts.
Don't bother looking for me. I'm not here.
No, these guys are the United Nations General Assembly.
Give 'em their props: The world may be a mess, but they don't stop trying to make it better. Guess they just aren't doing it fast enough for some people.
Gentlemen, gentlemen... honestly... enough of this petty bickering.

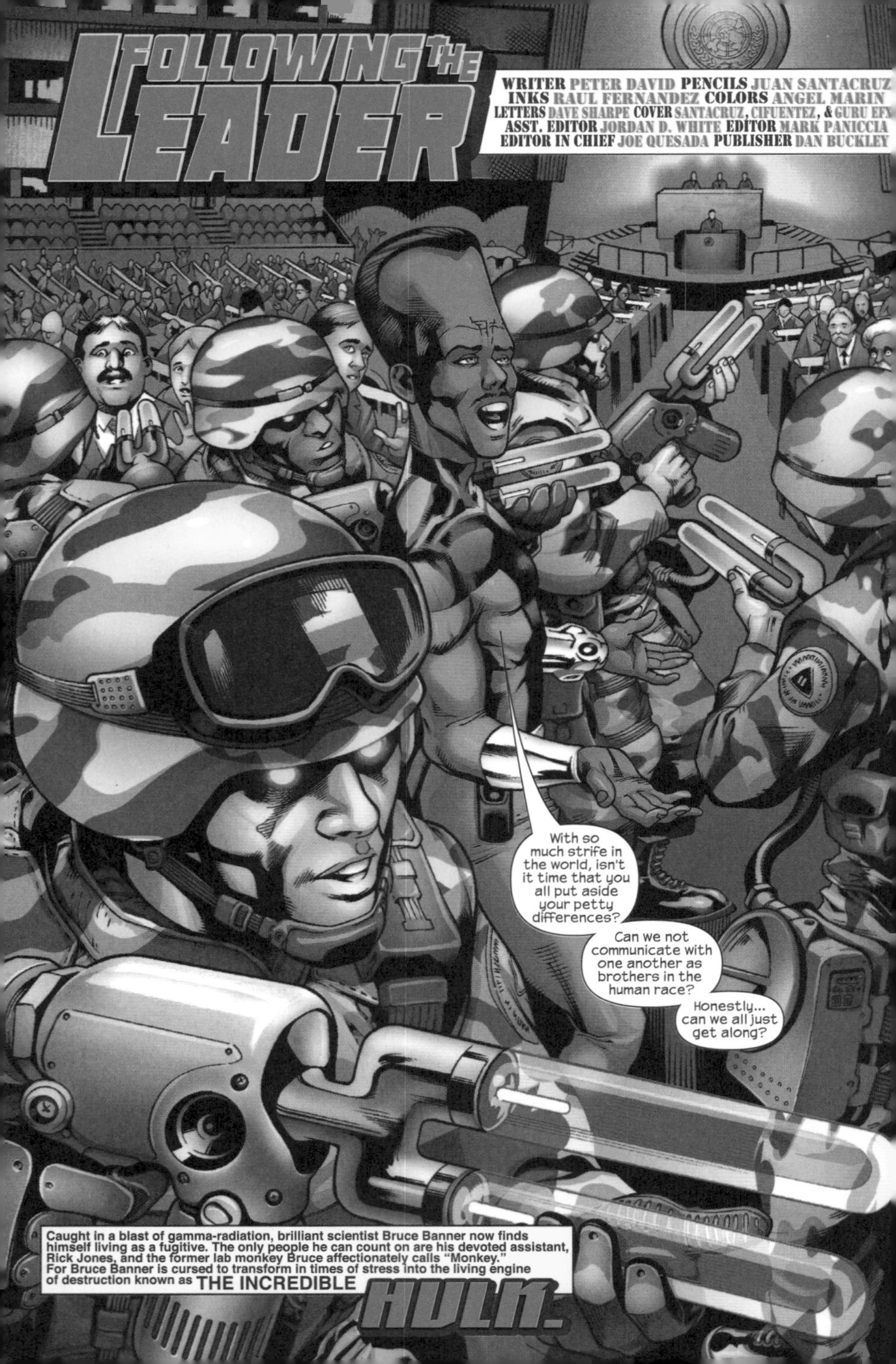

FOLLOWING THE LEADER
WRITER PETER DAVID PENCILS JUAN SANTACRUZ
INKS RAUL FERNANDEZ COLORS ANGEL MARIN
LETTERS DAVE SHARPE COVER SANTACRUZ, CIFUENTEZ, & GURU EFX
ASST. EDITOR JORDAN D. WHITE EDITOR MARK PANICCIA
EDITOR IN CHIEF JOE QUESADA PUBLISHER DAN BUCKLEY
With so much strife in the world, isn't it time that you all put aside your petty differences?
Can we not communicate with one another as brothers in the human race?
Honestly... can we all just get along?
Caught in a blast of gamma-radiation, brilliant scientist Bruce Banner now finds himself living as a fugitive. The only people he can count on are his devoted assistant, Rick Jones, and the former lab monkey Bruce affectionately calls "Monkey." For Bruce Banner is cursed to transform in times of stress into the living engine of destruction known as THE INCREDIBLE HULK.

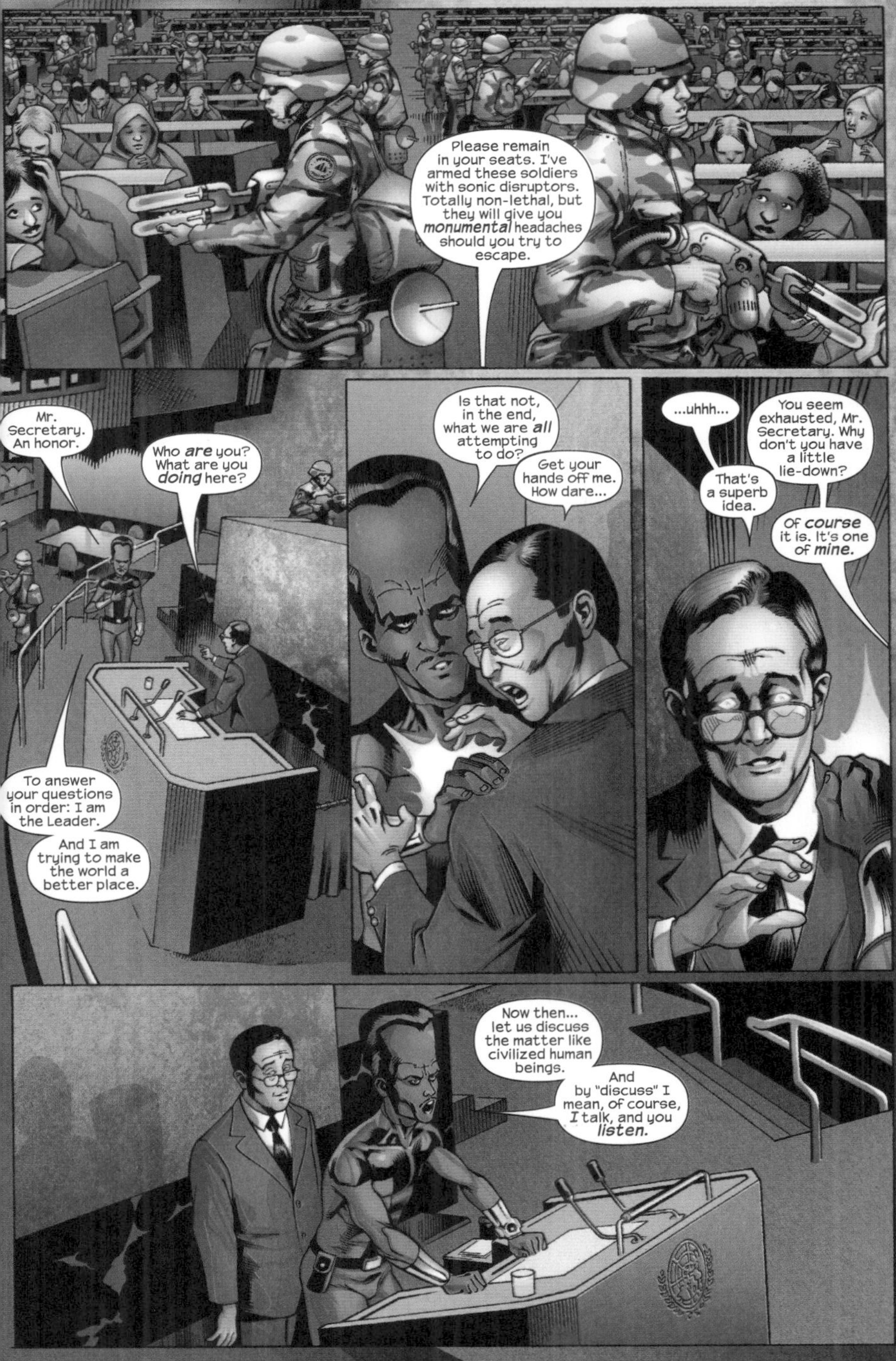

Please remain in your seats. I've armed these soldiers with sonic disruptors. Totally non-lethal, but they will give you *monumental* headaches should you try to escape.
Mr. Secretary. An honor.
Who *are* you? What are you *doing* here?
To answer your questions in order: I am the Leader.
And I am trying to make the world a better place.
Is that not, in the end, what we are *all* attempting to do?
Get your hands off me. How dare...
...uhhh...
You seem exhausted, Mr. Secretary. Why don't you have a little lie-down?
That's a superb idea.
Of *course* it is. It's one of *mine.*
Now then... let us discuss the matter like civilized human beings.
And by "discuss" I mean, of course, *I* talk, and you *listen.*

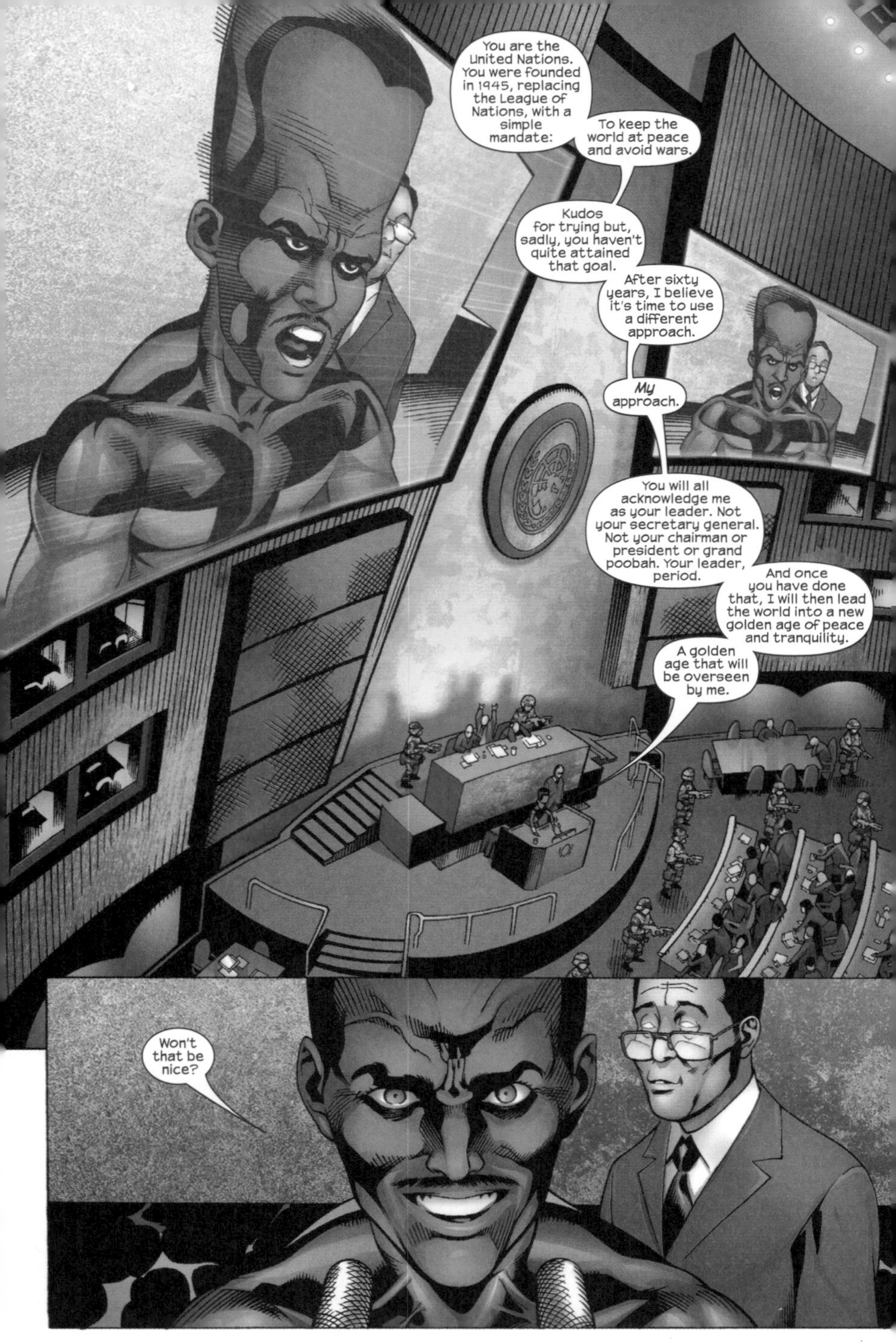
You are the United Nations. You were founded in 1945, replacing the League of Nations, with a simple mandate:
To keep the world at peace and avoid wars.
Kudos for trying but, sadly, you haven't quite attained that goal.
After sixty years, I believe it's time to use a different approach.
*My* approach.
You will all acknowledge me as your leader. Not your secretary general. Not your chairman or president or grand poobah. Your leader, period.
And once you have done that, I will then lead the world into a new golden age of peace and tranquility.
A golden age that will be overseen by me.
Won't that be nice?

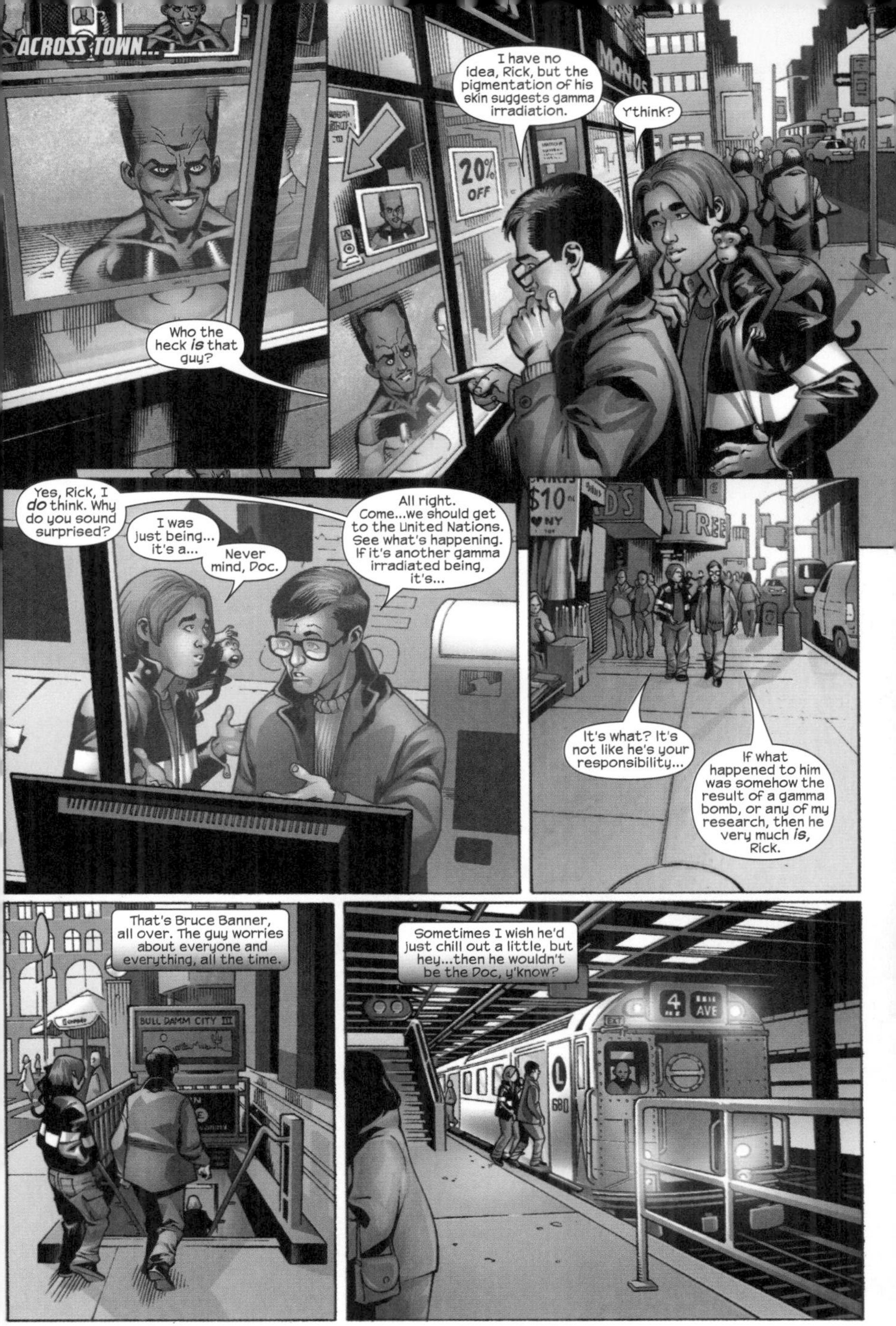
ACROSS TOWN...
Who the heck is that guy?
I have no idea, Rick, but the pigmentation of his skin suggests gamma irradiation.
Y'think?
20% OFF
Yes, Rick, I do think. Why do you sound surprised?
I was just being... it's a...
Never mind, Doc.
All right. Come...we should get to the United Nations. See what's happening. If it's another gamma irradiated being, it's...
$10
It's what? It's not like he's your responsibility...
If what happened to him was somehow the result of a gamma bomb, or any of my research, then he very much is, Rick.
That's Bruce Banner, all over. The guy worries about everyone and everything, all the time.
BULL DAMM CITY III
Sometimes I wish he'd just chill out a little, but hey...then he wouldn't be the Doc, y'know?
4 AVE
L
680

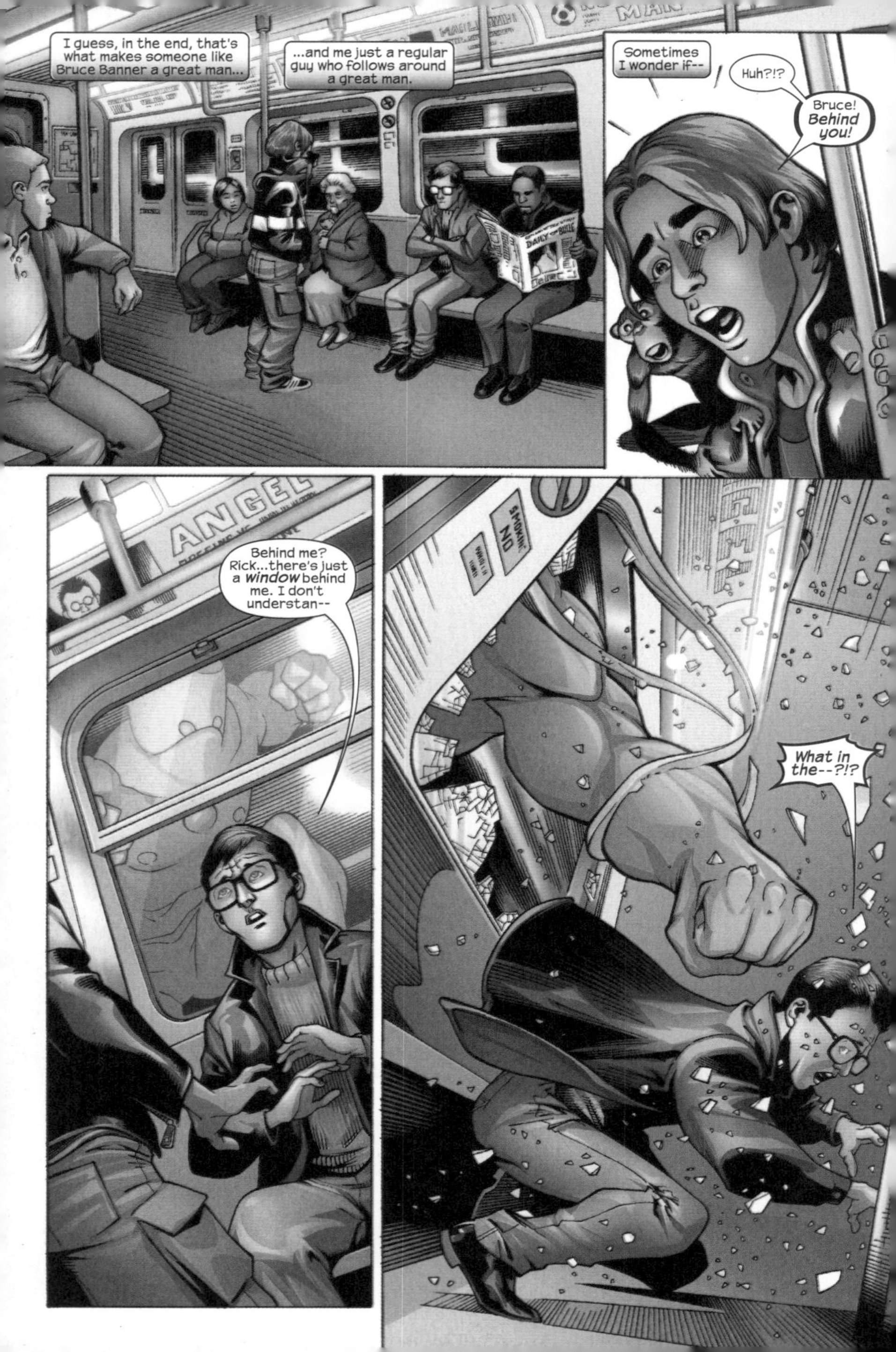

I guess, in the end, that's what makes someone like Bruce Banner a great man...
...and me just a regular guy who follows around a great man.
Sometimes I wonder if--
Huh?!?
Bruce! Behind you!
Behind me? Rick...there's just a window behind me. I don't understan--
What in the--?!?

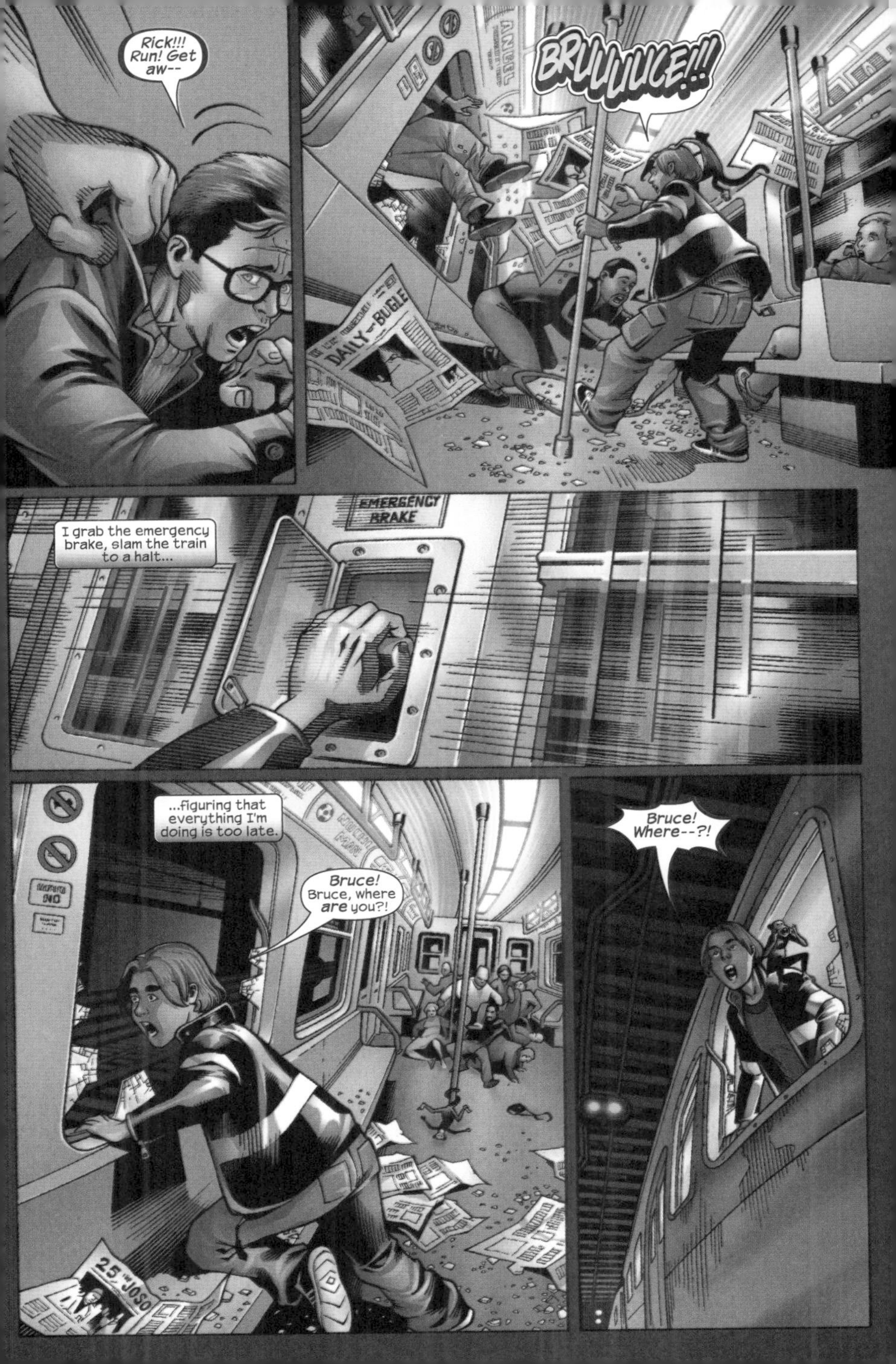

Rick!!! Run! Get aw--
BRUUUUCE!!!
I grab the emergency brake, slam the train to a halt...
EMERGENCY BRAKE
...figuring that everything I'm doing is too late.
Bruce! Bruce, where *are* you?!
Bruce! Where--?!

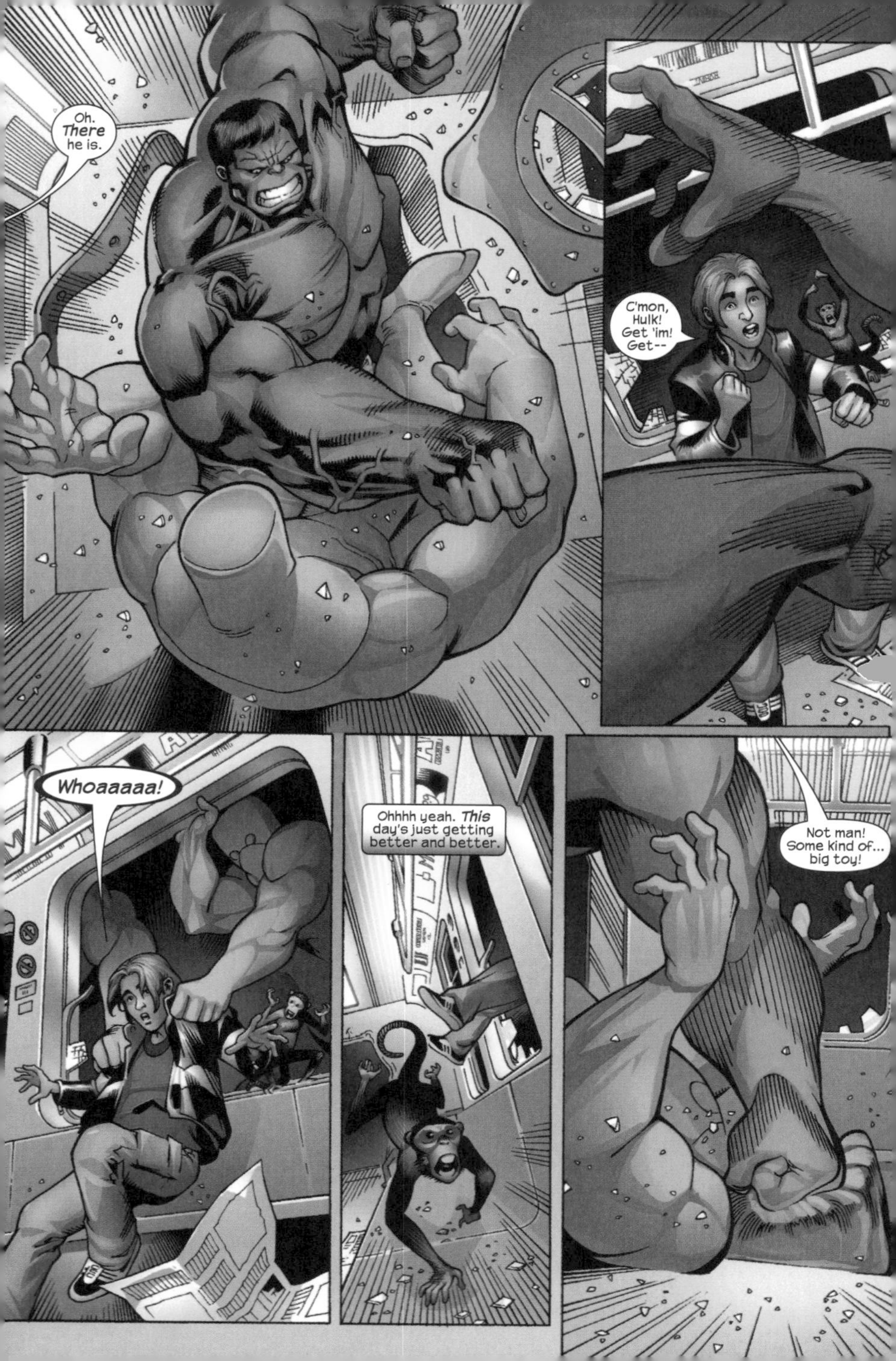
Oh. *There* he is.
C'mon, Hulk! Get 'im! Get--
Whoaaaaa!
Ohhhh yeah. *This* day's just getting better and better.
Not man! Some kind of... big toy!

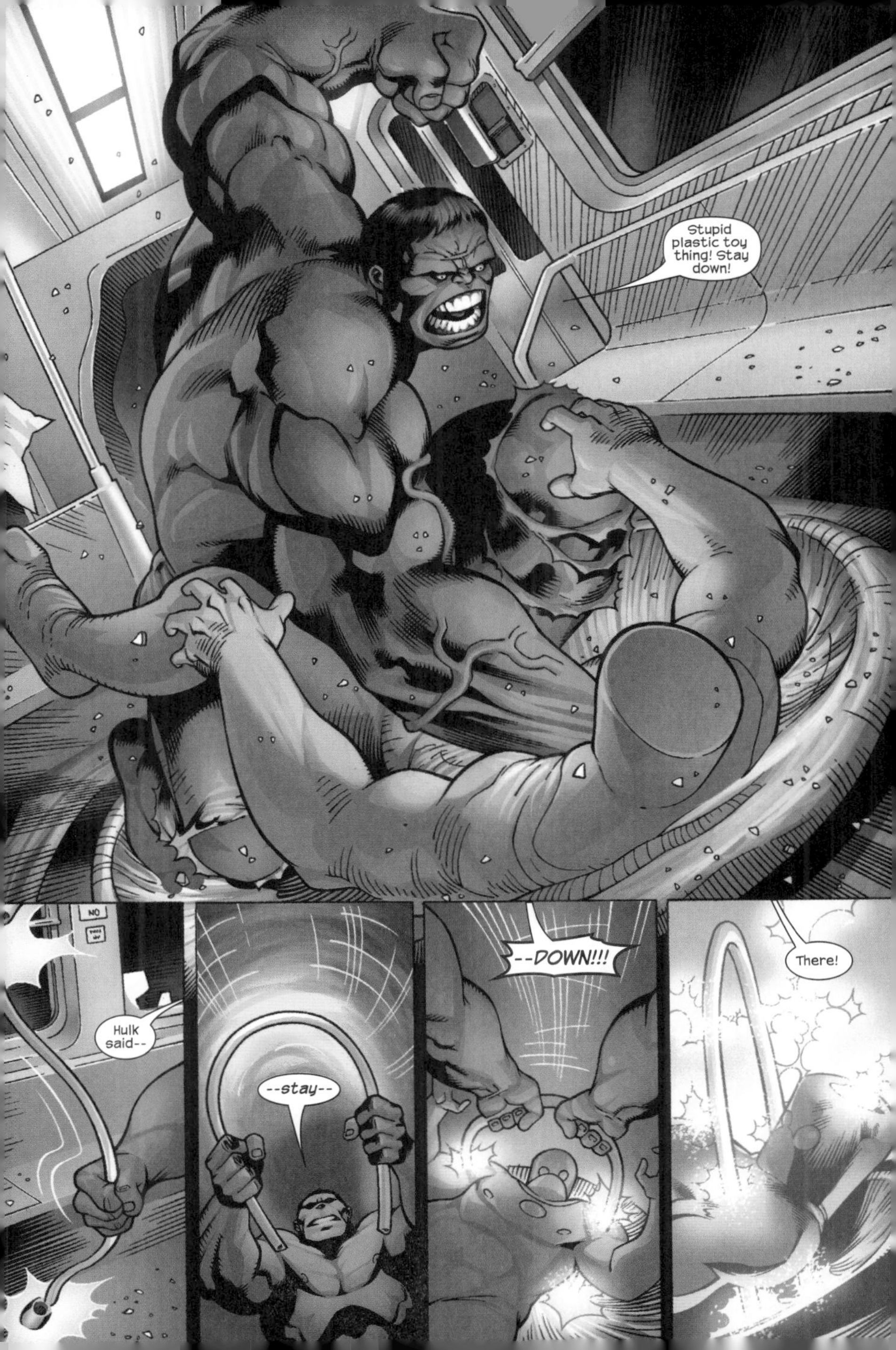
Stupid plastic toy thing! Stay down!
NO
Hulk said--
--stay--
--DOWN!!!
There!

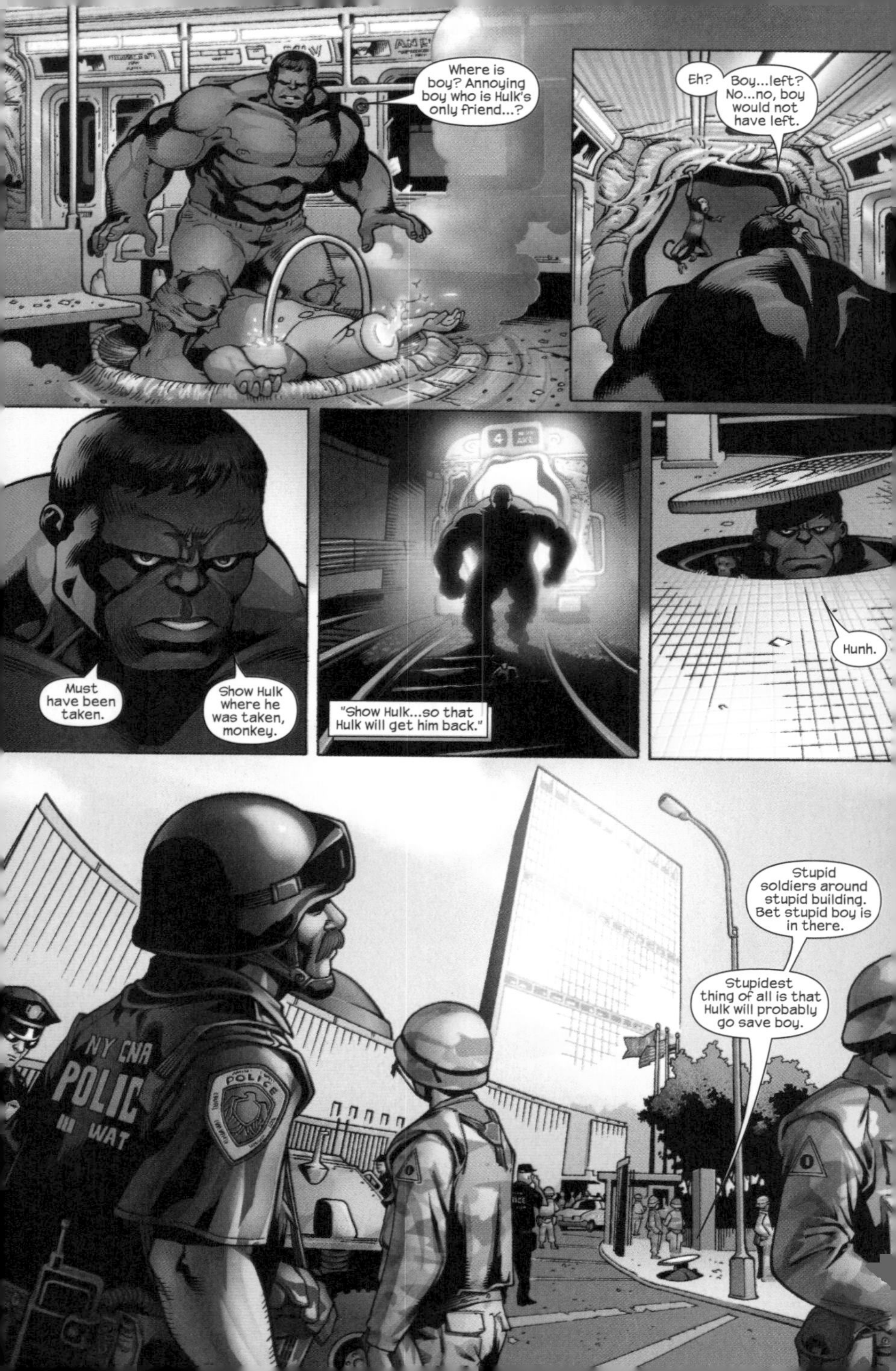
Where is boy? Annoying boy who is Hulk's only friend...?
Eh?
Boy...left? No...no, boy would not have left.
Must have been taken.
Show Hulk where he was taken, monkey.
"Show Hulk...so that Hulk will get him back."
Hunh.
NY CNA
POLIC
Stupid soldiers around stupid building. Bet stupid boy is in there.
Stupidest thing of all is that Hulk will probably go save boy.

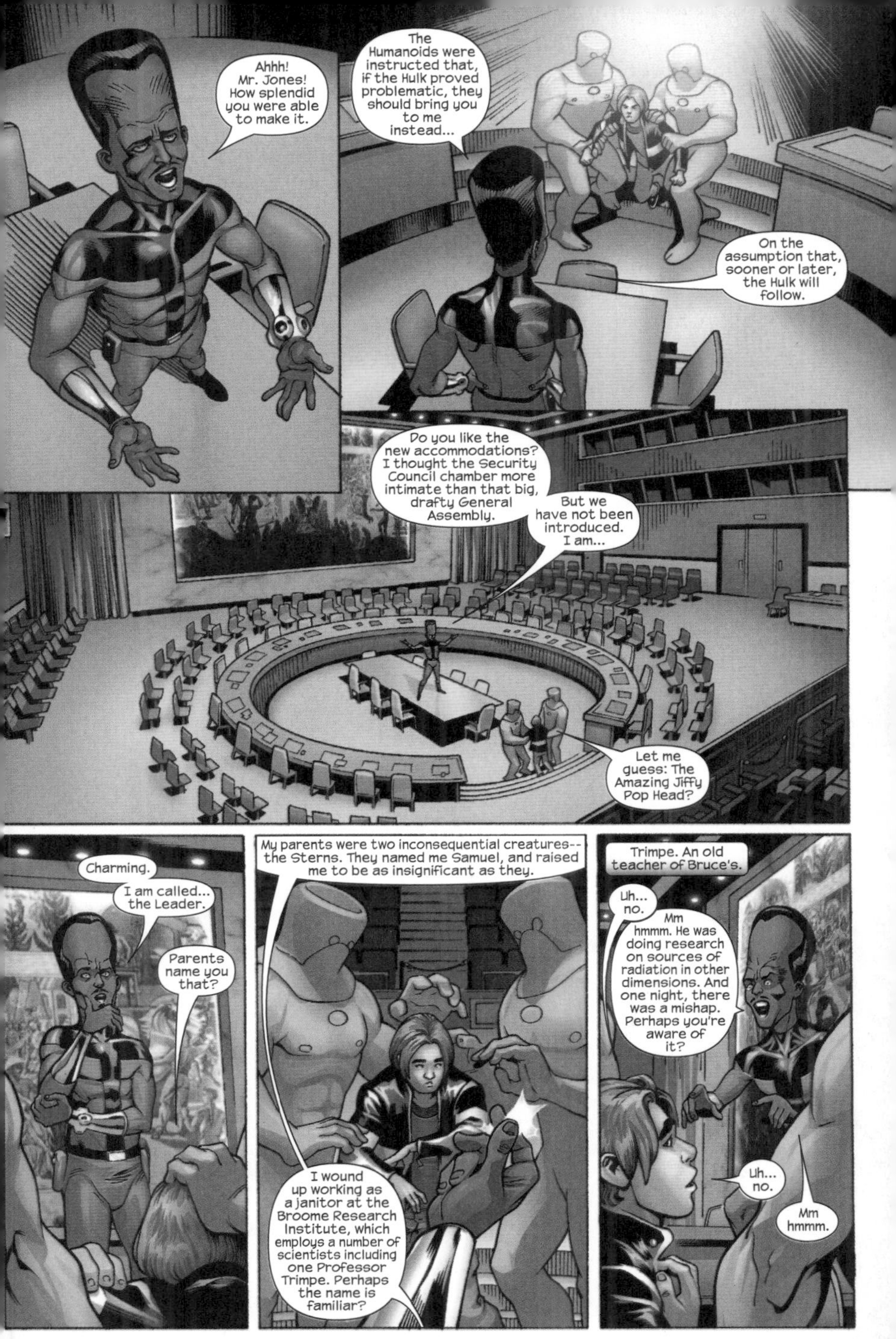

Ahhh! Mr. Jones! How splendid you were able to make it.
The Humanoids were instructed that, if the Hulk proved problematic, they should bring you to me instead...
On the assumption that, sooner or later, the Hulk will follow.
Do you like the new accommodations? I thought the Security Council chamber more intimate than that big, drafty General Assembly.
But we have not been introduced. I am...
Let me guess: The Amazing Jiffy Pop Head?
Charming.
I am called... the Leader.
Parents name you that?
My parents were two inconsequential creatures--the Sterns. They named me Samuel, and raised me to be as insignificant as they.
I wound up working as a janitor at the Broome Research Institute, which employs a number of scientists including one Professor Trimpe. Perhaps the name is familiar?
Trimpe. An old teacher of Bruce's.
Uh... no.
Mm hmmm. He was doing research on sources of radiation in other dimensions. And one night, there was a mishap. Perhaps you're aware of it?
Uh... no.
Mm hmmm.

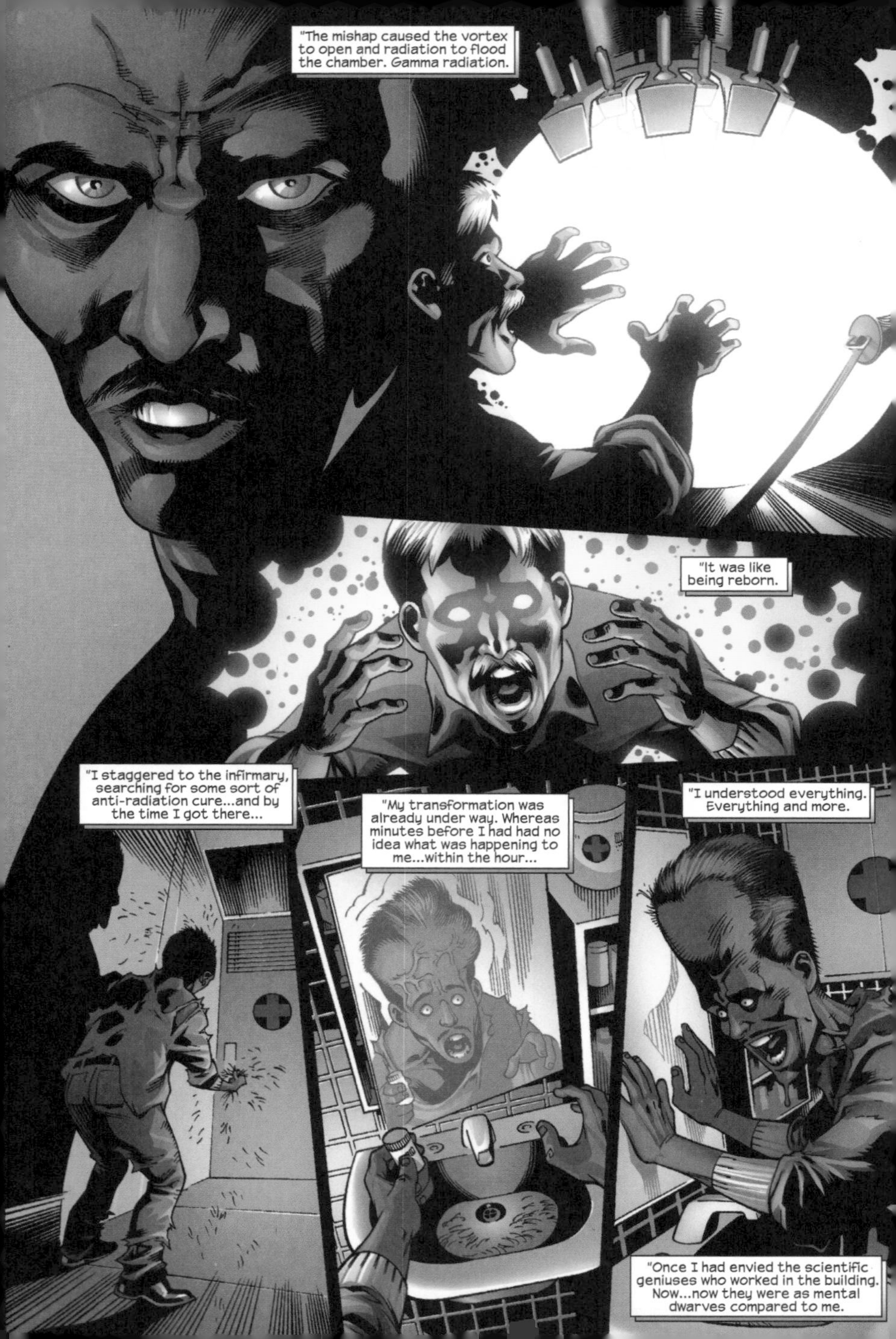
"The mishap caused the vortex to open and radiation to flood the chamber. Gamma radiation.
"It was like being reborn.
"I staggered to the infirmary, searching for some sort of anti-radiation cure...and by the time I got there...
"My transformation was already under way. Whereas minutes before I had had no idea what was happening to me...within the hour...
"I understood everything. Everything and more.
"Once I had envied the scientific geniuses who worked in the building. Now...now they were as mental dwarves compared to me.

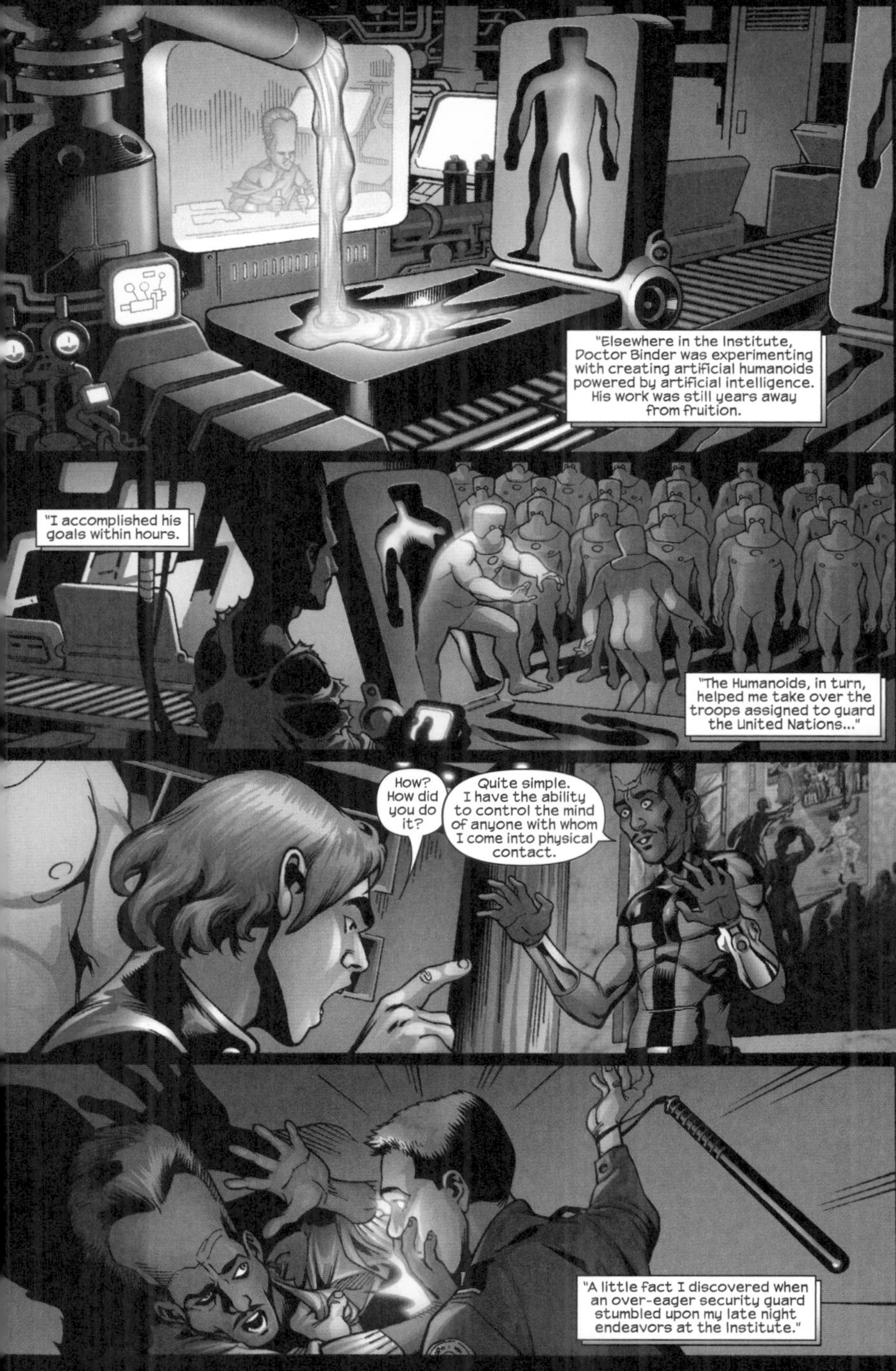
"Elsewhere in the Institute, Doctor Binder was experimenting with creating artificial humanoids powered by artificial intelligence. His work was still years away from fruition.
"I accomplished his goals within hours.
"The Humanoids, in turn, helped me take over the troops assigned to guard the United Nations..."
How? How did you do it?
Quite simple. I have the ability to control the mind of anyone with whom I come into physical contact.
"A little fact I discovered when an over-eager security guard stumbled upon my late night endeavors at the Institute."

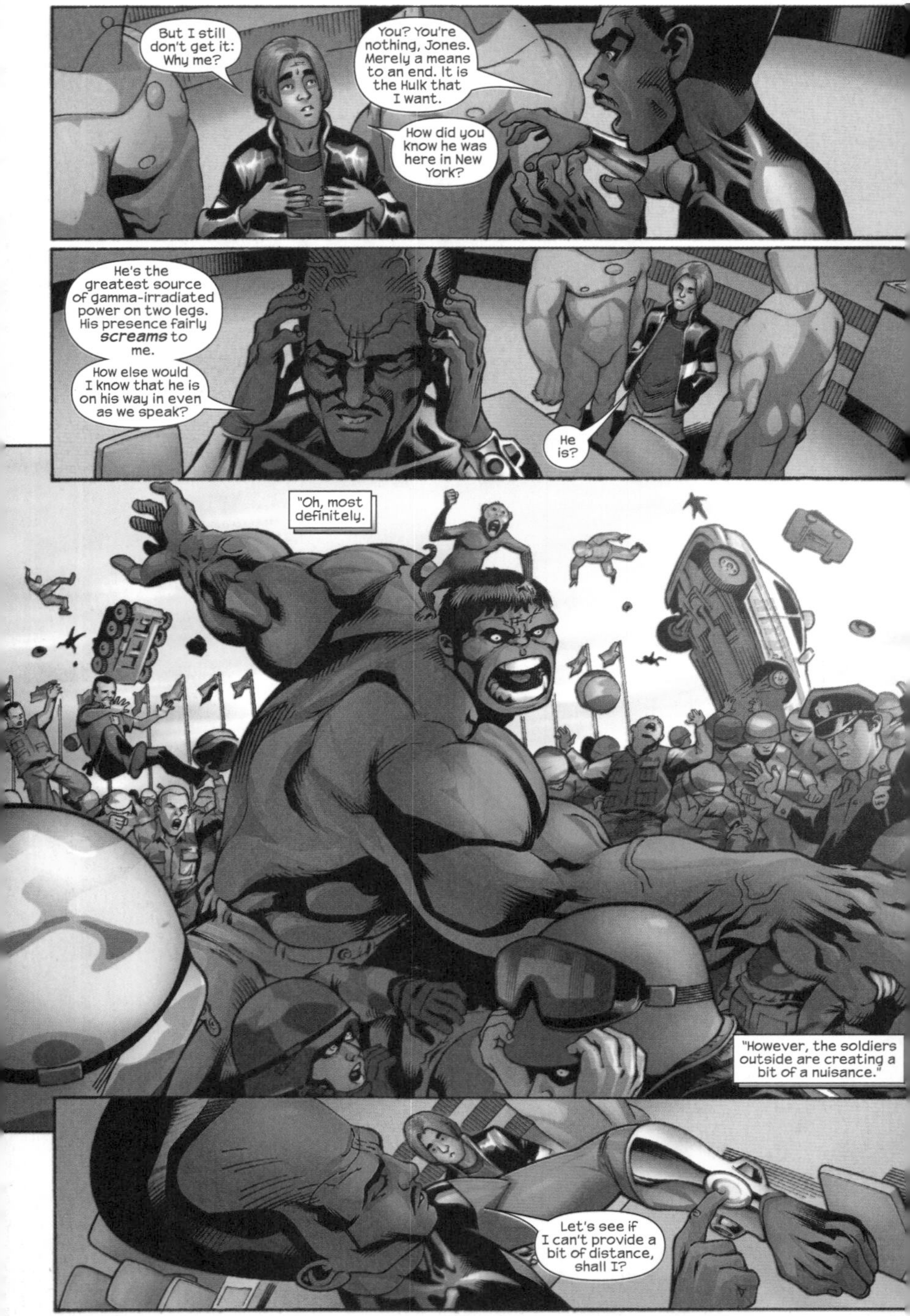

But I still don't get it: Why me?
You? You're nothing, Jones. Merely a means to an end. It is the Hulk that I want.
How did you know he was here in New York?
He's the greatest source of gamma-irradiated power on two legs. His presence fairly *screams* to me.
How else would I know that he is on his way in even as we speak?
He is?
"Oh, most definitely.
"However, the soldiers outside are creating a bit of a nuisance."
Let's see if I can't provide a bit of distance, shall I?

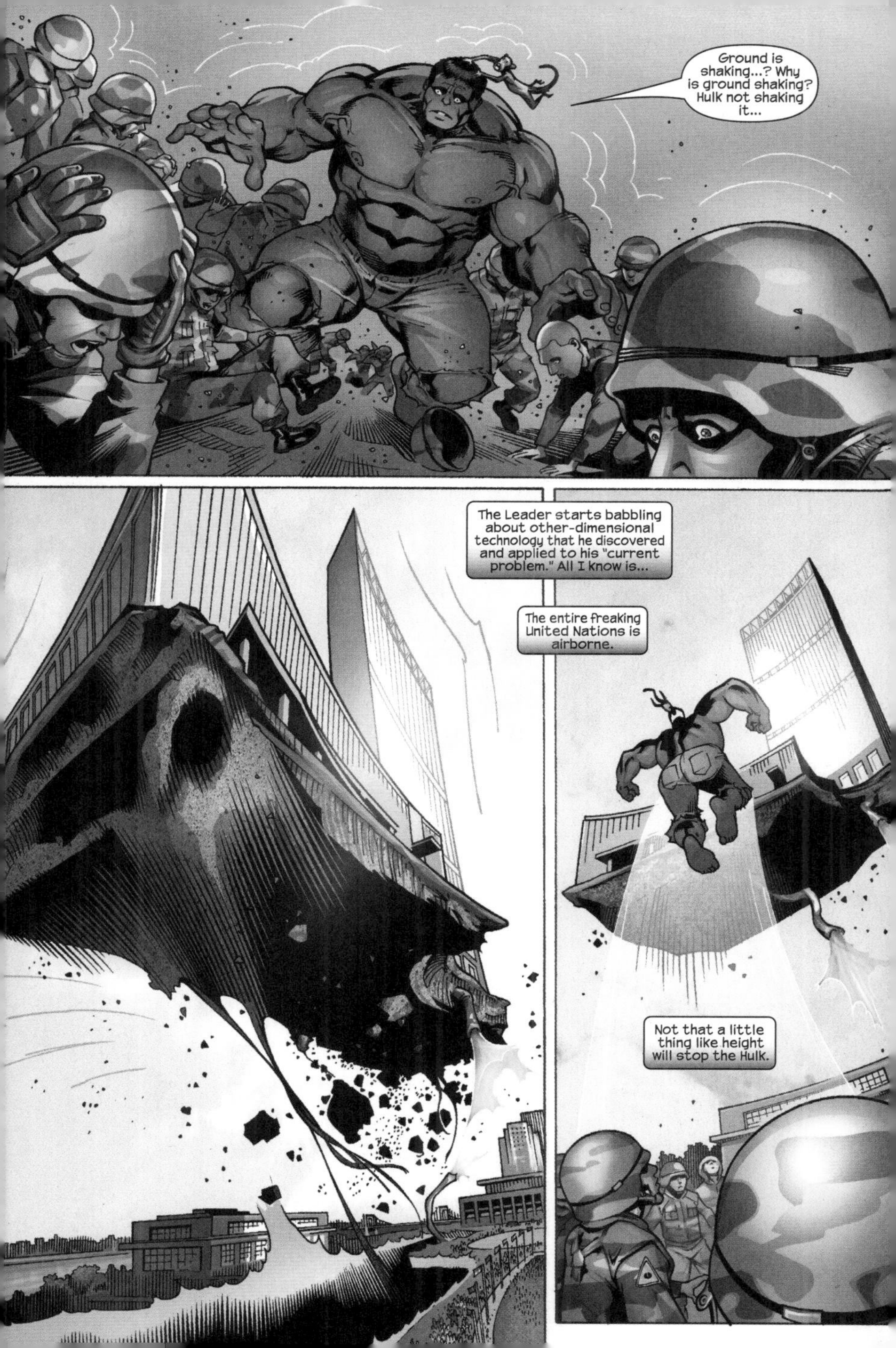
Ground is shaking...? Why is ground shaking? Hulk not shaking it...
The Leader starts babbling about other-dimensional technology that he discovered and applied to his "current problem." All I know is...
The entire freaking United Nations is airborne.
Not that a little thing like height will stop the Hulk.

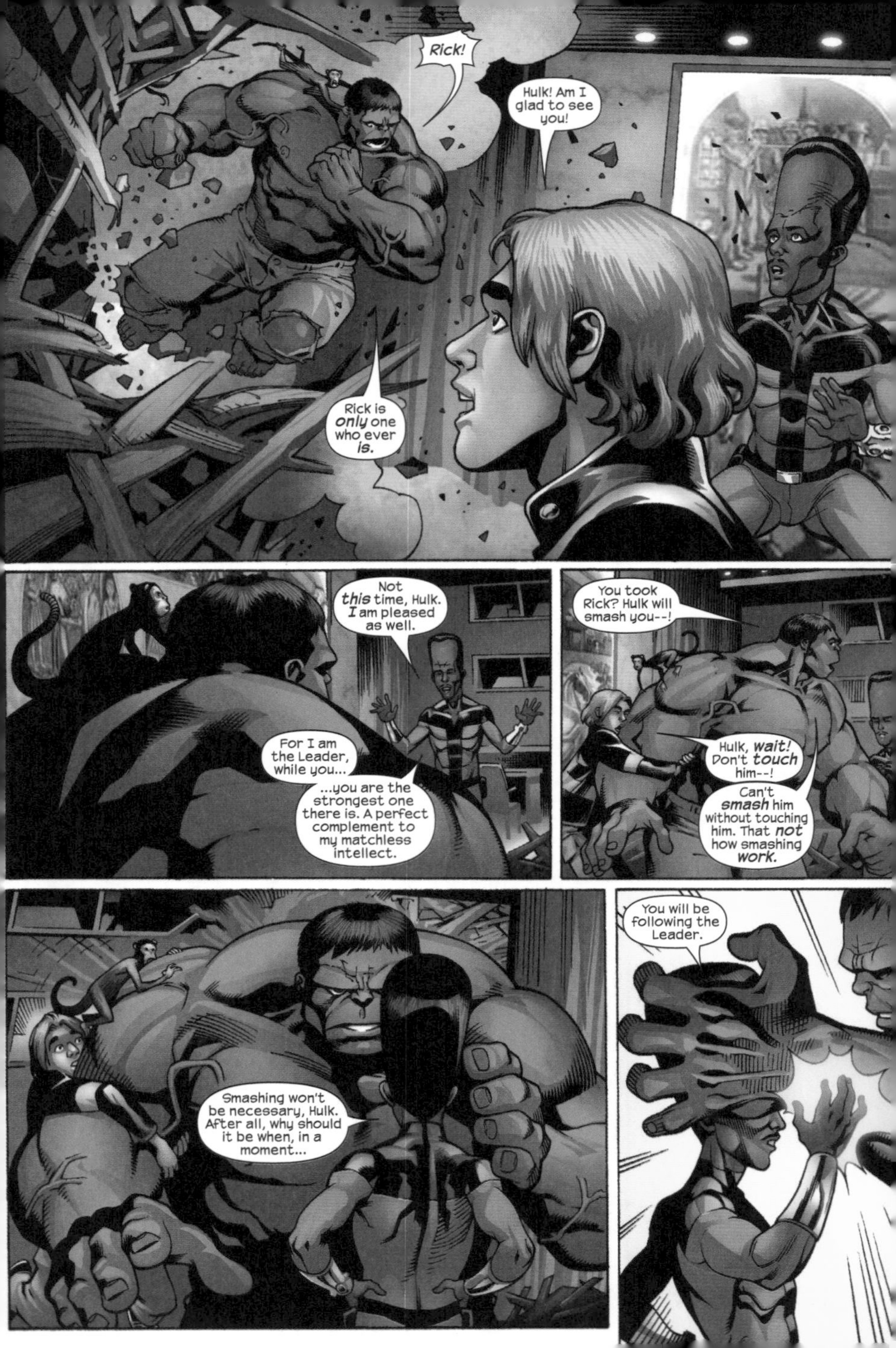

Rick!
Hulk! Am I glad to see you!
Rick is only one who ever is.
Not this time, Hulk. I am pleased as well.
For I am the Leader, while you...
...you are the strongest one there is. A perfect complement to my matchless intellect.
You took Rick? Hulk will smash you--!
Hulk, wait! Don't touch him--!
Can't smash him without touching him. That not how smashing work.
Smashing won't be necessary, Hulk. After all, why should it be when, in a moment...
You will be following the Leader.

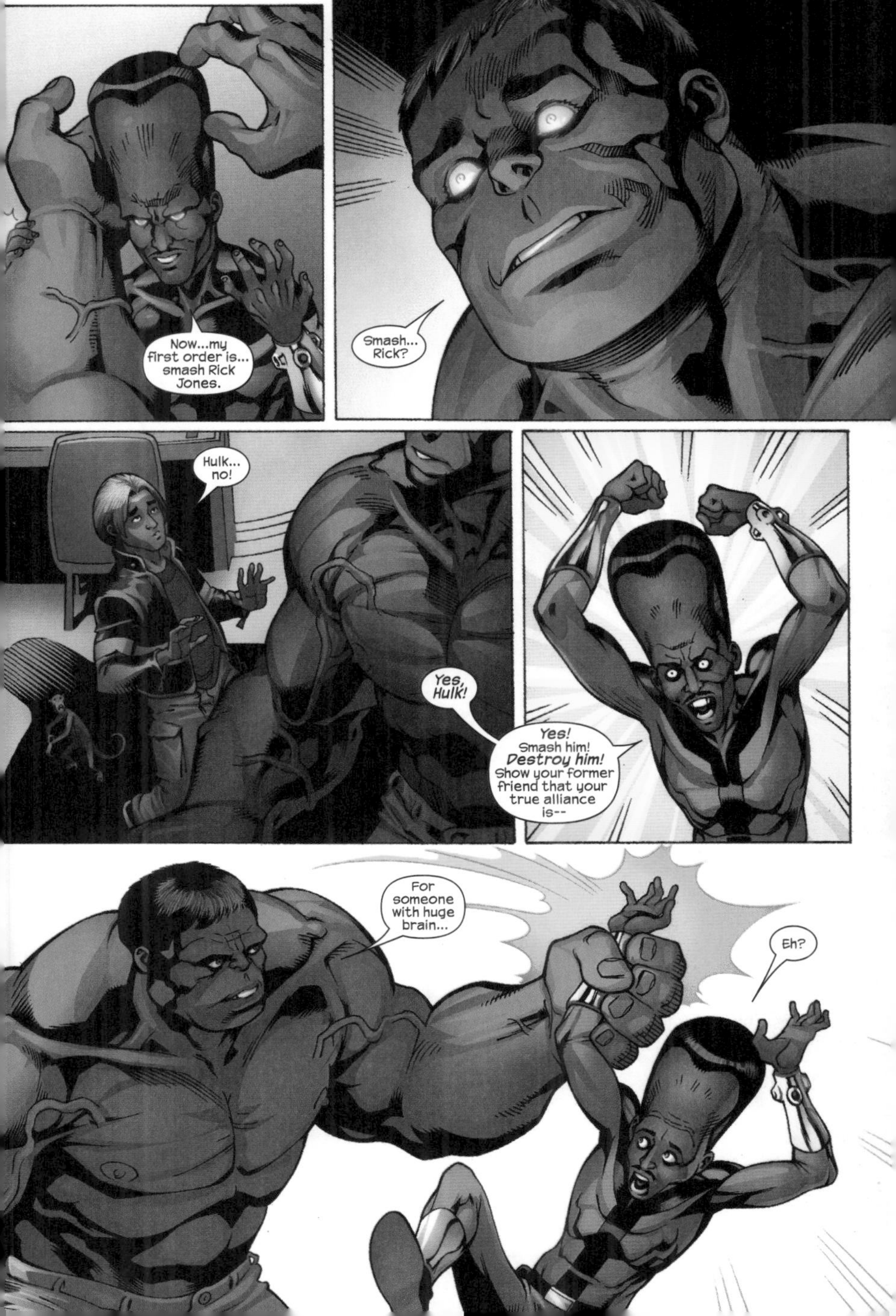
Now...my first order is... smash Rick Jones.
Smash... Rick?
Hulk... no!
Yes, Hulk!
Yes! Smash him! Destroy him! Show your former friend that your true alliance is--
For someone with huge brain...
Eh?

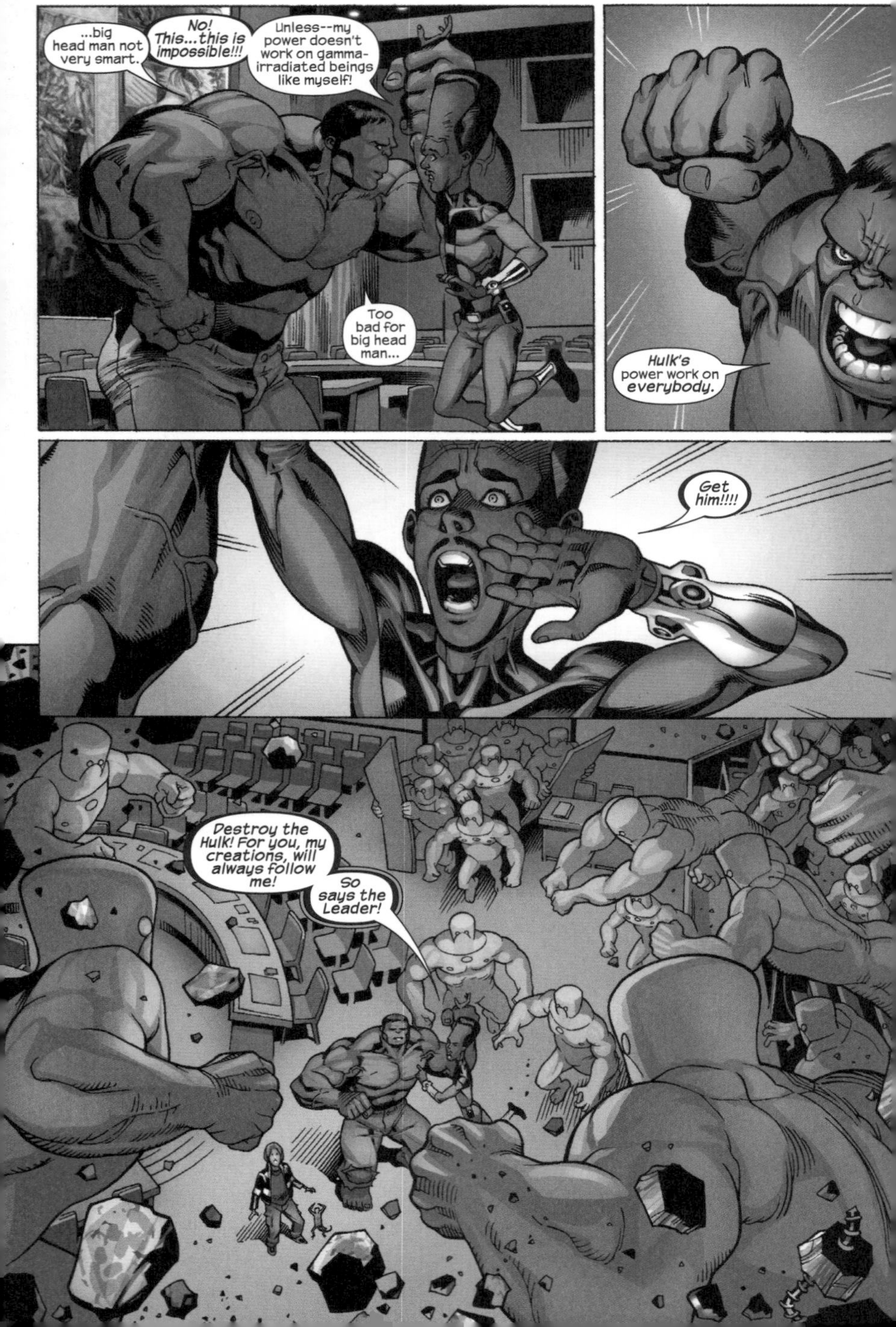
...big head man not very smart.
No! This...this is impossible!!!
Unless--my power doesn't work on gamma-irradiated beings like myself!
Too bad for big head man...
Hulk's power work on everybody.
Get him!!!!
Destroy the Hulk! For you, my creations, will always follow me!
So says the Leader!

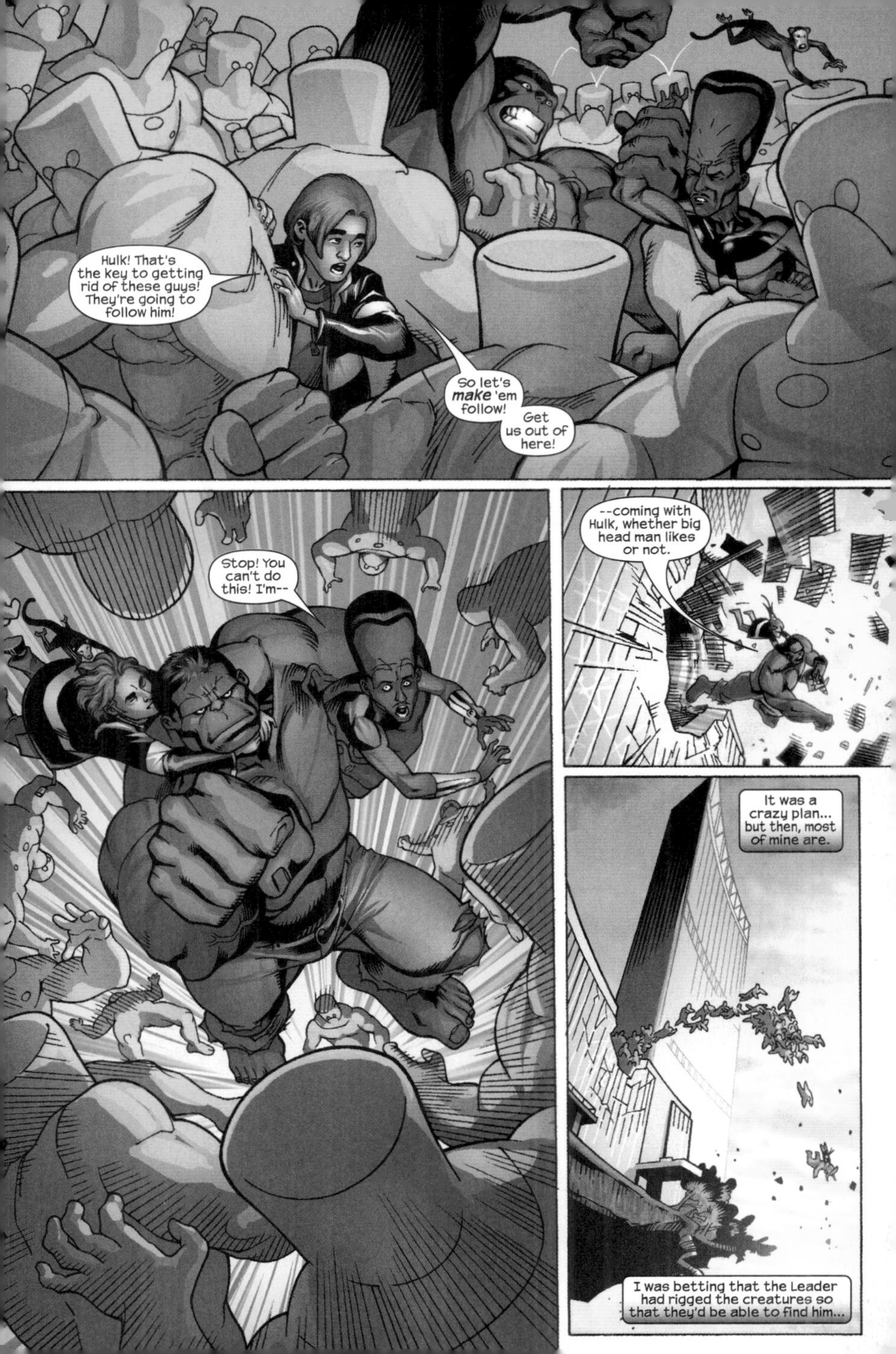
Hulk! That's the key to getting rid of these guys! They're going to follow him!
So let's *make* 'em follow!
Get us out of here!
Stop! You can't do this! I'm--
--coming with Hulk, whether big head man likes or not.
It was a crazy plan... but then, most of mine are.
I was betting that the Leader had rigged the creatures so that they'd be able to find him...

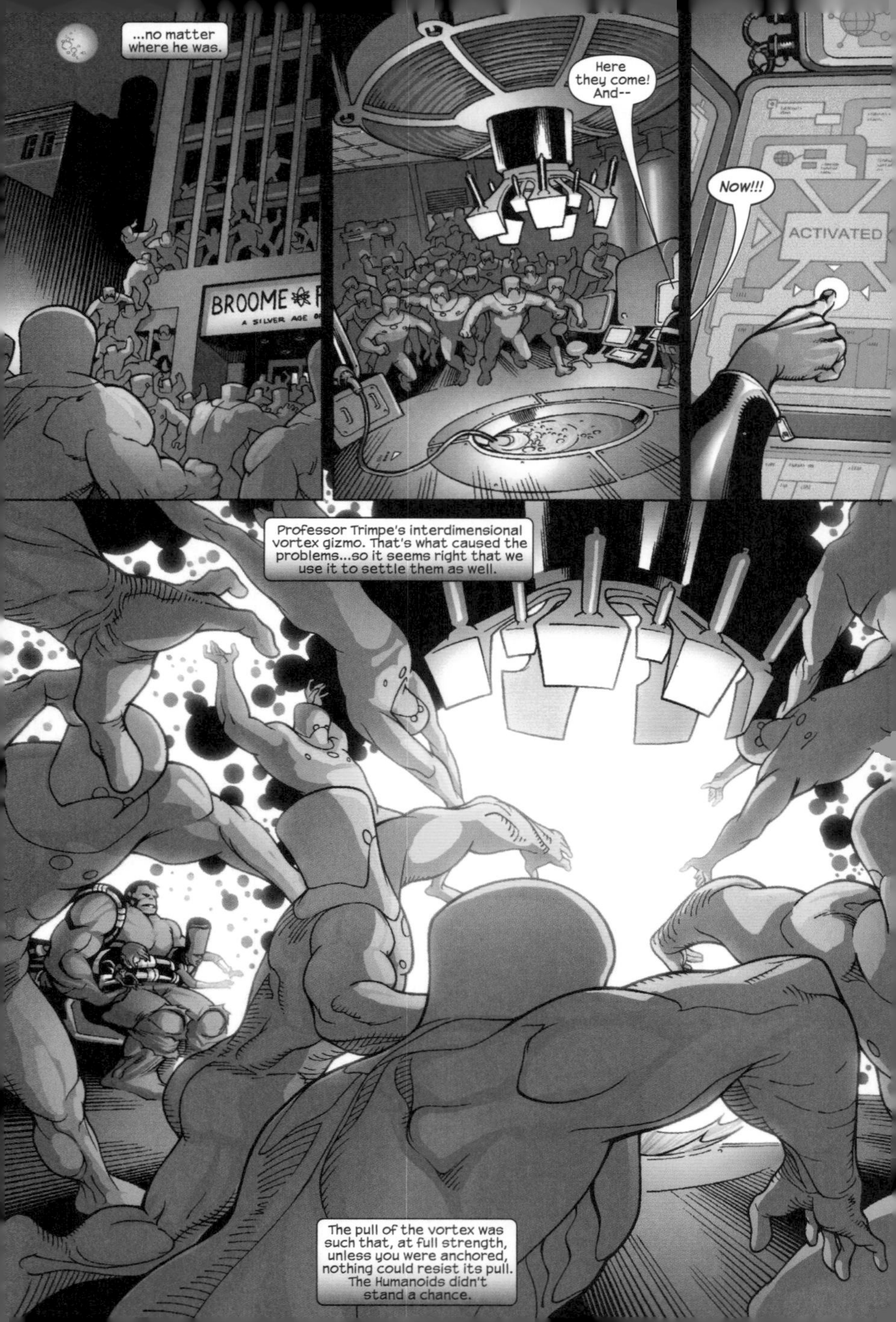
...no matter where he was.
BROOME
A SILVER AGE
Here they come! And--
Now!!!
ACTIVATED
Professor Trimpe's interdimensional vortex gizmo. That's what caused the problems...so it seems right that we use it to settle them as well.
The pull of the vortex was such that, at full strength, unless you were anchored, nothing could resist its pull. The Humanoids didn't stand a chance.

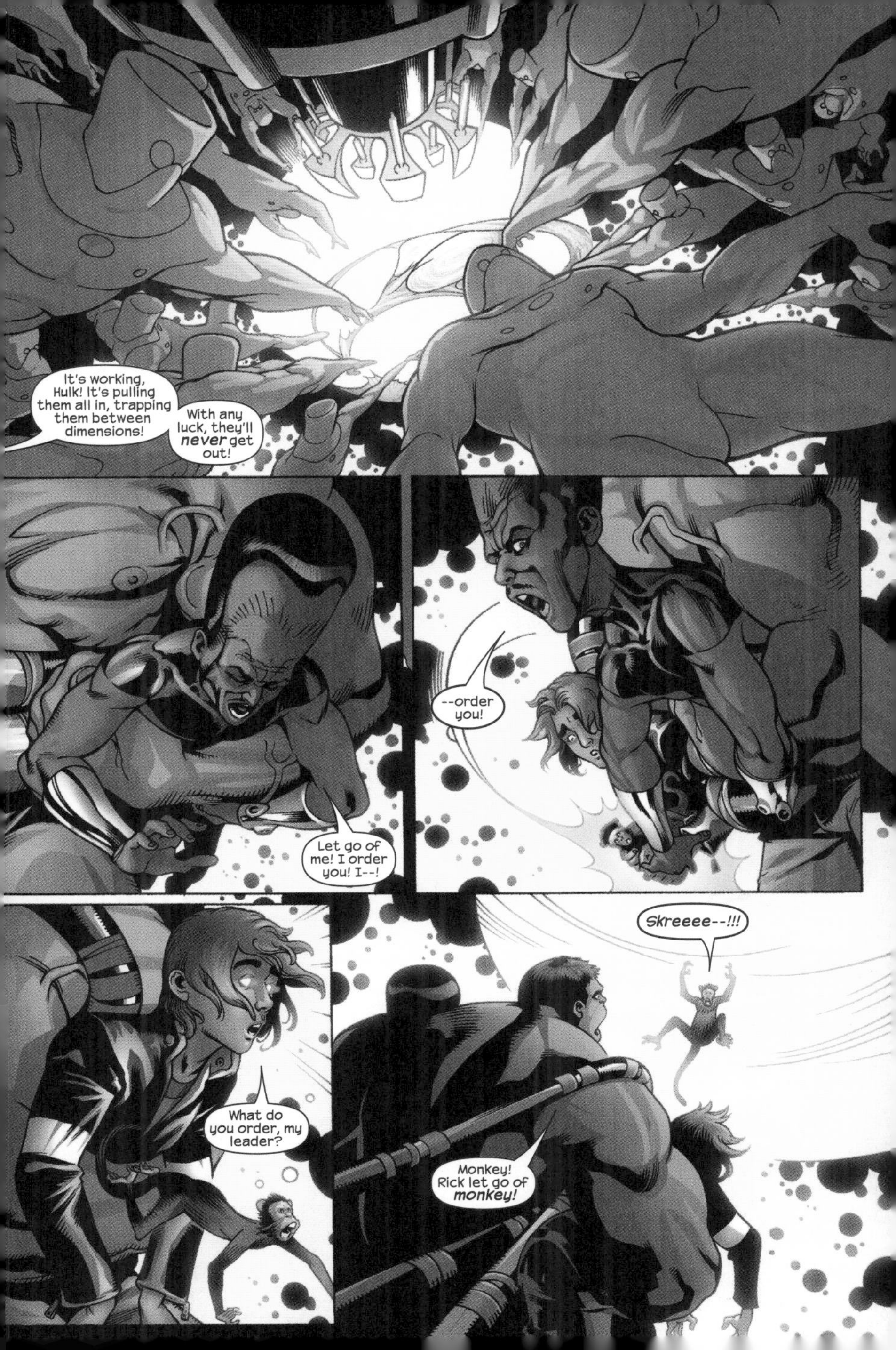
It's working, Hulk! It's pulling them all in, trapping them between dimensions!
With any luck, they'll **never** get out!
Let go of me! I order you! I--!
--order you!
What do you order, my leader?
Skreeee--!!!
Monkey! Rick let go of **monkey!**

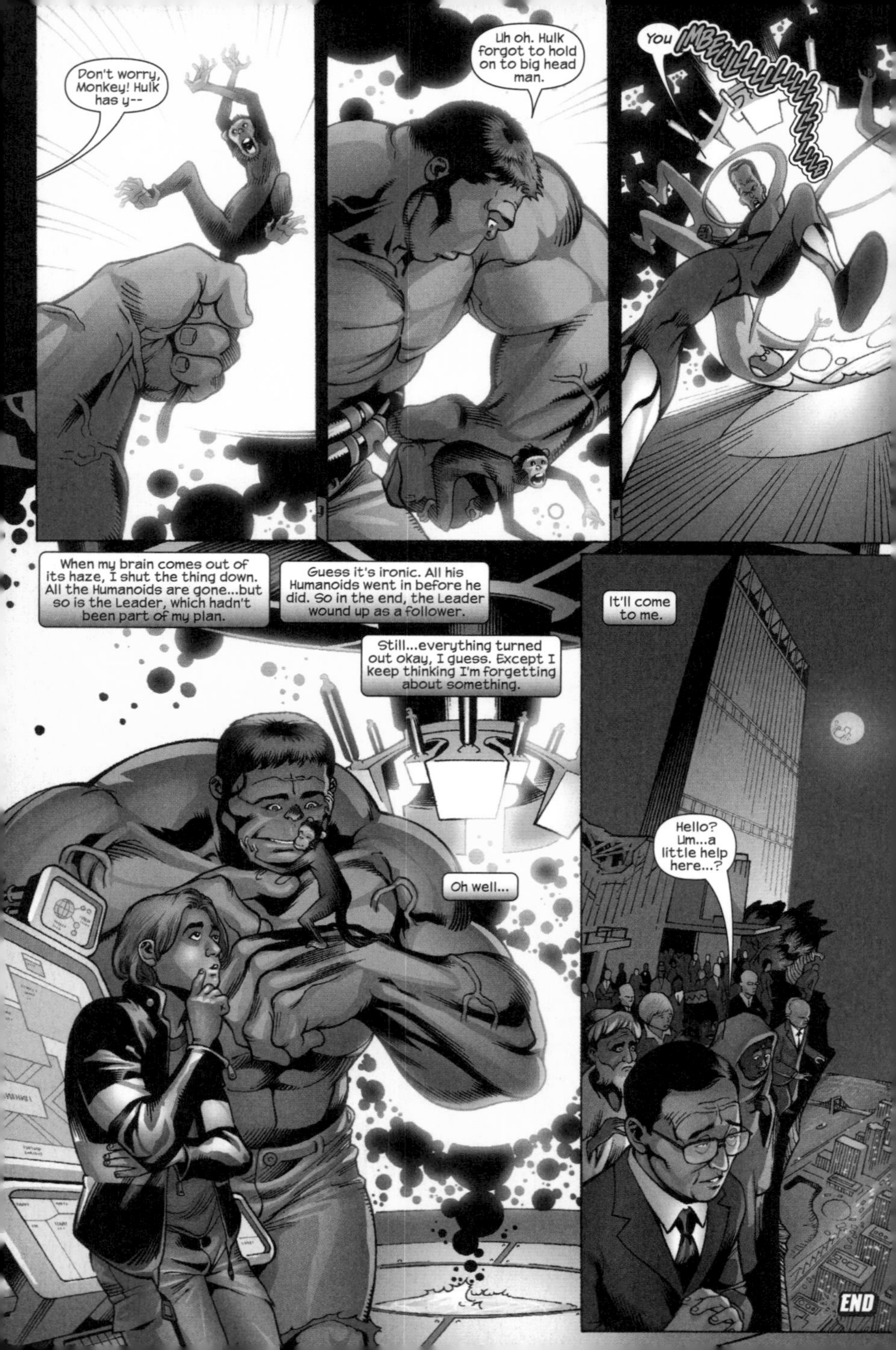
Don't worry, Monkey! Hulk has y--
Uh oh. Hulk forgot to hold on to big head man.
You IMBECILLLLLLLLLLLLLL
When my brain comes out of its haze, I shut the thing down. All the Humanoids are gone...but so is the Leader, which hadn't been part of my plan.
Guess it's ironic. All his Humanoids went in before he did. So in the end, the Leader wound up as a follower.
Still...everything turned out okay, I guess. Except I keep thinking I'm forgetting about something.
Oh well...
It'll come to me.
Hello? Um...a little help here...?
END

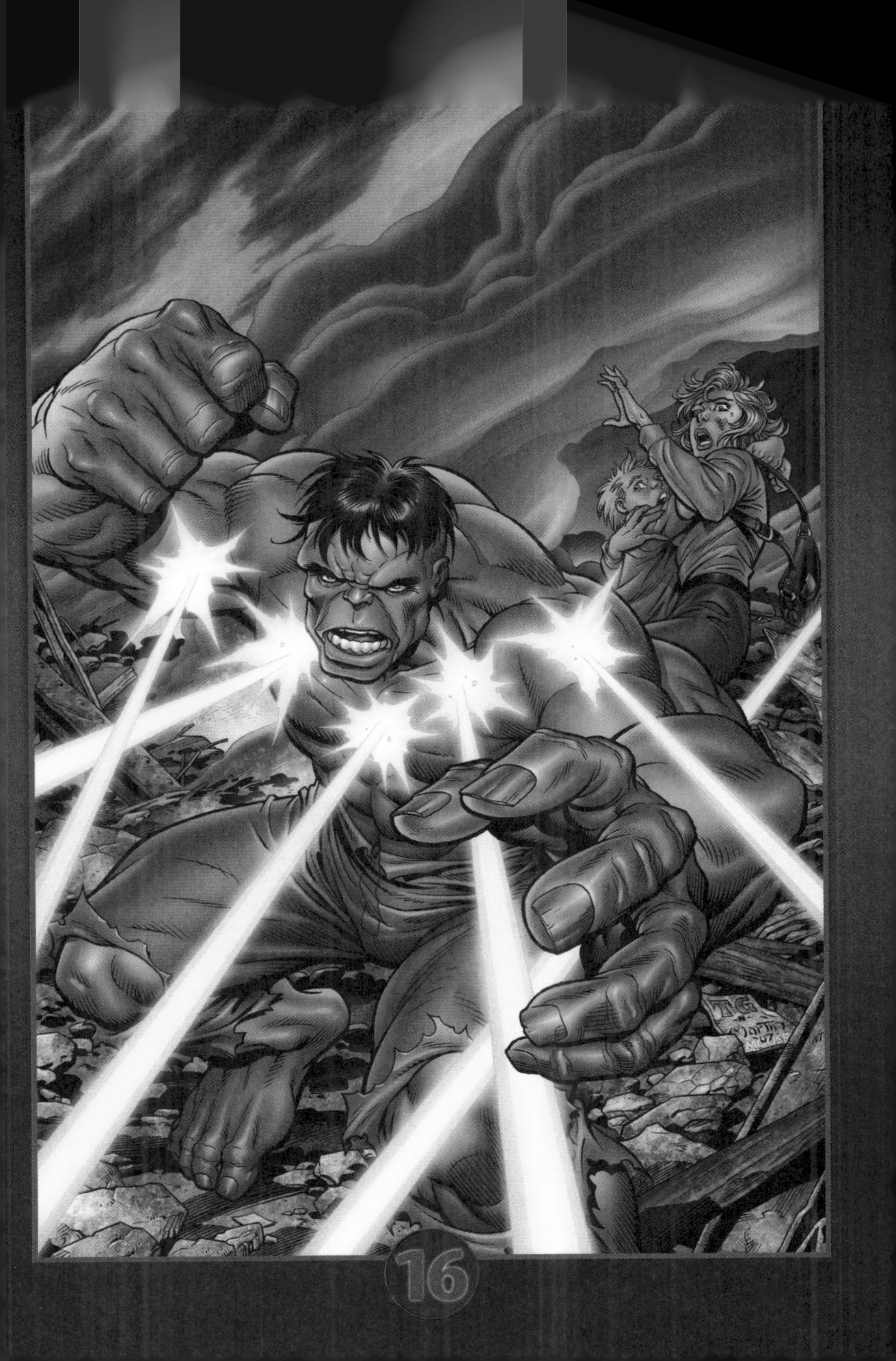

16

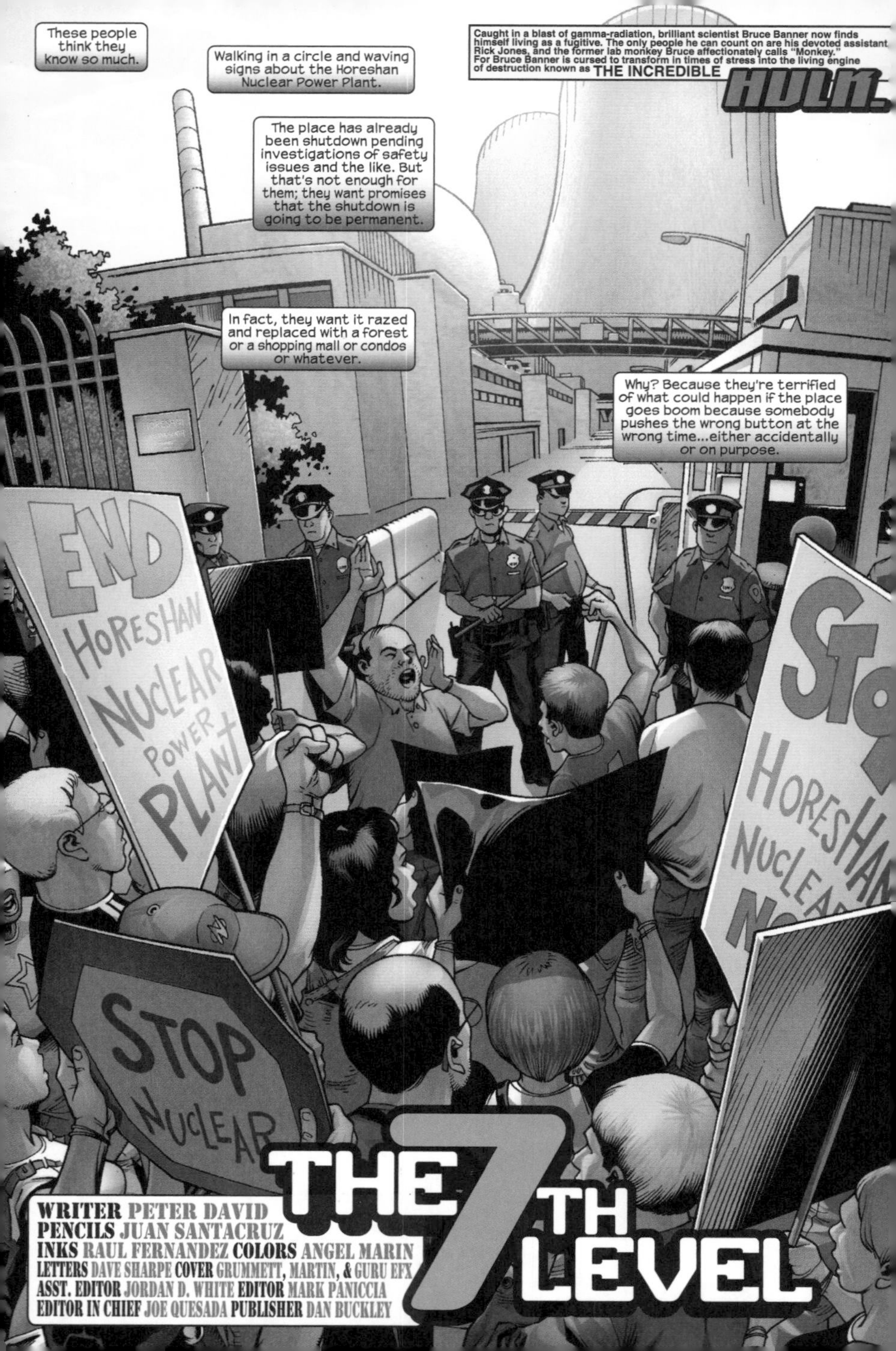

These people think they know so much.
Walking in a circle and waving signs about the Horeshan Nuclear Power Plant.
Caught in a blast of gamma-radiation, brilliant scientist Bruce Banner now finds himself living as a fugitive. The only people he can count on are his devoted assistant Rick Jones, and the former lab monkey Bruce affectionately calls "Monkey." For Bruce Banner is cursed to transform in times of stress into the living engine of destruction known as THE INCREDIBLE HULK.
The place has already been shutdown pending investigations of safety issues and the like. But that's not enough for them; they want promises that the shutdown is going to be permanent.
In fact, they want it razed and replaced with a forest or a shopping mall or condos or whatever.
Why? Because they're terrified of what could happen if the place goes boom because somebody pushes the wrong button at the wrong time...either accidentally or on purpose.
END HORESHAN NUCLEAR POWER PLANT
STOP HORESHAN NUCLEAR
STOP NUCLEAR
THE 7TH LEVEL
WRITER PETER DAVID
PENCILS JUAN SANTACRUZ
INKS RAUL FERNANDEZ COLORS ANGEL MARIN
LETTERS DAVE SHARPE COVER GRUMMETT, MARTIN, & GURU EFX
ASST. EDITOR JORDAN D. WHITE EDITOR MARK PANICCIA
EDITOR IN CHIEF JOE QUESADA PUBLISHER DAN BUCKLEY

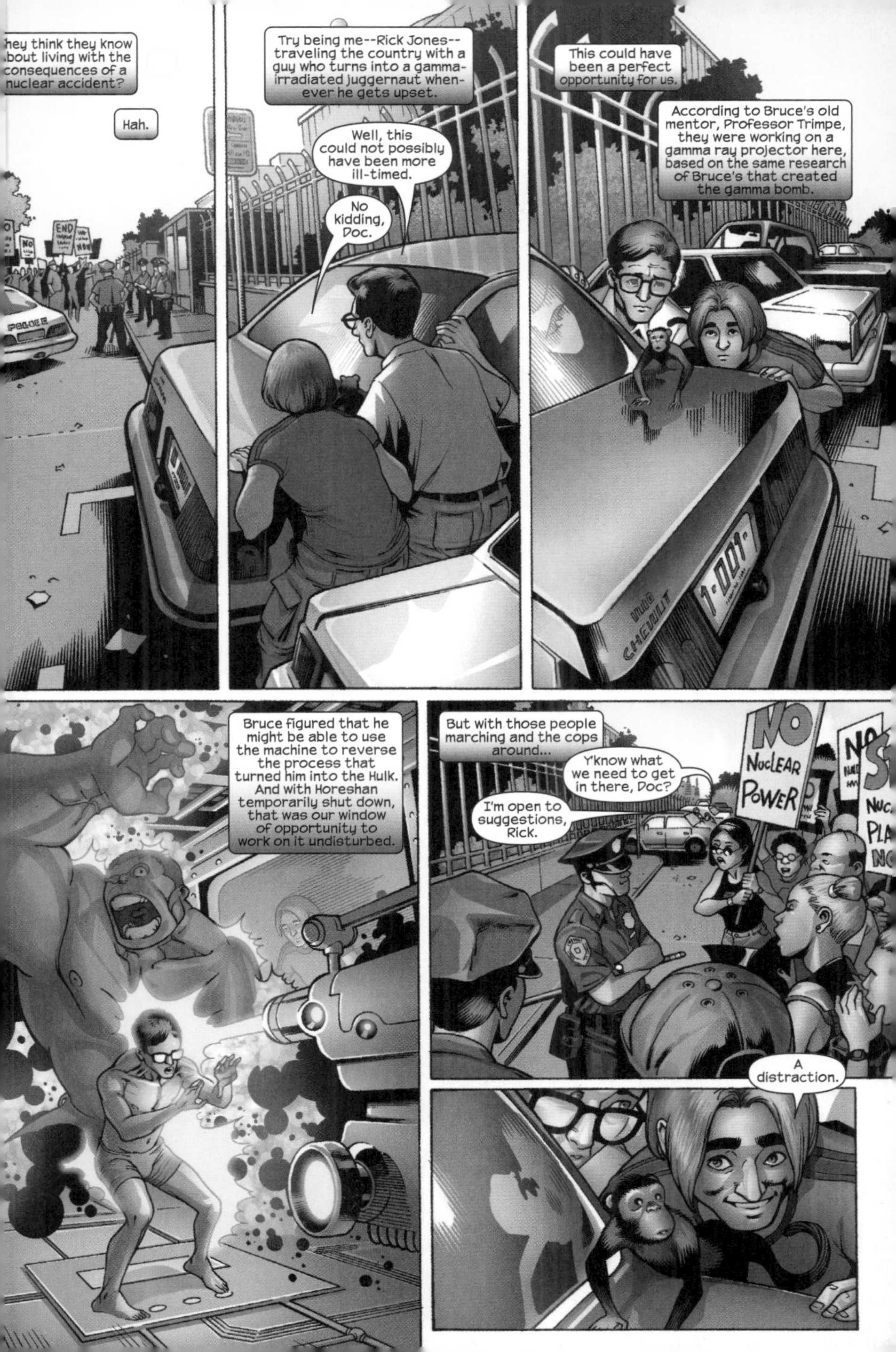

hey think they know
bout living with the
consequences of a
nuclear accident?
Hah.
Try being me--Rick Jones--
traveling the country with a
guy who turns into a gamma-
irradiated juggernaut when-
ever he gets upset.
Well, this
could not possibly
have been more
ill-timed.
No
kidding,
Doc.
This could have
been a perfect
opportunity for us.
According to Bruce's old
mentor, Professor Trimpe,
they were working on a
gamma ray projector here,
based on the same research
of Bruce's that created
the gamma bomb.
Bruce figured that he
might be able to use
the machine to reverse
the process that
turned him into the Hulk.
And with Horeshan
temporarily shut down,
that was our window
of opportunity to
work on it undisturbed.
But with those people
marching and the cops
around...
Y'know what
we need to get
in there, Doc?
I'm open to
suggestions,
Rick.
NO
NUCLEAR
POWER
A
distraction.

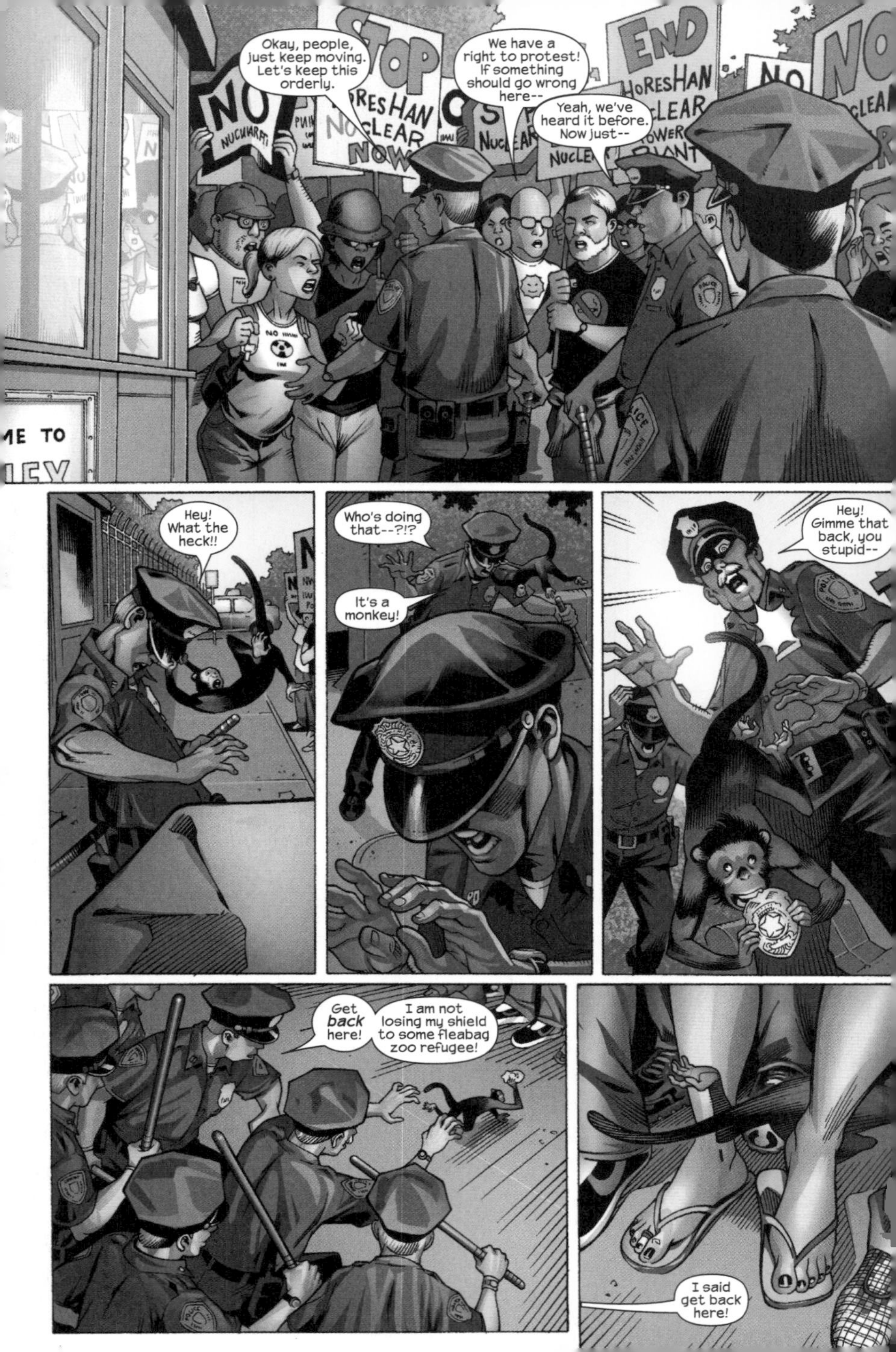

Okay, people, just keep moving. Let's keep this orderly.
We have a right to protest! If something should go wrong here--
Yeah, we've heard it before. Now just--
Hey! What the heck!!
Who's doing that--?!?
It's a monkey!
Hey! Gimme that back, you stupid--
Get back here!
I am not losing my shield to some fleabag zoo refugee!
I said get back here!

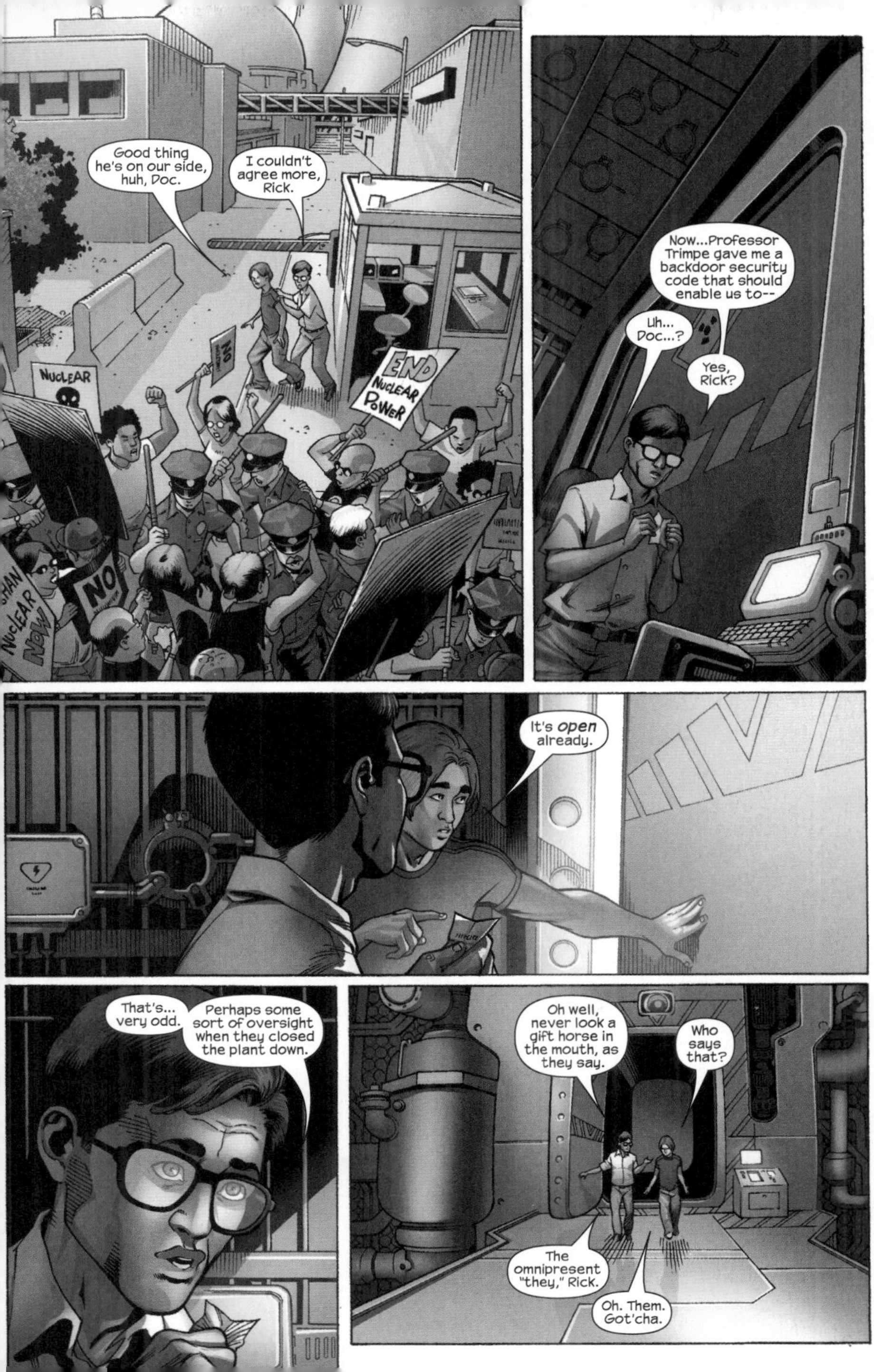
Good thing he's on our side, huh, Doc.
I couldn't agree more, Rick.
NUCLEAR
END NUCLEAR POWER
NO
NUCLEAR NOW
Now...Professor Trimpe gave me a backdoor security code that should enable us to--
Uh... Doc...?
Yes, Rick?
It's *open* already.
That's... very odd.
Perhaps some sort of oversight when they closed the plant down.
Oh well, never look a gift horse in the mouth, as they say.
Who says that?
The omnipresent "they," Rick.
Oh. Them. Got'cha.

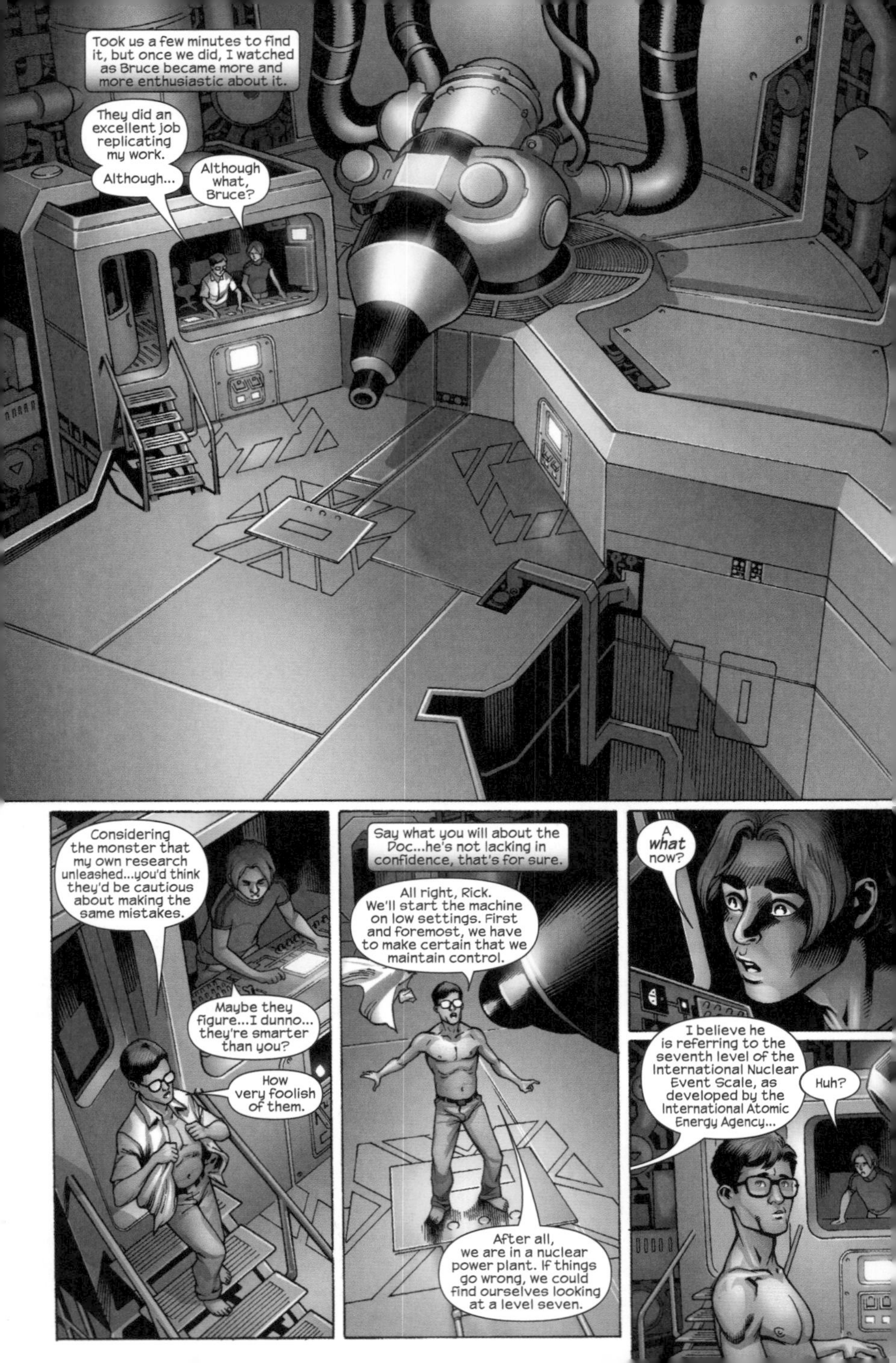
Took us a few minutes to find it, but once we did, I watched as Bruce became more and more enthusiastic about it.
They did an excellent job replicating my work.
Although...
Although what, Bruce?
Considering the monster that my own research unleashed...you'd think they'd be cautious about making the same mistakes.
Maybe they figure...I dunno... they're smarter than you?
How very foolish of them.
Say what you will about the Doc...he's not lacking in confidence, that's for sure.
All right, Rick. We'll start the machine on low settings. First and foremost, we have to make certain that we maintain control.
After all, we are in a nuclear power plant. If things go wrong, we could find ourselves looking at a level seven.
A *what* now?
I believe he is referring to the seventh level of the International Nuclear Event Scale, as developed by the International Atomic Energy Agency...
Huh?

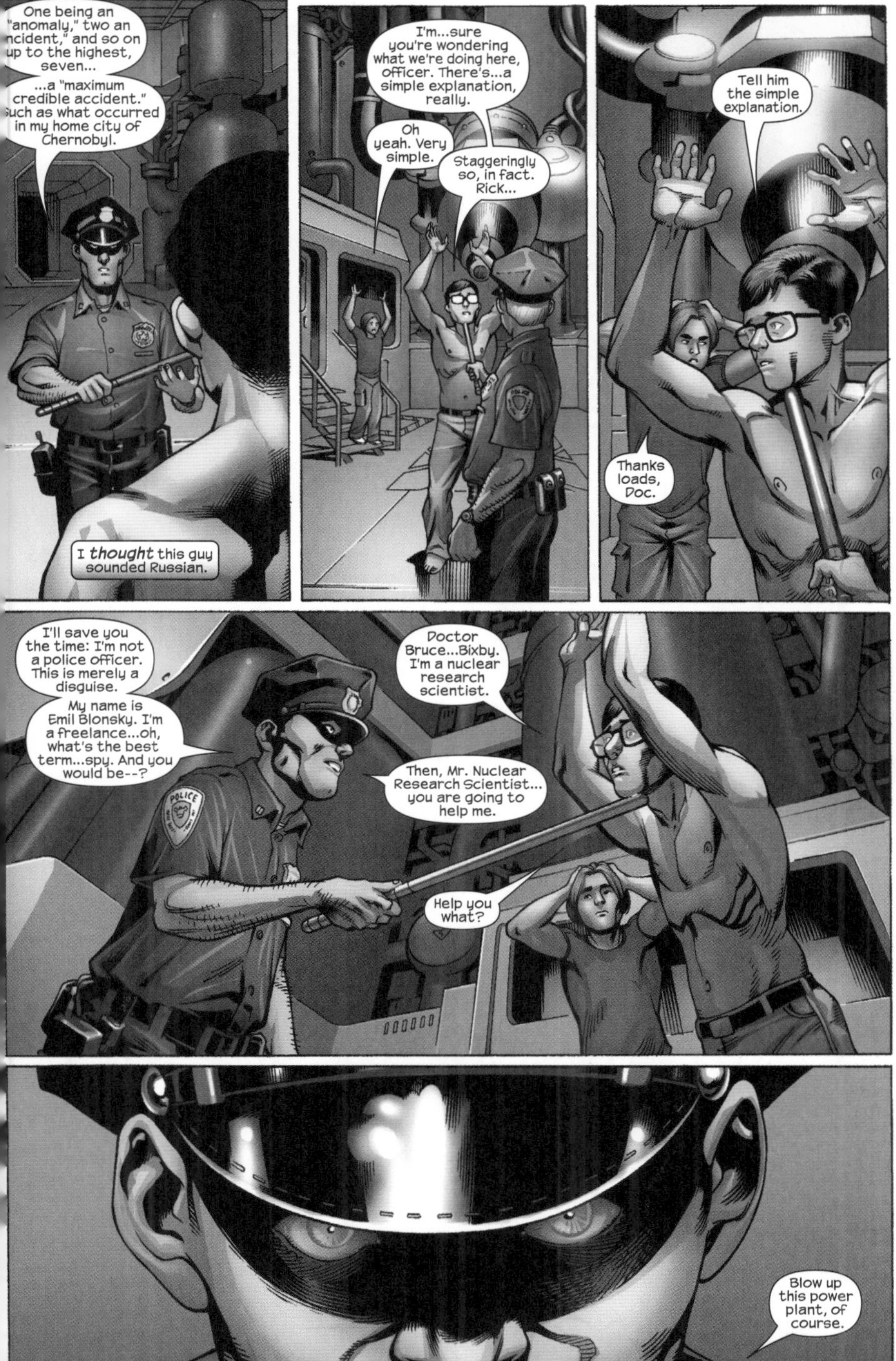
One being an "anomaly," two an incident," and so on up to the highest, seven...
...a "maximum credible accident." Such as what occurred in my home city of Chernobyl.
I *thought* this guy sounded Russian.
I'm...sure you're wondering what we're doing here, officer. There's...a simple explanation, really.
Oh yeah. Very simple.
Staggeringly so, in fact. Rick...
Tell him the simple explanation.
Thanks loads, Doc.
I'll save you the time: I'm not a police officer. This is merely a disguise.
My name is Emil Blonsky. I'm a freelance...oh, what's the best term...spy. And you would be--?
Doctor Bruce...Bixby. I'm a nuclear research scientist.
Then, Mr. Nuclear Research Scientist... you are going to help me.
Help you what?
Blow up this power plant, of course.

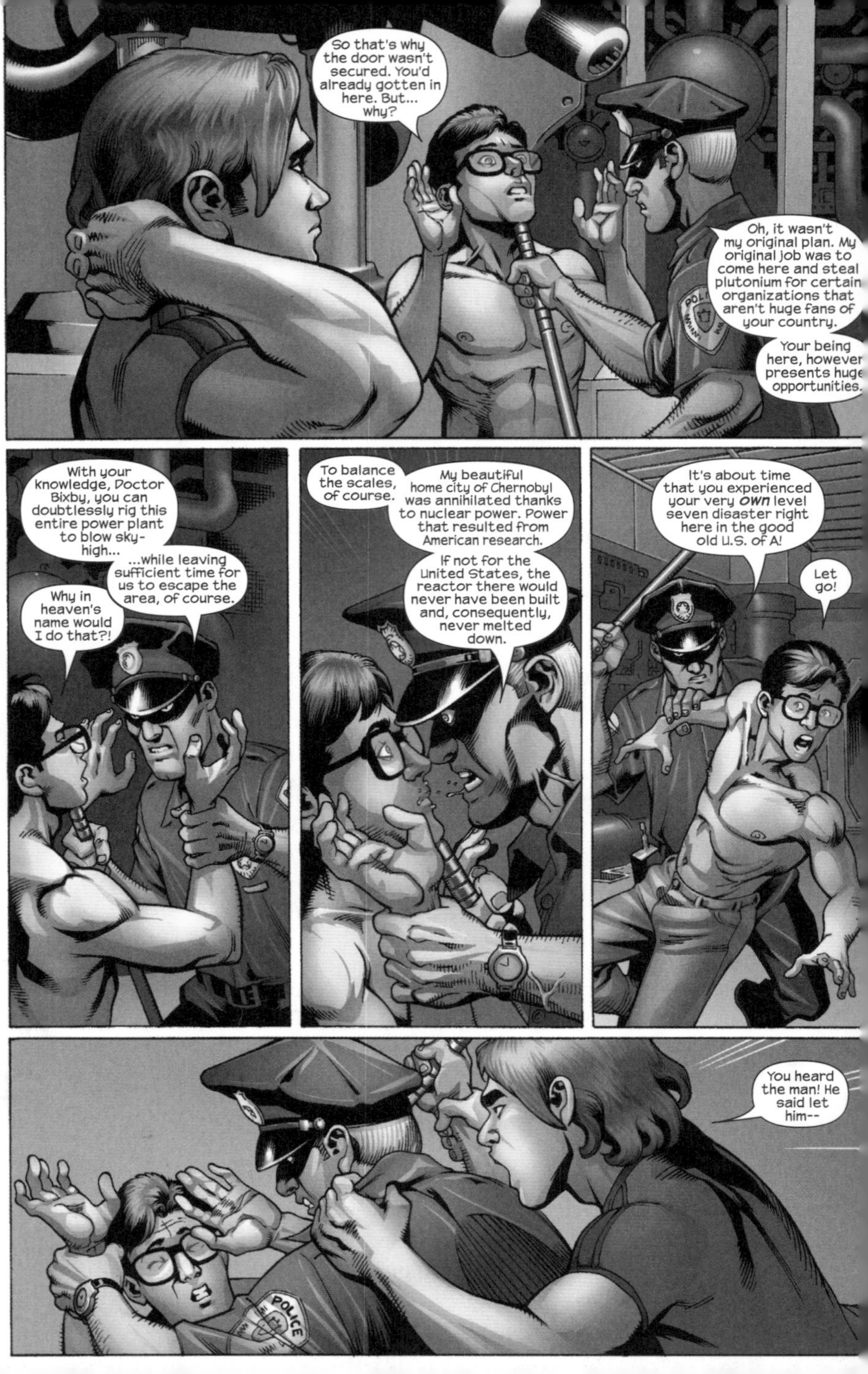

So that's why the door wasn't secured. You'd already gotten in here. But... why?
Oh, it wasn't my original plan. My original job was to come here and steal plutonium for certain organizations that aren't huge fans of your country.
Your being here, however presents huge opportunities.
With your knowledge, Doctor Bixby, you can doubtlessly rig this entire power plant to blow sky-high...
...while leaving sufficient time for us to escape the area, of course.
Why in heaven's name would I do that?!
To balance the scales, of course.
My beautiful home city of Chernobyl was annihilated thanks to nuclear power. Power that resulted from American research.
If not for the United States, the reactor there would never have been built and, consequently, never melted down.
It's about time that you experienced your very OWN level seven disaster right here in the good old U.S. of A!
Let go!
You heard the man! He said let him--

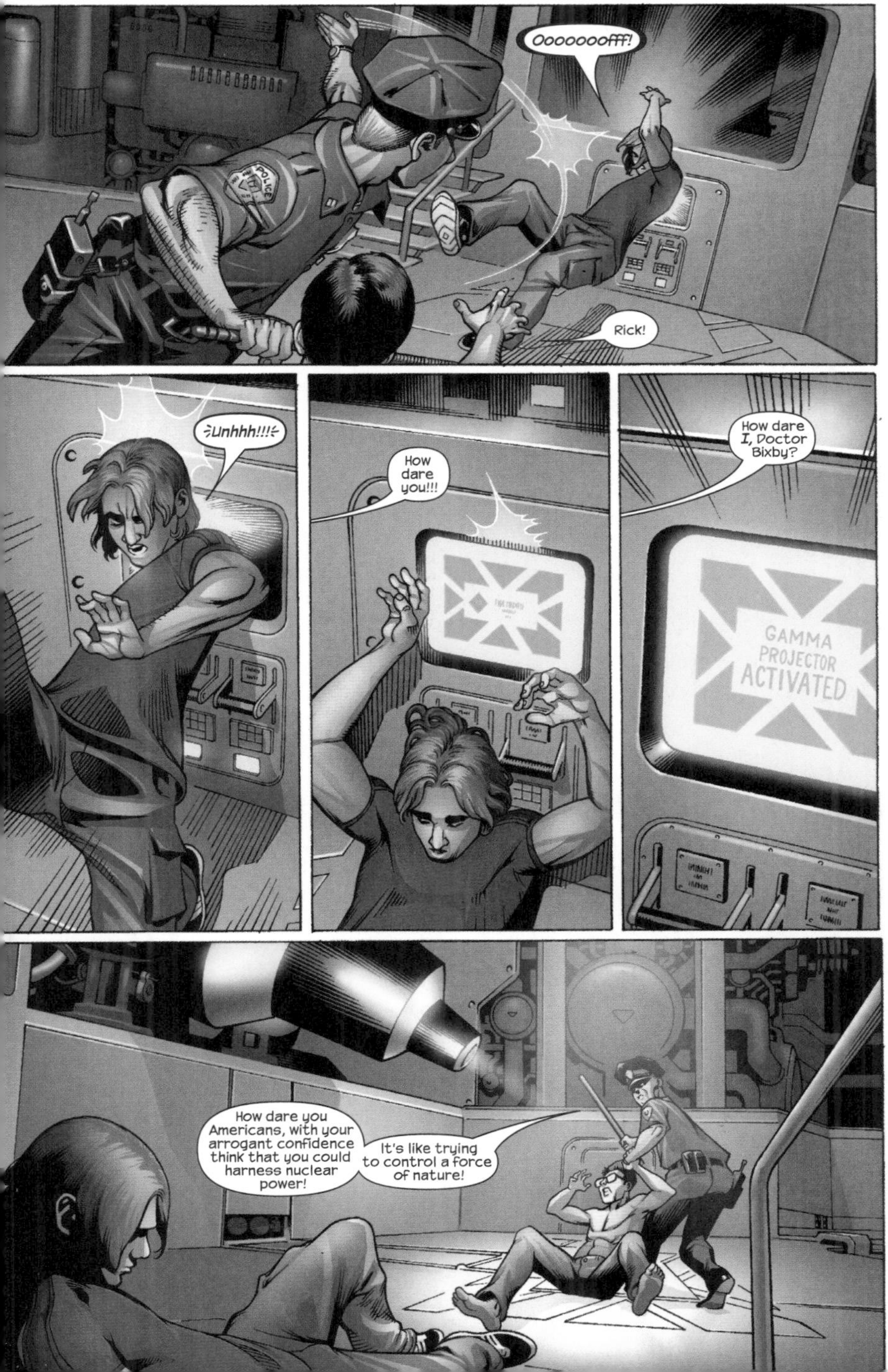
Ooooooofff!
Rick!
Unhhh!!!
How dare you!!!
How dare I, Doctor Bixby?
GAMMA PROJECTOR ACTIVATED
How dare you Americans, with your arrogant confidence think that you could harness nuclear power!
It's like trying to control a force of nature!

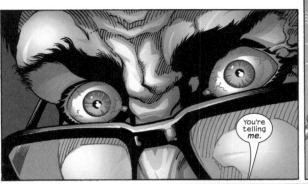

You're telling *me*.

What...

ARRRRHAAAAAHHH

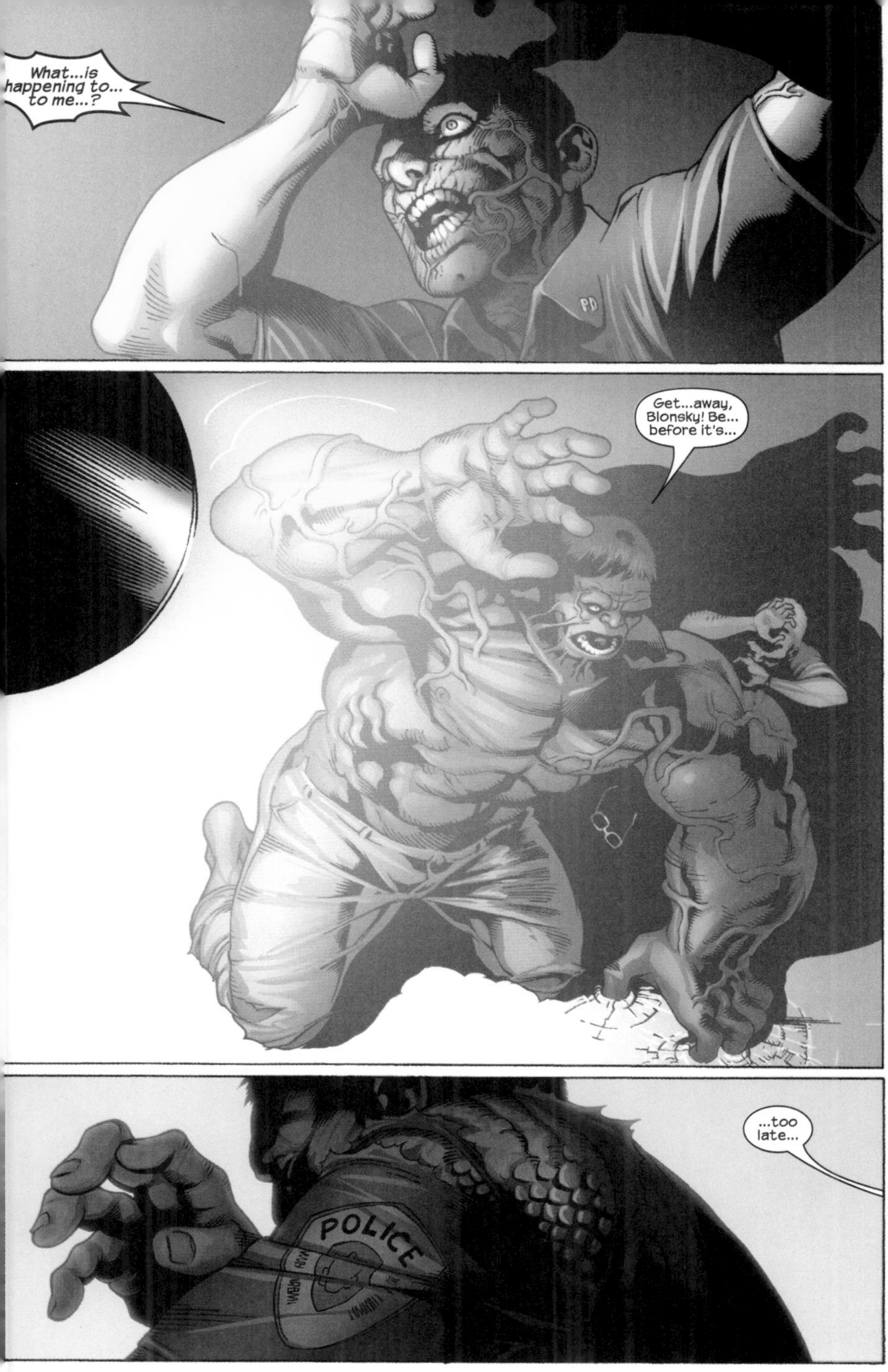
What...is happening to... to me...?
Get...away, Blonsky! Be... before it's...
...too late...
POLICE

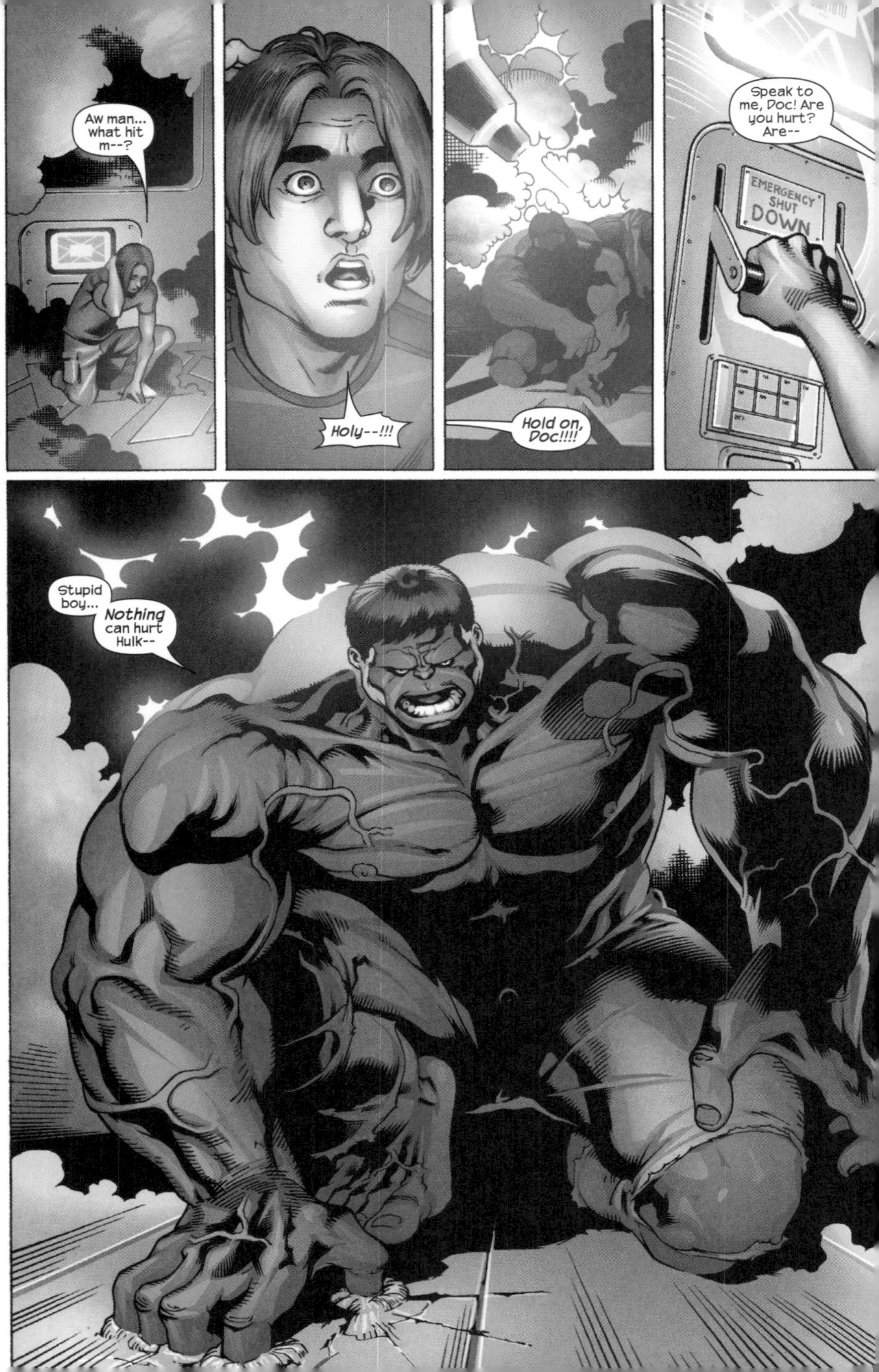

Aw man... what hit m--?
Holy--!!!
Hold on, Doc!!!!
Speak to me, Doc! Are you hurt? Are--
EMERGENCY SHUT DOWN
Stupid boy... *Nothing* can hurt Hulk--

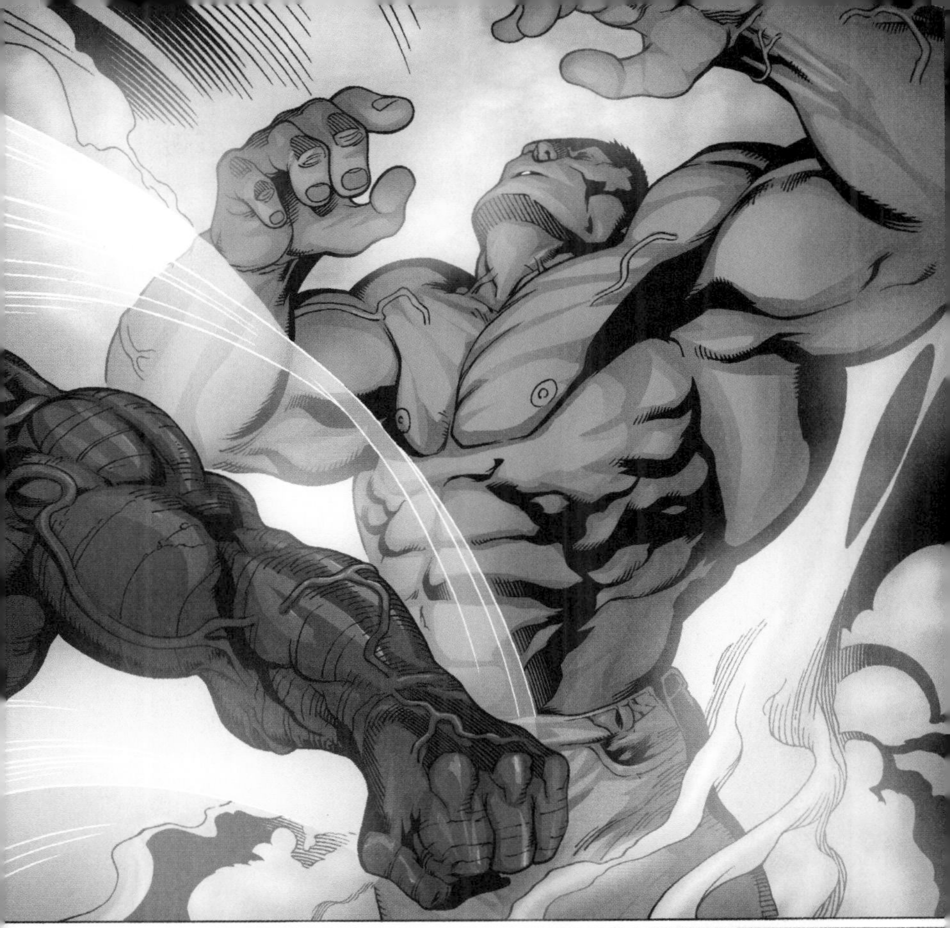

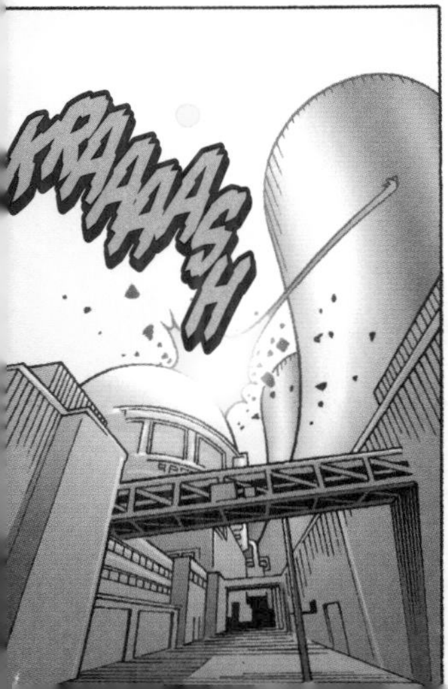
KRAAASH

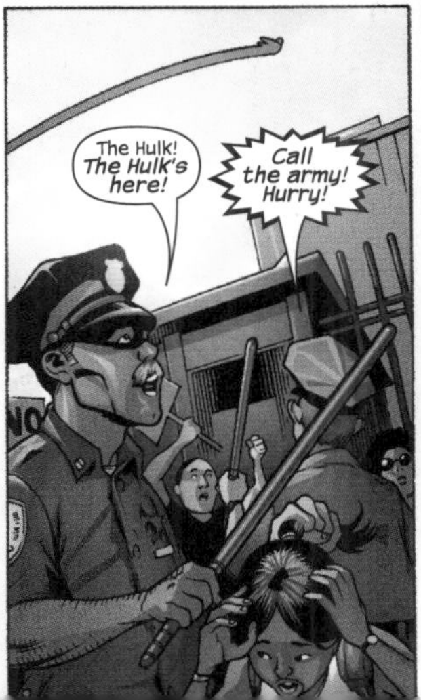
The Hulk! The Hulk's here!
Call the army! Hurry!

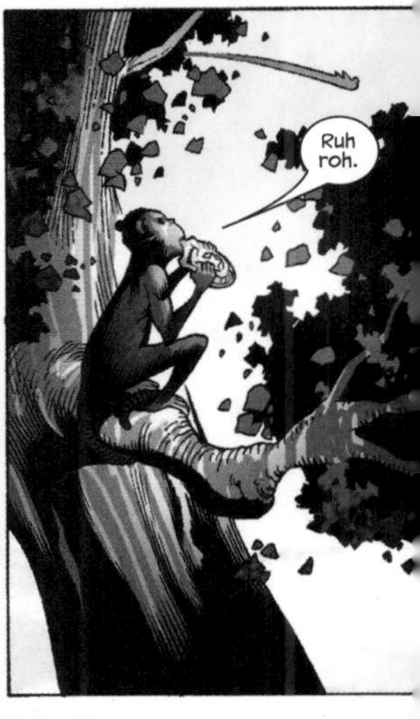
Ruh roh.

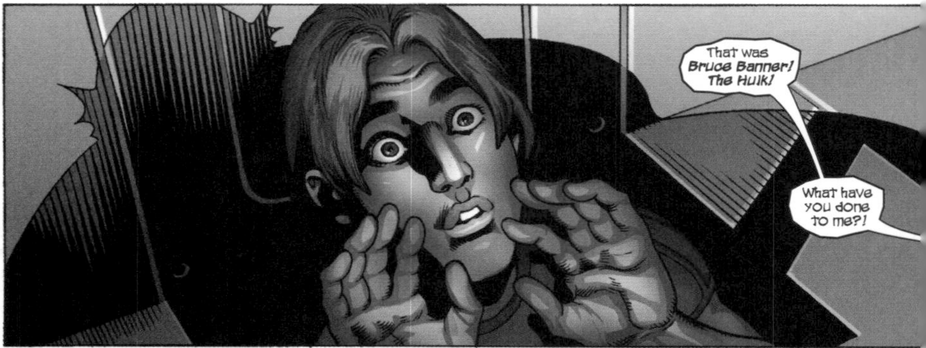
That was Bruce Banner! The Hulk!
What have you done to me?!
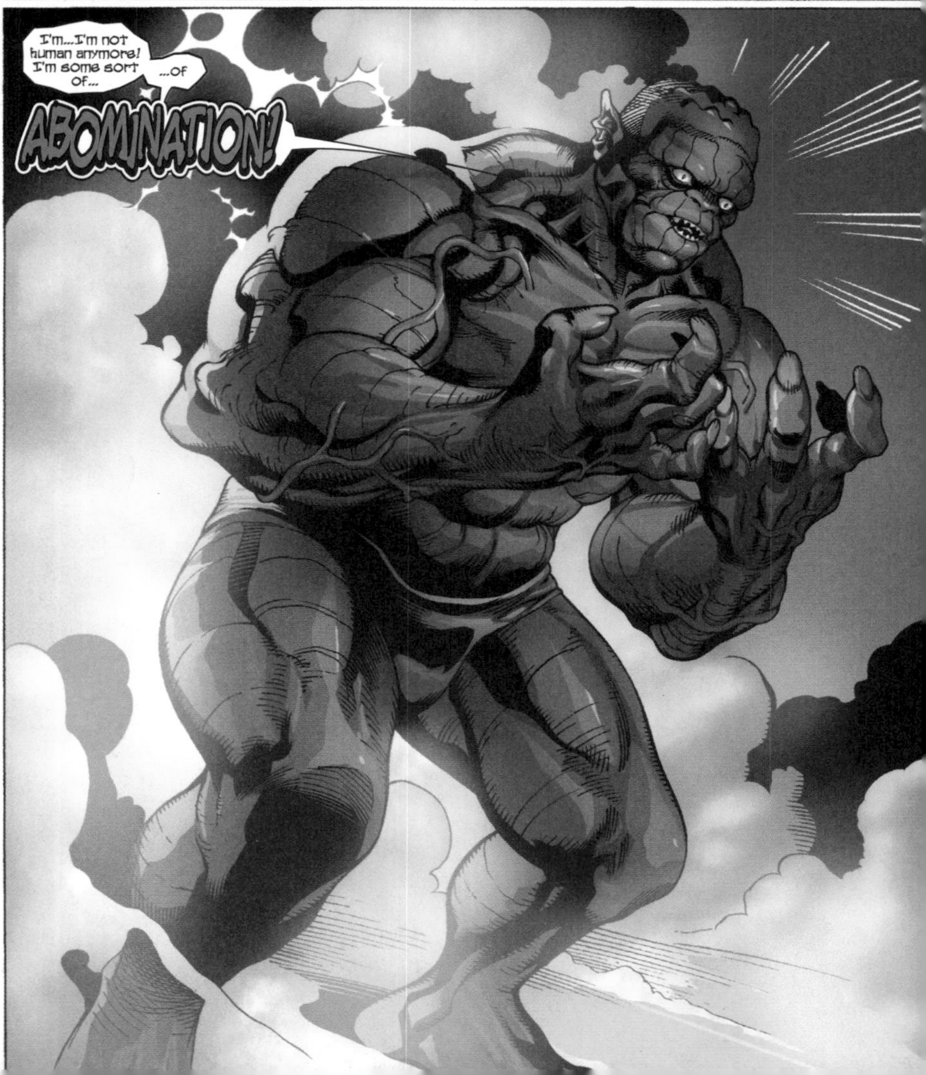
I'm...I'm not human anymore! I'm some sort of...
...of
ABOMINATION!

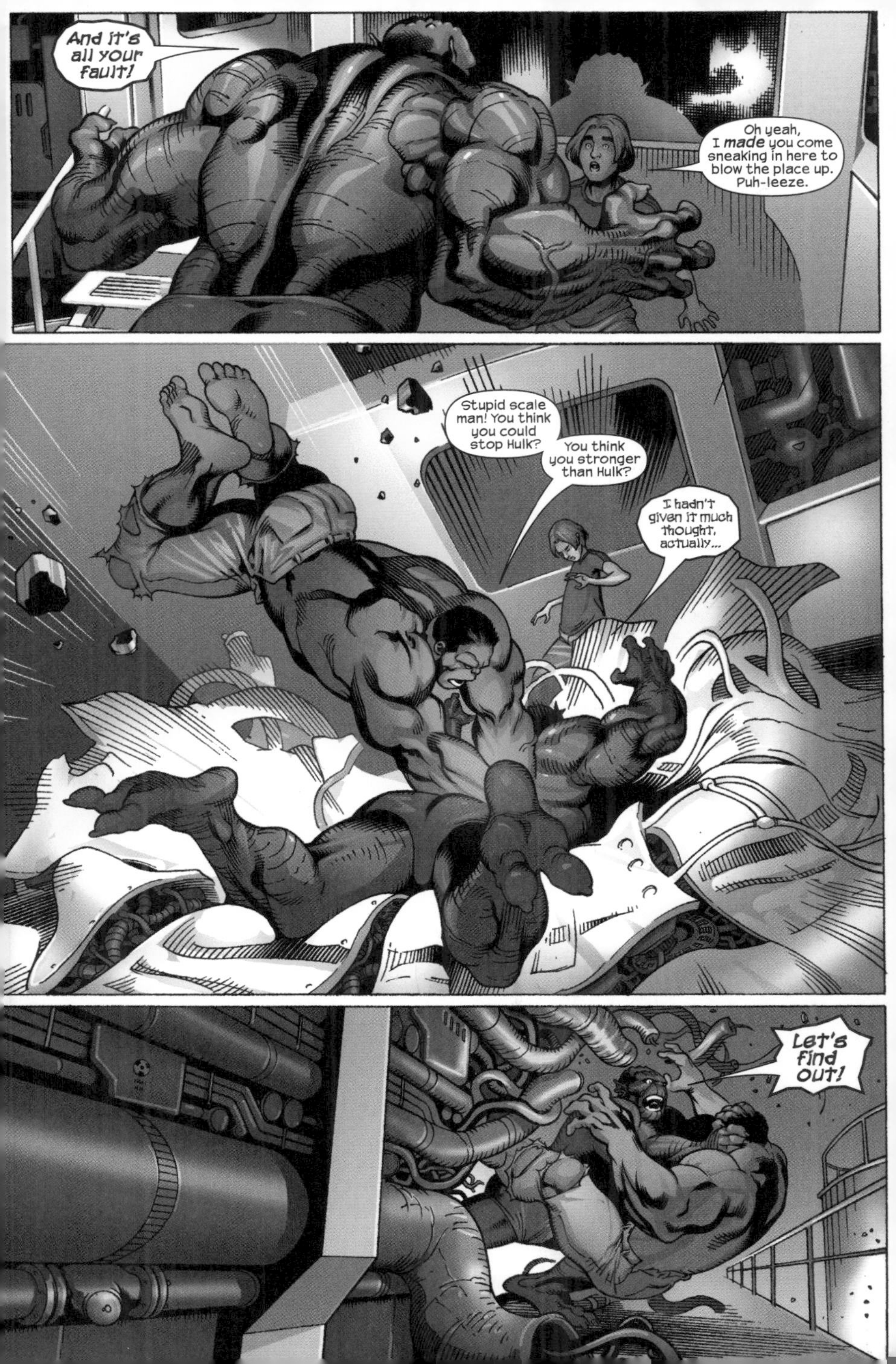
And it's all your fault!
Oh yeah, I made you come sneaking in here to blow the place up. Puh-leeze.
Stupid scale man! You think you could stop Hulk?
You think you stronger than Hulk?
I hadn't given it much thought, actually...
Let's find out!

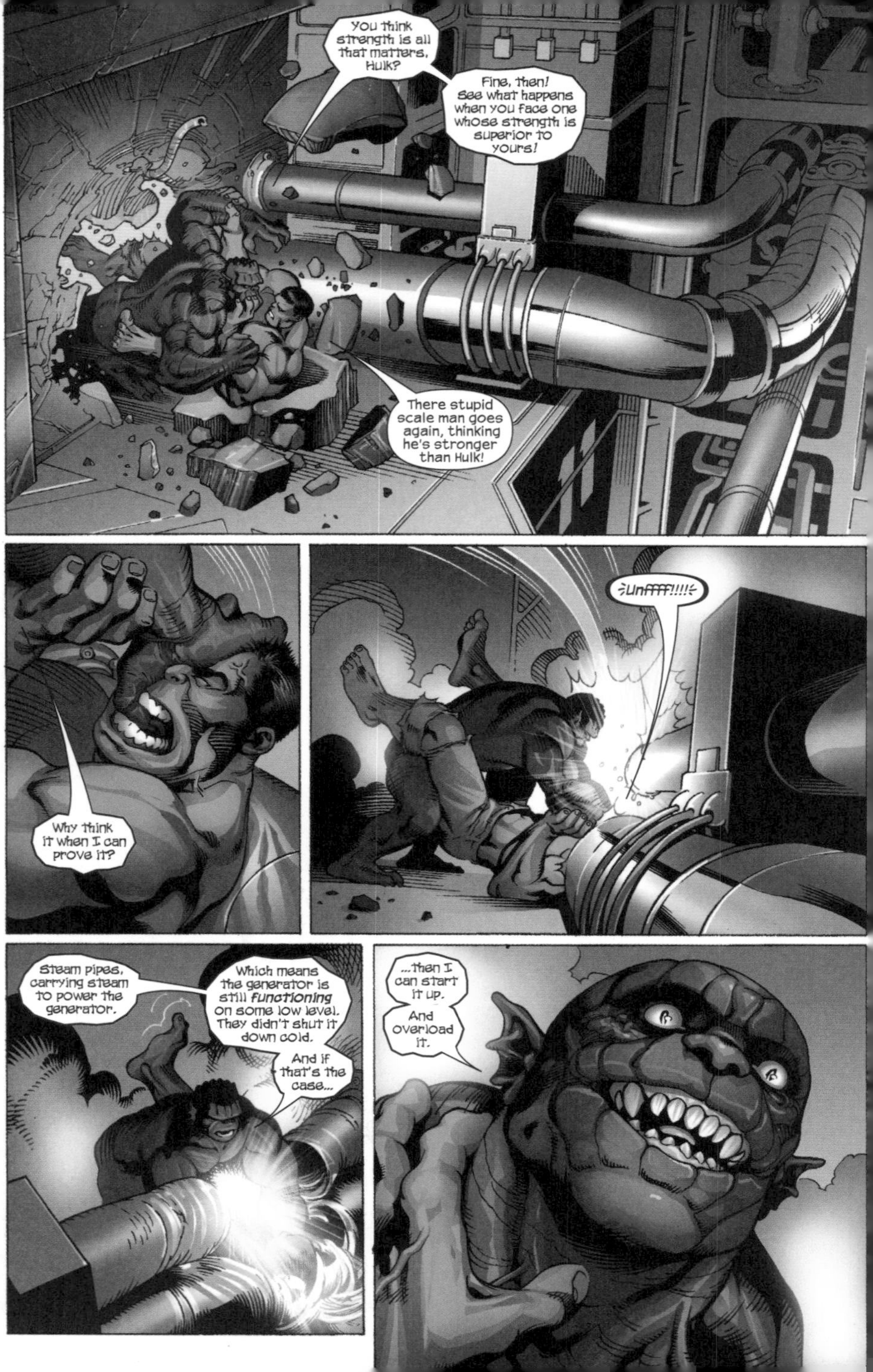
You think strength is all that matters, Hulk?
Fine, then! See what happens when you face one whose strength is superior to yours!
There stupid scale man goes again, thinking he's stronger than Hulk!
Why think it when I can prove it?
UNFFFF!!!!
Steam pipes, carrying steam to power the generator.
Which means the generator is still functioning on some low level. They didn't shut it down cold.
And if that's the case...
...then I can start it up.
And overload it.

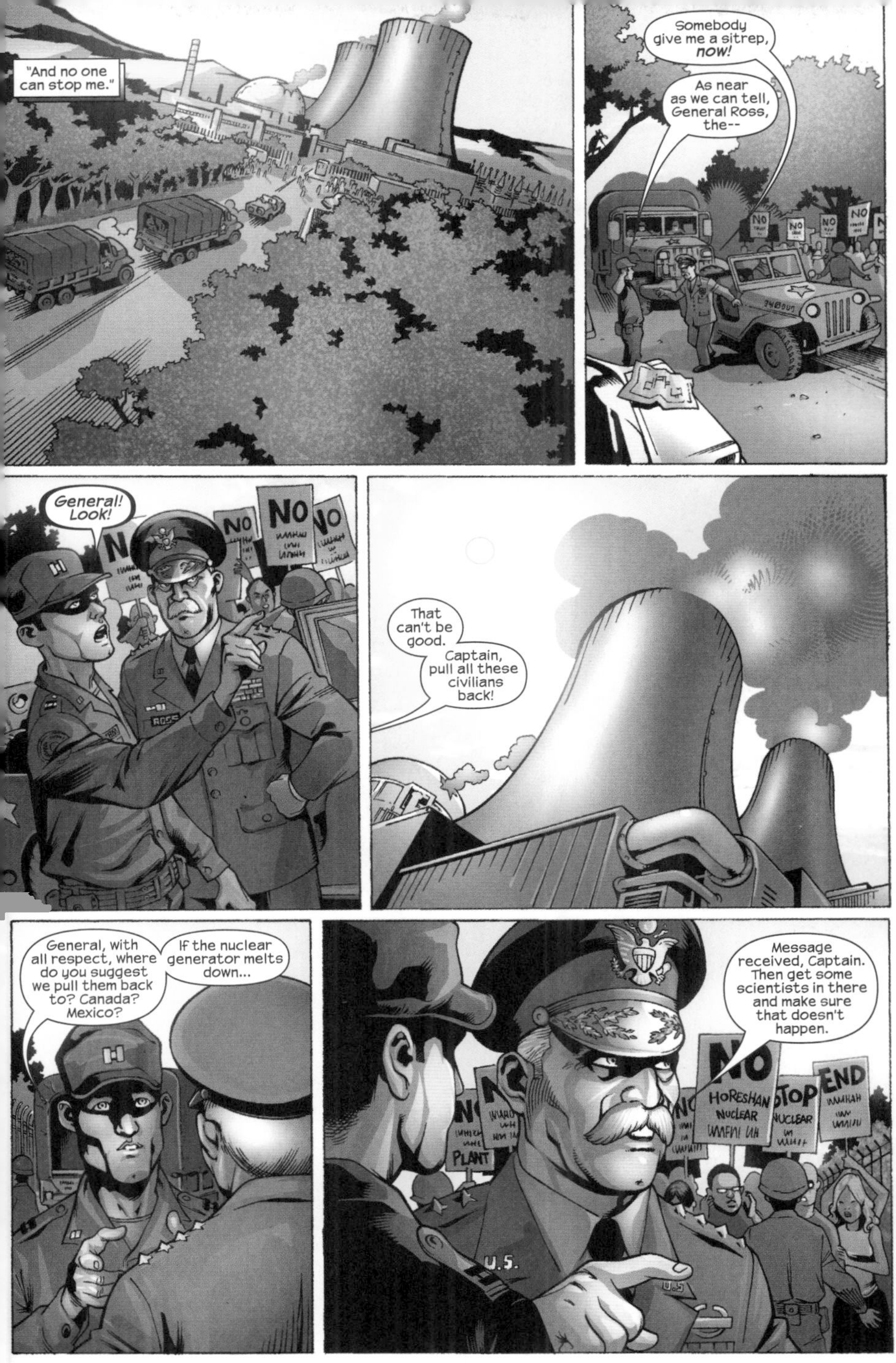
"And no one can stop me."
Somebody give me a sitrep, *NOW!*
As near as we can tell, General Ross, the--
*General! Look!*
NO
NO
NO
That can't be good.
Captain, pull all these civilians back!
General, with all respect, where do you suggest we pull them back to? Canada? Mexico?
If the nuclear generator melts down...
Message received, Captain. Then get some scientists in there and make sure that doesn't happen.
NO
PLANT
NO HORESHAN NUCLEAR
STOP NUCLEAR
END
U.S.

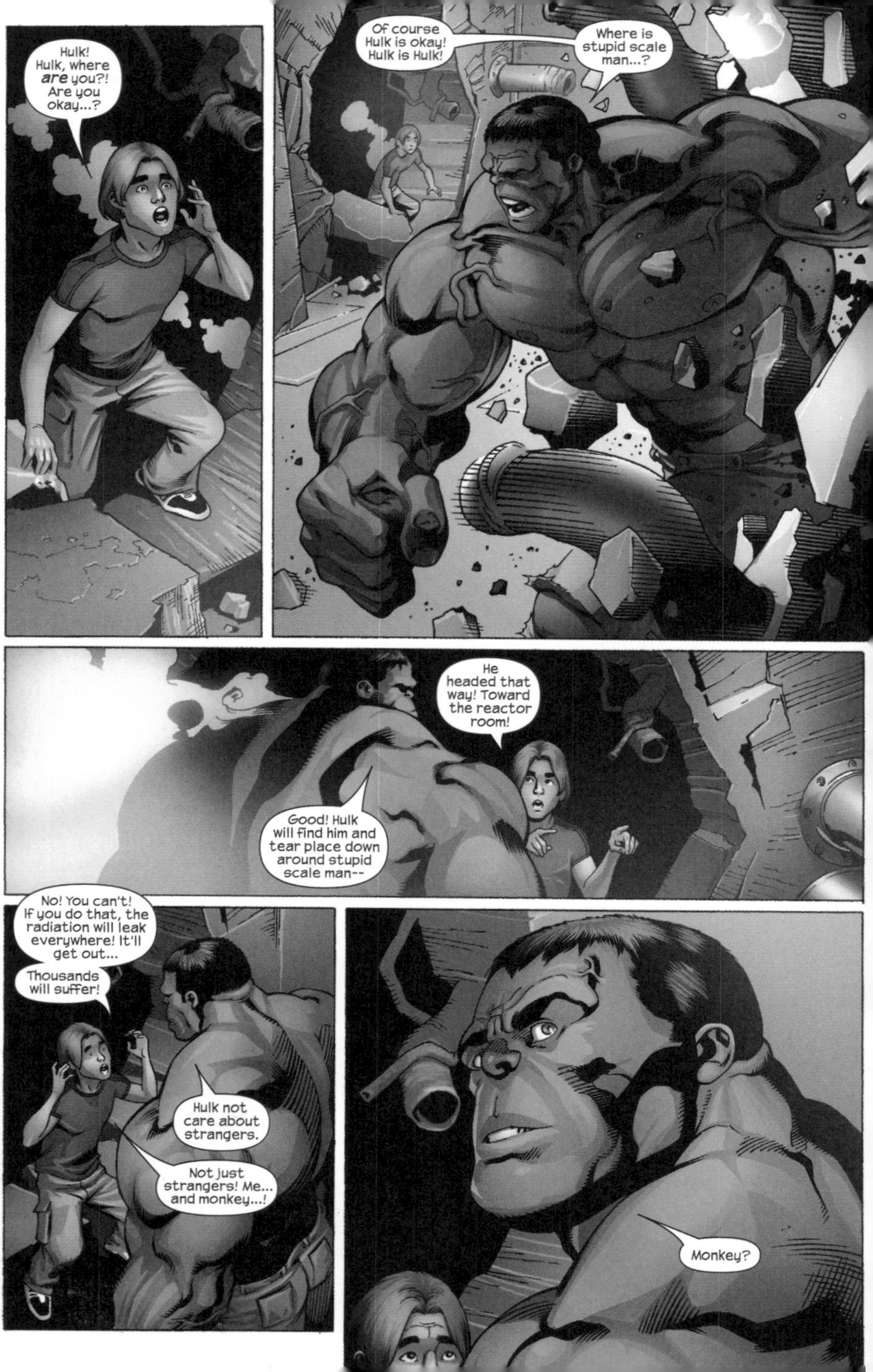

Hulk! Hulk, where *are* you?! Are you okay...?
Of course Hulk is okay! Hulk is Hulk!
Where is stupid scale man...?
He headed that way! Toward the reactor room!
Good! Hulk will find him and tear place down around stupid scale man--
No! You can't! If you do that, the radiation will leak everywhere! It'll get out...
Thousands will suffer!
Hulk not care about strangers.
Not just strangers! Me... and monkey...!
Monkey?

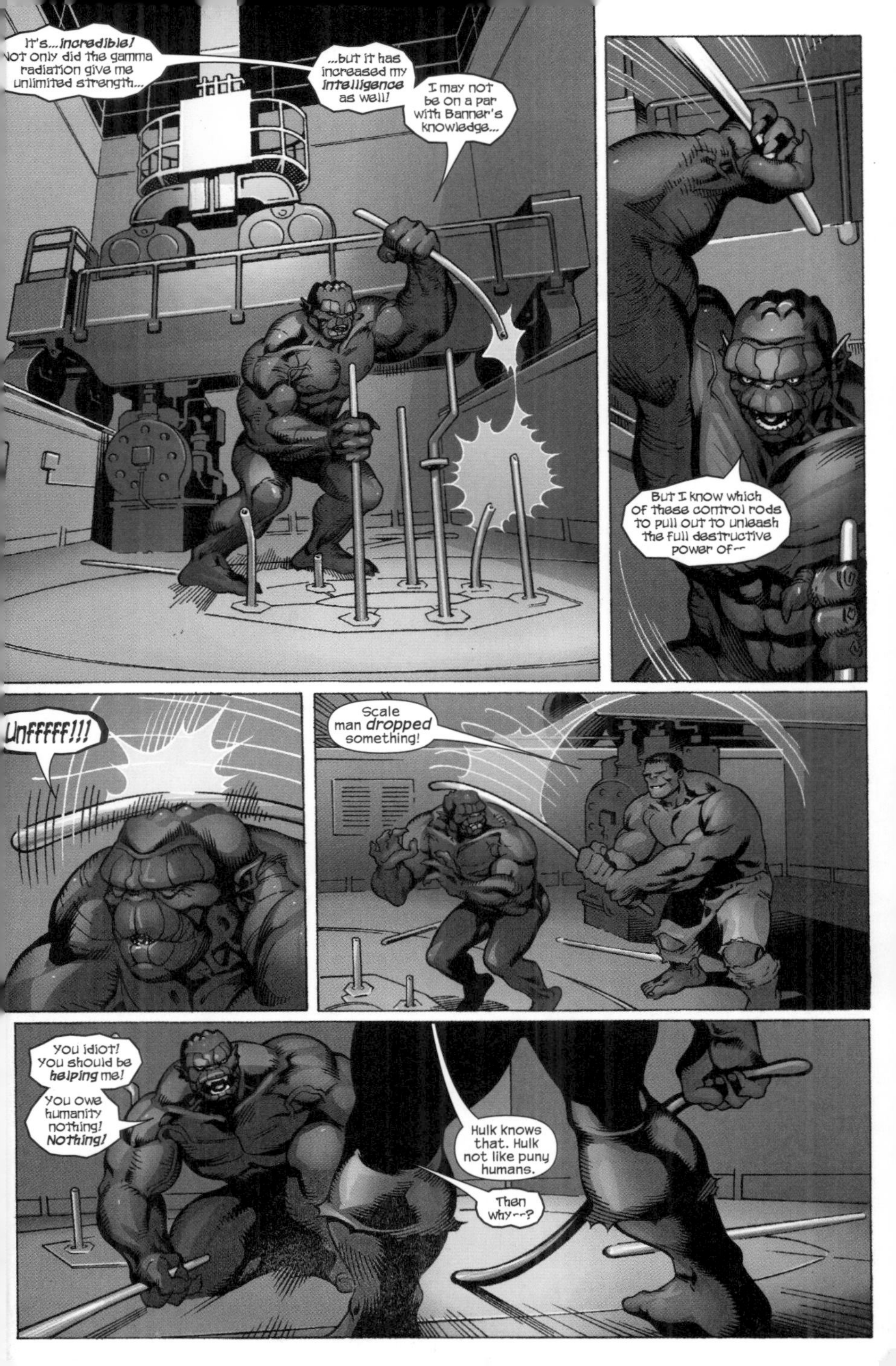
It's...incredible! Not only did the gamma radiation give me unlimited strength...
...but it has increased my intelligence as well!
I may not be on a par with Banner's knowledge...
But I know which of these control rods to pull out to unleash the full destructive power of--
Unffffff!!!
Scale man dropped something!
You idiot! You should be helping me!
You owe humanity nothing! Nothing!
Hulk knows that. Hulk not like puny humans.
Then why--?

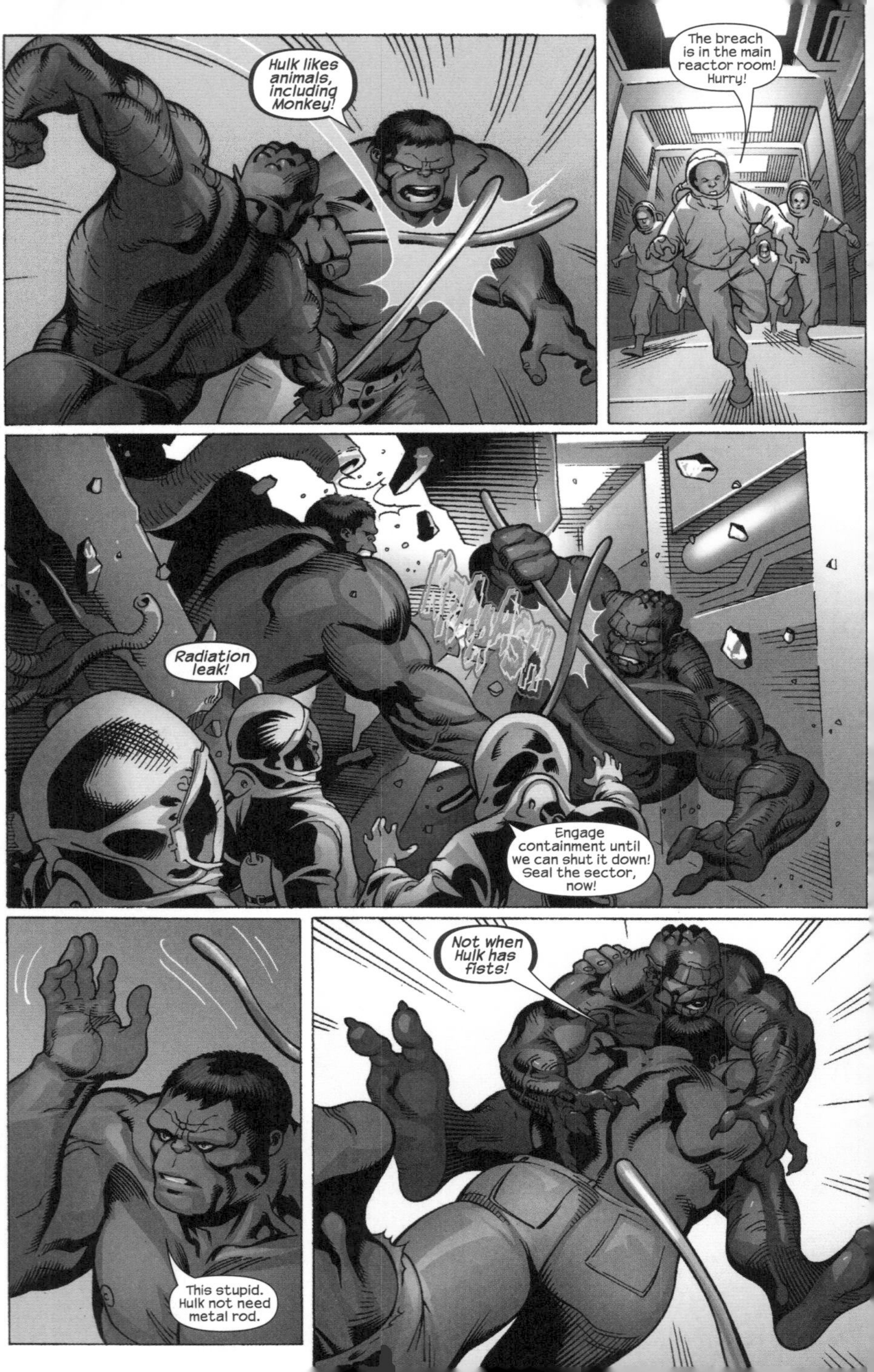
Hulk likes animals, including Monkey!
The breach is in the main reactor room! Hurry!
Radiation leak!
Engage containment until we can shut it down! Seal the sector, now!
This stupid. Hulk not need metal rod.
Not when Hulk has fists!

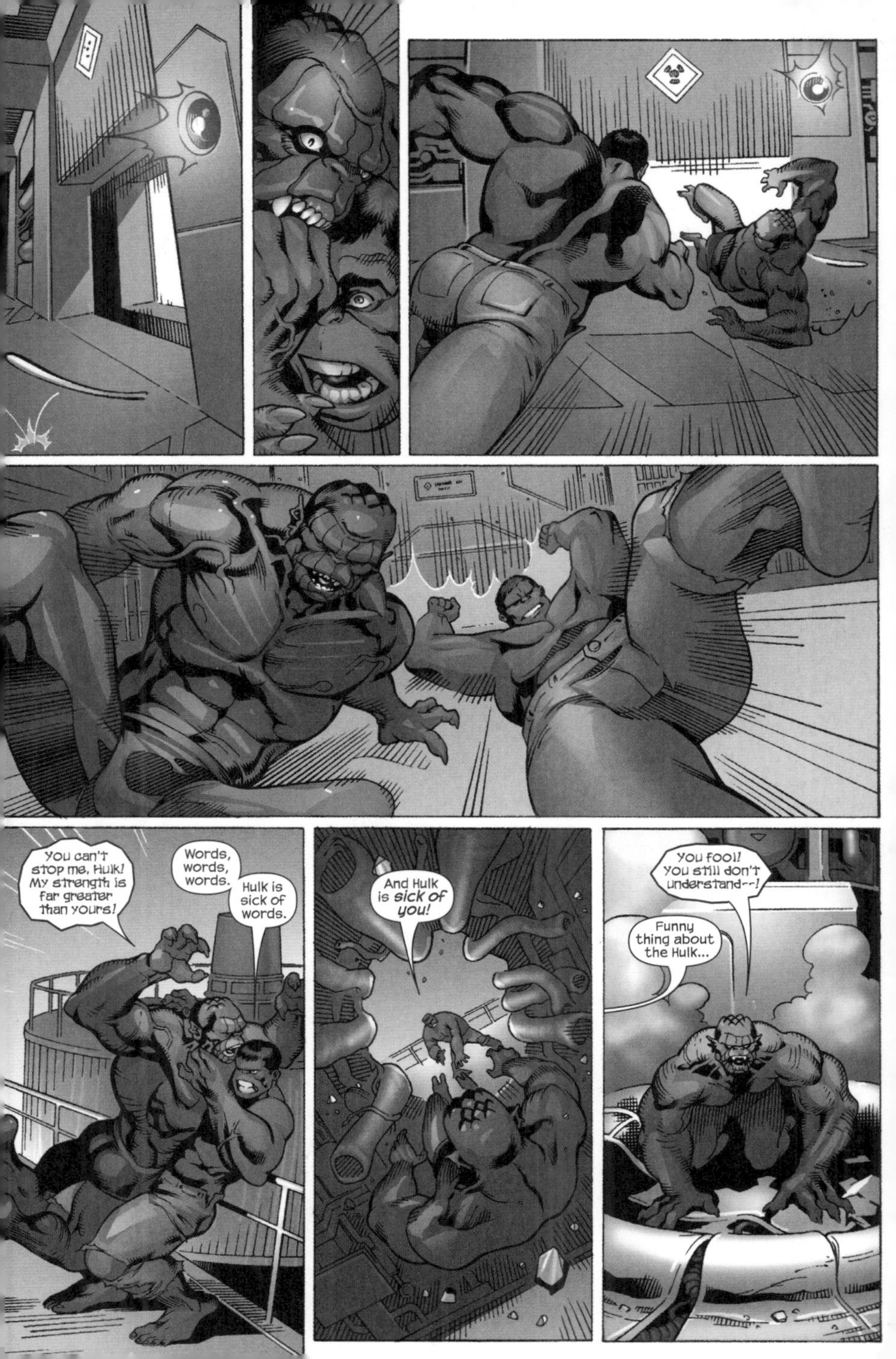

You can't stop me, Hulk! My strength is far greater than yours!
Words, words, words.
Hulk is sick of words.
And Hulk is sick of you!
You fool! You still don't understand--!
Funny thing about the Hulk...

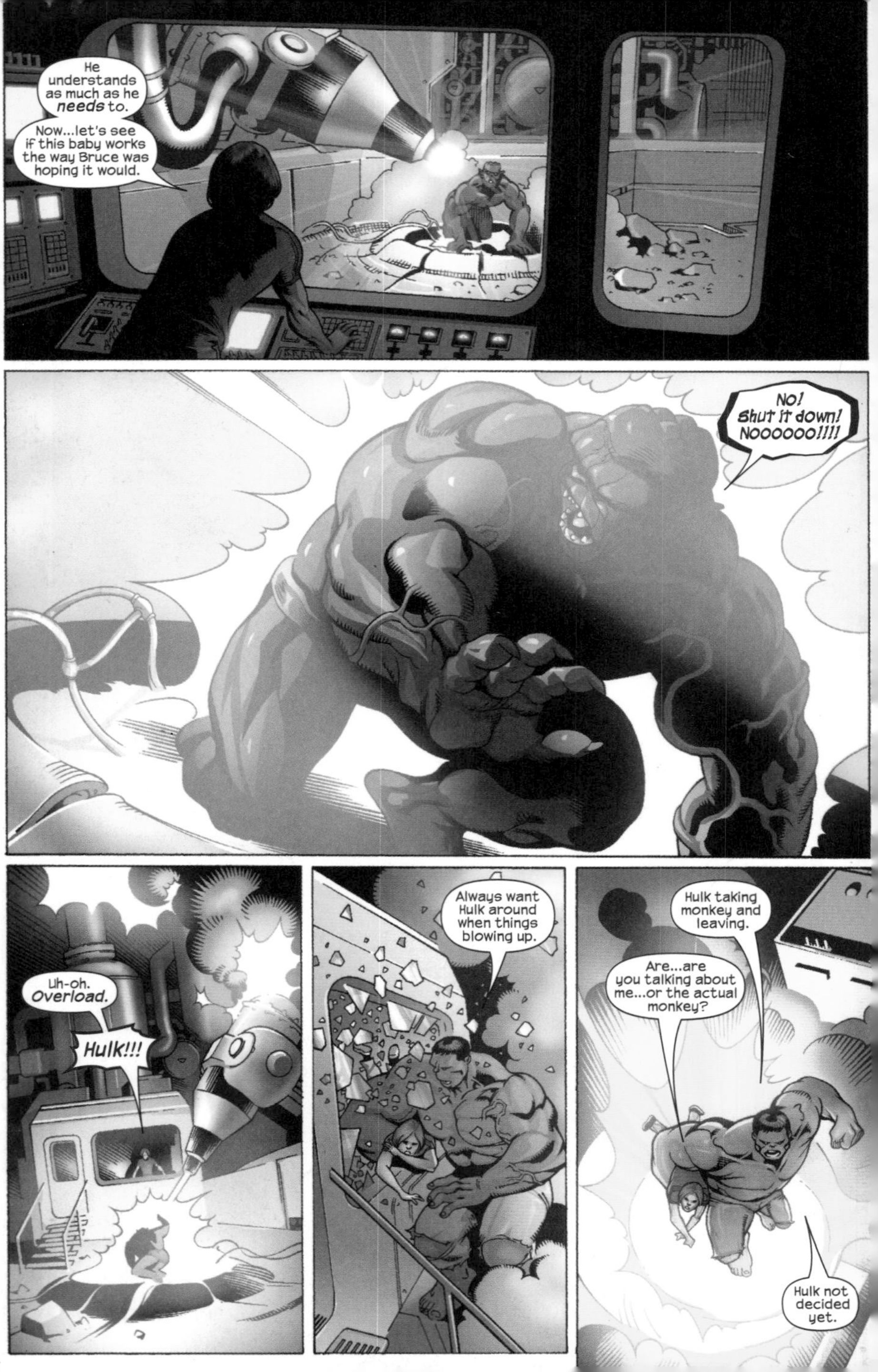
He understands as much as he *needs* to.
Now...let's see if this baby works the way Bruce was hoping it would.
No! Shut it down! NOOOOOO!!!!
Uh-oh. *Overload.*
Hulk!!!
Always want Hulk around when things blowing up.
Hulk taking monkey and leaving.
Are...are you talking about me...or the actual monkey?
Hulk not decided yet.

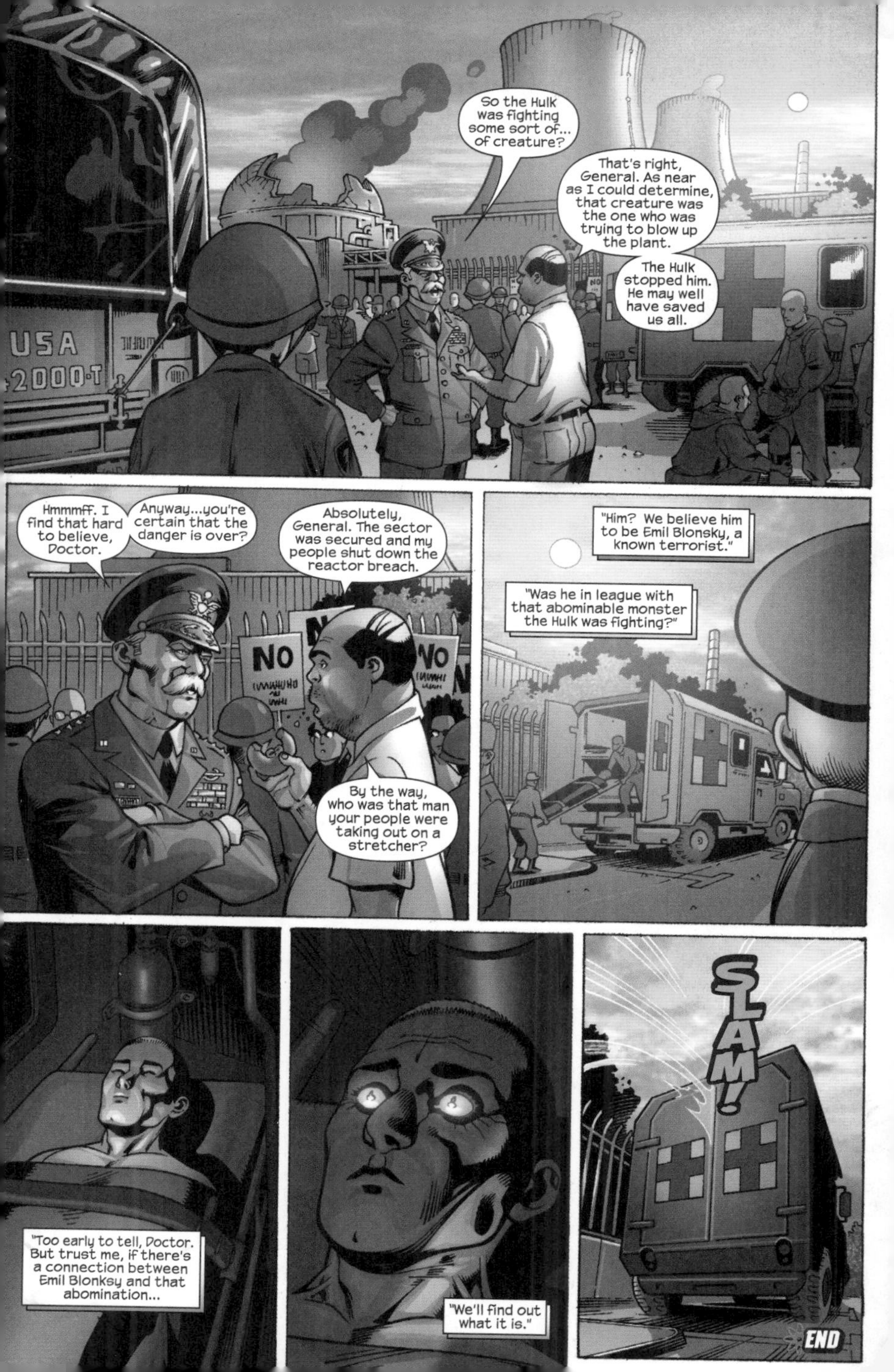
So the Hulk was fighting some sort of... of creature?
That's right, General. As near as I could determine, that creature was the one who was trying to blow up the plant.
The Hulk stopped him. He may well have saved us all.
USA
2000-T
Hmmmff. I find that hard to believe, Doctor.
Anyway...you're certain that the danger is over?
Absolutely, General. The sector was secured and my people shut down the reactor breach.
NO
NO
By the way, who was that man your people were taking out on a stretcher?
"Him? We believe him to be Emil Blonsky, a known terrorist."
"Was he in league with that abominable monster the Hulk was fighting?"
"Too early to tell, Doctor. But trust me, if there's a connection between Emil Blonksy and that abomination...
"We'll find out what it is."
SLAM!
END

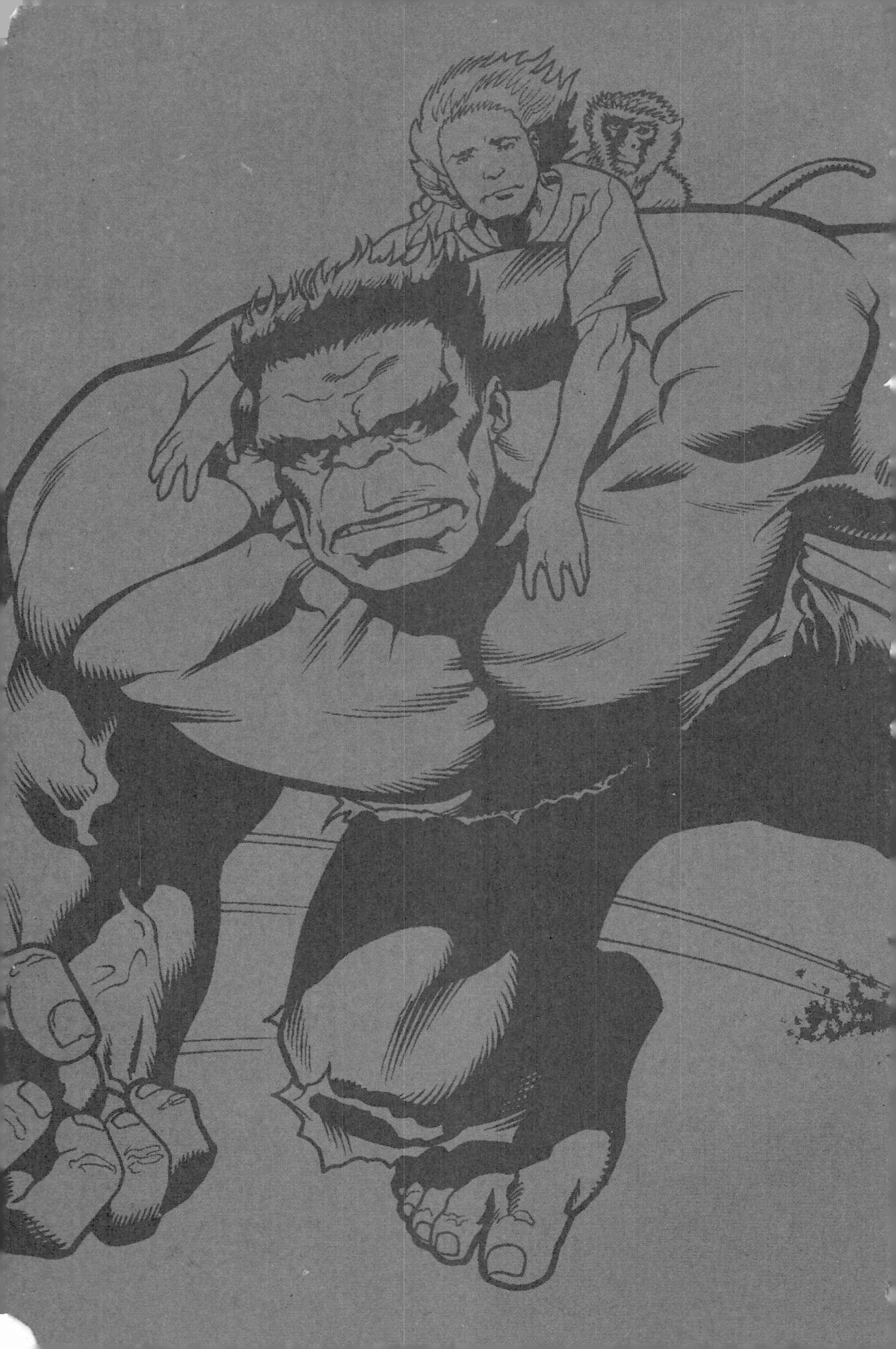